THE ORDER OF THE STAR

Also by Evelyn Hart from Severn House:

THE GREEN FIELDS BEYOND

THE ORDER OF THE STAR

Evelyn Hart

This first world edition published in Great Britain 1997 by
SEVERN HOUSE PUBLISHERS LTD of
9–15 High Street, Sutton, Surrey SM1 1DF.
This title first published in the U.S.A. by
SEVERN HOUSE PUBLISHERS INC of
595 Madison Avenue, New York, N.Y. 10022.

Copyright © 1997 by Evelyn Hart

All rights reserved.
The moral right of the author has been asserted.

British Library Cataloguing in Publication Data

Hart, Evelyn
 The order of the star
 1. Hong Kong – Fiction
 I. Title
 823.9'14 [F]

 ISBN 0 7278 5258 2

All situations in this publication are fictitious and
any resemblance to living persons is purely coincidental.

Typeset by Palimpsest Book Production Limited,
Polmont, Stirlingshire, Scotland.
Printed and bound in Great Britain by
Hartnolls Ltd, Bodmin, Cornwall.

'To the memory of a beloved grandmother'

Overture

1923

Chapter One

The Port of Yokohama was *en fête*. Louise Winter stood on the pier built by her late husband James, one of the original settlers. Head held high, her small stoutish figure as upright as ever, she felt an immense pride that the event was to celebrate the arrival of her daughter Camille.

It seemed the whole town had turned out to greet Camille in a personal tribute from the people for one who had been born and brought up in their famous International City. A triumphal arch had been erected on the exit from the dock in honour of the visit. It was decorated in bunting and flowers with the words written large: THE TREATY PORT WELCOMES HER DAUGHTER STAR OF OPERA.

There was a band. Flags were out everywhere on the route to the civil reception to be given in the Town Hall by the Mayor. It rivalled the gala for the Duke of Connaught's visit in 1906 when Camille, then one of the flag wavers, was fourteen. It was now 1923 and she was world famous.

Louise had been prepared for the occasion, but Camille was taken by surprise. She was used to such receptions in Europe and the United States, but here, in her home town in Japan, she had not expected it. For a moment she could not imagine who the music, the waving and cheering crowds were for, until, as she walked down the gangway closely followed by Nanna carrying her little daughter Izolda, she recognised the familiar figure of the station-master who had seen her off by train all those years ago; she had been seventeen and leaving Japan to attend finishing school in England prior to going to Paris for singing training. Now, with a deep bow and beaming smile, the old man handed her a posy of flowers.

Mother and daughter embraced warmly, and, delighted to meet her granddaughter for the first time, Louise took Izolda from Nanna. *God Save the King* was played, and off through the triumphal arch they swept in a limousine to the civil reception through streets lavishly decorated with flags. There, waiting to be met, were a host of old friends including Camille's first singing teacher Florrie Mendelson, Hilary Tait (a school friend) and, thrill upon thrill, her very first beau, American Bertie Poole, who rushed up, all six foot two of him, to hug her and introduce his wife from Boston. In the crowd were Louise's immediate neighbours on the Bluff, Kirkland and Katie Wilson together with another neighbour, a Mr Orange, also an original settler and contemporary of James Winter's. Even Mazo, Camille's old dressmaker, and Dentici, the first Italian baker to the Port, were hovering around in the background to greet her. It was an unforgettably heart-warming day for Louise. And Camille had been tremendously touched and made happy by it all.

Now it was a Saturday, three weeks since Camille's arrival, and the family's departure for Australia was imminent. Louise too, was going with them. It was a heavily oppressive early autumn morning with an unpleasantly hot wind which a sudden storm and deluge of rain in the night had done nothing to alleviate. Louise sat in her garden in the shade of

The Order of the Star

the leafy wisteria arbour waiting for her daughter to come out and join her. Briskly she fanned herself with an old ivory-bound fan. Beads of sweat lay on her temples. The grey wig, which she had worn since her hair had fallen out in handfuls when she had been ill with sprue on a visit to her son Jimmy in China, felt heavy and hot on her head. Her hair had grown under the wig and was now white and silky fine. The trichologist had advised that it would benefit to uncover, but to go white overnight and let the world see it? Too much of a shock for her and everyone else! One day maybe . . . She kept on putting that day off and the months grew into years.

While waiting, Louise's thoughts wandered further. It was surprising how little the Treaty Port had changed since James's death in 1909. There were only a few modern buildings in the town, and hardly any new ones up here on the Bluff. There was the reclaimed land below the cliffs which spoiled the wide stony sweep of Dare's Beach but which as yet had not been built over. There were the cars and chauffeurs instead of the broughams and coachmen. The roads were as potholed as ever even though most were tarmacadamed and therefore less dusty.

In the Great Foreign Cemetery, quite near to James's grave, there was now a granite Memorial to the eighty-four British, American and French men, who had some personal association with Yokohama, killed in the 1914–18 War. Many of her old friends still lived up on the Bluff, including Dr Wheeler who continued to do his rounds among his old patients, unsteady on his pins though he was. *She* would never desert him as long as he lived! His wife was part of her bridge four – Saturday – they were playing this afternoon. Their son George, school friend of her boy Jimmy, had won the VC in Mesopotamia. That had made the dear couple, who were now in their nineties, very proud.

Though on her arrival Camille had looked a bit peaky from the 'flu, the roses were now back in her cheeks. The stay for a week down on the coast in their summer house had seen to that. They were packed and ready to go on the morrow. She herself had declared she would never leave 'Akamatsu' again when she had returned from Paris during the first year of the war, but to hear her famous daughter in *Madame Butterfly*, well, that was too strong a lure for any mother to resist! Also she would like to meet Joel again, last seen in Paris, her very favourite man for Camille after Bertie. However, it had not worked out like that . . .

How quickly the visit was going. The first of September already; gracious, Camille's wedding day. Was it really nine years since she had married Commander Richardson in Sheerness? There had been no mention of the anniversary at breakfast this morning. Was the marriage over? She did not know and would not ask, but it looked suspiciously like it with all the separations after Izolda's birth in 1920. Camille had taken up her career again with Joel as conductor and they were always on tour. Louise, with her Christian beliefs, did not approve of divorce, but times had changed and, as she had predicted right from the start, Camille and the stiff Commander – he was a Captain RN now but she would always think of him as the Commander who had wooed her daughter in Wei-chu where the China Fleet lay at anchor – were incompatible. Joel would have been a far more suitable husband; just the right temperament for Camille. During their touring together both in Europe and America it would seem from Camille's letters they had got on famously. She reckoned they had grown famous together, the conductor

The Order of the Star

and the lead soprano. Well, Camille had not said anything about a divorce in the offing and it was pure conjecture on Louise's part. It would be interesting, though to watch the two in Australia . . .

The garden was looking particularly colourful in spite of the heat. The original cuttings she had taken from Captain Owston's banksia roses, the first to be grown in Yokohama, were flowering profusely, and the well-watered begonias were making a great splash. A garden-boy did most of the work these days under the watchful eye of Hambei, who had something wrong with his back and was bent nearly double. The dear old man still liked to hold the weeding basket for her, though. They were such old friends.

An ancient and grumpy Ishii polished the car installed in the stables. It was a vehicle which he regarded with a certain amount of awe. He watched with distrust as the chauffeur drove it to the front porch. He had once told her that he could tolerate it when it was stabled and static, but not when it moved and belched disgustingly from behind! Faithful Ishii, James's groom long before she had come into the picture. Shogira, the head house-boy, was still with her as she hoped he always would be as well as wonderful Hatsu who was helping Nanna look after Izolda. It filled her cup of happiness to have daughter and granddaughter to stay . . . Ah, here they came . . .

Wearing a dress of sheerest green chiffon made from a bale in her father's factory, silk lining glistening through the flimsy material, the jade colour of which matched her eyes and the emerald of her engagement ring on her finger, Camille stepped through the French windows of Akamatsu with Izolda. Nanna followed. James, who had been married to a Japanese lady, the daughter of a Samurai, before being widowed and then marrying Louise, had some twenty years later had the house built on the Bluff for Louise to remind her of her American roots in southern Georgia. Izolda was put down for her morning's sleep in the cot Hatsu had placed a short distance away under the shade of a pine tree. Immediately Izolda sat up.

"Lie down, Izarling," Camille said firmly, using her pet name for her daughter, and laid her down on her tummy a second time. "You know perfectly well you are sleepy; if you do not go to sleep now you'll be tired this afternoon and there will be tears." Camille tucked the sheet over the small figure and saw that the adored rag doll her father had given her in Shanghai was beside her. She stayed bending over the cot and patting her daughter to sleep while humming a tune so melodic that it seemed to Louise the very birds must stop their flutterings on the lawn to cock their heads and listen. Soon eyelids drooped, and Camille joined Nanna sitting beside her mother in the arbour.

"Phew, it's hot!" Camille exclaimed, pushing a strand of her long titian hair back from her face. She secured it with a hairpin into the rest of her abundant locks, dressed high. She sat down on the marble bench scattered with cushions. "I used to avoid this spot as a child; in fact it used to frighten me with its shadows, I don't know why. Today I'm grateful for its shade." She rubbed her neck where she had a slight heat rash, and then picked up her embroidery from the sewing basket on the table. The chain from the Chinese coin piece she habitually wore had irritated the skin and she had not put it on that morning but had dabbed her neck with camomile lotion and left the necklace on her dressing-table. The good luck charm had been given her by a previous beau in Wei-chu and she had worn it by day ever since; she felt

The Order of the Star

naked and rather vulnerable without it, particularly when she thought back to the terrible scene with DD in Shanghai as she passed through on her way to Japan so that he could see Izolda and they could have a talk. He had refused point blank to even consider a divorce. He said it would ruin his career. She gave a little involuntary shiver at the remembrance of the row.

"The arbour is the coolest place right now and gives us protection from this scorching wind." Louise fanned herself vigorously.

"It was so hot and stuffy all night, wasn't it, Nanna darling?" Camille said banishing her unpleasant thoughts, "I heard you get up to see to Izolda in the storm. You must be fatigued. Why don't you go in and have a little lie down?"

"I'm seldom tired," Nanna smiled. She held up her needle to the light to thread it. "Oh dear, my hands *are* sticky. Is it always as hot as this at this time of year, Mrs Winter?"

"Should start to cool down now, Nanna. I reckon we are in for another storm – that'll fix it," Louise foretold. She looked up at the darkening sky. "It will be quite a relief to be on the high seas tomorrow. Ah good, here come the drinks. Thank you, Shogira."

"My ladies stay in garden today," the grey-haired head-boy ordered as he poured three glasses of fresh lemon with crushed ice. "This hot-time; *jishin*-time." Louise and Camille exchanged quick glances at the word.

"I shall be going to bridge as usual this afternoon; please see the car is ordered," Louise said evenly.

"Very good, lady." Shogira placed the beaded net on the jug and disappeared soft-footed over the lawn and into the house.

"Delicious," Nanna sipped the drink, "so refreshing."

"How I miss Papa here; I keep expecting him to walk out from the study door. Strange to think he would have been in his late seventies."

"Neither can I figure him being as old as I am; he was always boyish at heart."

"Mother, you're not *old*!"

"I sure feel it sometimes."

At that moment across the lawn towards them came Hatsu, waddling along in her peculiar pigeon-toed shuffle, almost as if her long cotton kimono restricted her steps. With the years she had put on so much weight that she appeared nearly as wide as she was tall, her fat little arms looking like a dwarf's.

"What is it, Hatsu?" Camille asked, seeing the troubled expression on her amah's ivory-seamed face.

"There are portents." Hatsu's heavily-lidded eyes blinked rapidly. "Look at birds hopping on lawn. They should be resting in leafy shade of trees in heat of day, as our little one here is resting. I feel *kami* catfish are cross, angry like day thou wast a child that bad morning. I *smell* them!"

"What is Hatsu saying?" Nanna asked.

"She is telling us the catfish in the ground are angry," Camille explained. With their mutual *mono-no-aware* insight, born from her early childhood days with the amah, Camille now caught Hatsu's apprehension. Nervously she made a daisy button-stitch, and unsatisfied with it, unpicked it and started again.

"Catfish? Never heard of such a thing. What nonsense," Nanna sniffed unperturbed.

"We have listened to thy tales of catfish and *jishin* portents many times, Hatsu," Louise took up briskly. The electric

The Order of the Star

tension between Camille and Hatsu needed earthing. She glanced up at the sky again. There was no doubt it was foreboding, torrid; the atmosphere heavy in a drifting lurid fog of heat despite the wind which whipped the air away before one's face, making it difficult to breathe. Odd sort of day. Better to take the usual precautions . . . Be on the safe side. "Since thou art alarmed, Hatsu, thou shalt stay in the garden today with Camille and the child when I go to my bridge, and we will sleep out this night on our camp-beds as we did that night after thou saved Camille when she was not much younger than Izolda is now. For that we will ever be grateful to thee."

"Oh blast! I've run out of green silk," exclaimed Camille. "I'd better nip into the house and fetch some more."

"Let me go, Mrs Richardson."

"It's all right, Nanna. You won't be able to find the colour I want."

"Thou stayest. I find!" Hatsu ordered as Camille got to her feet. She put a restraining hand on her erstwhile charge's arm. The two looked at each other.

"Why not leave it for the moment – go on to another colour, honey," Louise suggested.

"I can't, Mother. It's the last bit . . . I won't be a second," and she ran lightly towards the house.

Twisting her dimpled hands before her, Hatsu's blinking gaze followed Camille's figure as if hypnotised. Both Louise and Nanna's eyes also rested on her. She was somehow particularly radiant that morning. Her green dress, as diaphanous as pictures of Ophelia, blew against her in the hot wind to outline her slimness. With willowy grace she glided up the steps to the verandah and slipped into 'Akamatsu'. Still twisting her hands before her in agitation, Hatsu moved away from the arbour to the cot where she stood peering down at the sleeping child.

At that exact moment the noontide muzzle-loading cannon by the Union Club below the Bluff boomed across the harbour. The gun that had not failed to blast out the Saturday hour since the first settlers had arrived, gave the signal that told the Europeans in the Port it was time to down work in offices, banks or factories and make their way to the Club for a drink.

In the split second after the boom, even as the sound of the gun was still reverberating round the harbour – the earthquake struck.

Chapter Two

Even before the earthquake struck, Hatsu had snatched up sleeping Izolda into her tubby arms. With her precious burden she waddled for the centre of the lawn. Nanna and Louise leapt to their feet the instant that the ground began to shake. They made for the grass as the arbour trellis-work with its wisteria vines collapsed with a sigh.

Camille, in the drawing-room, searching around in the sewing-box for her embroidery silk, and Shogira, setting the table for lunch in the dining-room, were the only people indoors.

"Camille, *come out! Where are you?*" Louise shouted as she ran for the house. "Camille, please come! You *must* come quickly! *Camille* . . . Cam—" Louise was barely half way when she stopped dead, the unended name dying on her lips in a gasp of horror. She stood rooted to the spot as she watched her home collapse with a splintering, soughing groan before her. Timbers buried themselves in a suffocating dust, leaving jagged gaps with hollow walls supporting tottering chimneys. At the same moment one side of the garden slid down the cliff to the paddy-fields below, taking the thatched summer house, Camille's *no-ken-do* tree she had loved to climb as a child to write her poetry, and all the pines, with it, leaving the remains of the house sickeningly near the displaced edge. Izolda's empty cot stood drunkenly by a gaping precipice.

Amidst an underground roaring rumble they stood there: Louise, Nanna and Hatsu, who tightly held the sleepy child. They stood shuddering, transfixed, on the heaving, pulsing, uneven lawn, unable to speak or call, unable to do more than try and keep their balance. At any moment they expected the earth to split open under them and engulf them at the very point on which they stood.

Dumb and helpless with fear as to what had happened to Camille, Louise watched the nightmare of timbers and plaster showering into the ruins of her house, the ground under her feet lurching as violently as waves in a heavy sea. For fully four minutes of what seemed an eternity of shocked disbelief, she stood there.

Then, as abruptly as it had come, the earthquake ceased. Louise, the first to recover, shouted to the servants clustered round the outbuildings which appeared only slightly damaged though the outside kitchen, where the charcoal stove had been glowing hotly under the dishes being prepared for lunch, was on fire. Some stayed to damp it down, others came running to her agonised calls, and like stupefied automatons, together with Louise and Nanna, began to tear at the ruins with their hands in a desperate bid to find Camille and Shogira.

Black clouds of ominous smoke, dropping swirling pieces of live torch-lit smuts, swept over the garden carried by the fierce wind from the growing inferno of the city below. Down there, in that first shattering strike, the flimsy houses had fallen like matchsticks onto the embers in the hearths of thousands of households cooking their midday meal.

Stopping for a moment to wipe her face, her heart

pounding, her breath coming in gasps, Louise looked up to see Kirkland Wilson staggering in over the broken fence between their two properties. She took in the nasty-looking gash on his head.

"Katie's . . . dead," he managed, the words coming strangled from his harrowed face. "Killed . . . in the verandah . . . Fallen chimney, I think . . . We were escaping from the house. You all right? All of you?" he looked round vaguely.

"Camille and Shogira are in here," she pointed.

"Oh, God!" He plunged headlong into the wreckage, ignoring his personal sorrow and shock as, after an uncanny thirty minutes' quiet, once more the lacerated earth trembled, shook, vomited, and hellishly swayed in a fresh upheaval of tortured turmoil. All the while more timbers and plaster fell.

They found Shogira first. His body was badly crushed. The servants laid him on the inner lawn by the fallen arbour where the grass was humped as if invaded by an army of giant moles. There he lay, Louise's best of friends, an expression of mild surprise on his grey face.

Mr Orange arrived from the other side of the property together with one or two more to join in the frantic search for Camille. Then the emerald of her dress became visible deep amongst the timbers. Kirkland called for a saw, the men sweating away to cut her free.

They lifted her out, her figure so young and lissome in the dainty dress. Gently they laid her on the grass beside the faithful old head servant.

"Camilla, my baba," moaned Hatsu crouched beside her and rocking, rocking backwards and forwards on her heels, "Camilla, thou – we – knewest . . ."

Kneeling beside her daughter, Louise straightened Camille's dress about her slender form and arranged her hair. She folded her daughter's hands over her breasts, observing the gleaming emerald engagement ring on her finger. The husband had been tardy in giving it to her, had he not? He was always short of money and they could not have managed at first had she not given Camille a generous allowance from James' fortune. Dear God. Would there be anything left now? In the end DD had bought the ring with a lump sum the Navy had given him for a buoy he invented.

There was no shadow of suffering on the tranquil, still face she kissed, no knowledge of the grief and fear of the living gathered around her, of the anguish of a mother, of frightened Nanna holding the unaware child, of grief-stricken Hatsu rocking and bending beside her, of Kirkland suddenly aged beyond belief, of the despairing servants standing by talking amongst themselves in hushed whispers. She lay there, her body broken, upon the bed of green, her dress torn, her long hair released and flowing over her shoulders as it used to cascade as a child. It was more titian-coloured than ever in the livid light of sun through fire: the colour of autumn, her favourite season. Camille lay resting, peaceful, innocent of the horror taking place. Very quietly she lay, utterly beautiful.

That she could no longer enchant with her eyes and tilt of head, sing to vast, entranced audiences, love, laugh, rejoice in the seasons; that she could no more seize life with both hands; that she could no longer hold on to every minute, could no more charm and enthuse others with her zest for life – was quite inconceivable.

It was impossible to comprehend that Camille was dead.

The Order of the Star

In that terrible moment of disbelief and yet knowledge, for a moment Hatsu ceased her moaning and looked up at her mistress. And in that glance Louise saw that Hatsu, in her intuitive *mono-no-aware* closeness with Camille, had always feared that it would end thus.

Stunned, inactive, wordless, tearless, waiting for something – she knew not what – while three bodies (grey-haired Katie Wilson brought there too), lay by the ruined arbour, Louise's shocked mind veered away from the terrible present to the other earthquake: the day 'Akamatsu's roof had pancaked off the house doing only comparatively minor damage; the day they had camped out in the garden all night as small shocks continued, Katie and her little daughter Helen with them, her childless sister-in-law Maude Winter keeping the children amused – four of them, Edouard, Jimmy, Camille and Helen Wilson. Edouard had died of meningitis as a strong young man; now Camille. How many more tragedies would she have to suffer before her turn came? That other day of earthquake when James and his elder brother Baldwin had come running up from their offices, they had been overjoyed to find each other and their families safe. That was the day when Hatsu had saved Camille in the house by shielding her charge with her own body under the nursery table. Today Hatsu had held another child in her protective arms, but she had not been able to save Camille a second time.

Now, with the continuing shocks, more masonry from the ravaged walls fell with plops, crashes and rising dust into the shell of Louise's home, making it too dangerous to attempt to salvage any of her possessions, and she restrained the servants from trying to do so. They stood around in the chaos of the garden, aimless and miserable, every now and then throwing terrified glances at the billows of reddened smoke streaking overhead.

"Lady," tremblingly Hambei tottered up to Louise, "look over cliff. See, our villages are burning. They be in ruin, all in ruin . . ."

Louise looked and saw the destruction with more fires catching on. "You must go to your homes and families and do what you can to save life. Tell all the servants to go, and quickly," Louise said, forcing herself to think practically.

Obeying, they came up to her one by one, there on the lawn. They took her hands and kissed them in farewell before going off down the tortured Bluff road, bent Hambei and rheumy Ishii among them. Only Hatsu flatly refused to leave. She knelt on beside Camille, her body rocking and moaning.

"Stop it, old woman!" Hambei, seeing she was not following, turned back to admonish sharply. "Is there not trouble enough come upon us without thou adding to it with thy wailings. Obey our lady and come with us to our fishing village. Maybe by the sea it is not so bad." He shook her forcibly by the shoulder.

"There is nothing you can do here. I think you should go, Hatsu-san," Louise said gently. With tears pouring down her cheeks, Hatsu gave Camille a final glance before coming up and kissing Louise's hands.

"Little one, Lady," she sobbed, "take care of little one," and slowly she shuffled her way into the upheaval outside to follow reluctantly in the wake of the others.

'The little one' – where was Nanna? Louise looked desperately round and saw her by the fruit trees at the end of the garden, carrying Izolda as far away as she could from the grim scene. "Mummy on gound," she heard the

The Order of the Star

cheerful prattle. "Mummy on gound," the baby's finger pointed.

More neighbours, some with cuts and bruises, all with frightened faces, came over the severed gates to enquire and to tell of other tragedies, other shattered houses, others killed, many badly hurt. They grouped together, discussing whether to go or stay, and if to go, where? They with Louise, all of them that fearsome day, knew that this was no ordinary earthquake. This was a cataclysm.

Most of the gathering moved off. Kirkland and Mr Orange stayed on with Louise, who found a stump to sit on by the bodies. Still she could not believe it, could not believe that Camille was truly dead. The earthquake rumbled and vibrated sending the chimneys that were left crashing into the ruins. Mr Orange and Kirkland discussed in hushed voices what to do next.

By early afternoon some sailors arrived with stretchers. "We've orders to take the bodies to the Naval Hospital grounds, Ma'am, where we're digging temporary graves. There's quite a crowd gathering there. The heat up here is terrible, Sir, you should be leaving."

They picked up Camille's limp form and placed it on a stretcher, and once more Louise arranged the tattered dress around her daughter and stroked her shining hair. She put out a shaking hand to gently touch the pale cheek, but she could not bear to kiss her again and feel the coldness which had already set in. And they covered her. Camille in the newly dug shallow grave. There would not even be a coffin to protect her from the earth, only a winding sheet. At the thought of that, Louise very nearly did faint. "Mr Orange and I will go with the sailors," Kirkland said at her side. He took her arm to steady her. "We'll assess how bad the fire is and get advice on what we should do. Stay here with Nanna, Louise."

"We'll be back as soon as we can," Mr Orange said, coughing as smoke billowed over. "In the meantime, have a look round and see if there is any way we could go down the cliffs from here."

Louise watched them go. Mr Orange was a good bit older than Kirkland and was trailing along behind the latter who was urging him to hurry. When they vanished round a corner she walked to the gaping edge by the house and peered dubiously over into a sheer landslide drop. No way down by the inner cliffs. She saw the flames flaring out from the Kirin Brewery on the way to Sumuko's (James's first wife's,) village. After the 1894 earthquake, James had sent Shogira over to see if Sumuko's family was safe, and found all well. Now it looked as if the village was being engulfed. Louise moved on, picking her way along the side of the garden with its wreckage of pine trees. Clumps of earth and stones gave way further and avalanched at her feet with the oscillating ground. The cot was there, a leg broken. She snatched up the sheet. What did she want it for? Ah yes, to tie up the gash in Kirkland's head. As she grasped the sheet something fell out. She was just about to bend down to see what it was when Nanna appeared holding Izolda by the hand. "Keep away from the edge, Nanna," Louise cautioned. She made her way gingerly towards them. They went together to the safer outhouses at the back which were untouched other than that the kitchen was half burnt. A tiny spark of hope lit up Louise's ravaged face: she could live there! They found a basket and collected a packet of biscuits and a few tins of canned milk.

Kirkland returned alone, panting, his face blackened by

The Order of the Star

smuts. He looked ghastly. He was not a young man, though a good bit younger than Mr Orange who, unable to keep up the pace, he had left behind. In fact Kirkland was older than she, over seventy, while she was only sixty-seven. Fancy that – sixty-seven, her husband and two children dead before her . . . "Oh, I see you've gotten a bandage," she said vaguely. "I was going . . ." she indicated the sheet.

"They tidied me up at the hospital. Dreadful scenes; bodies, wounded . . . They took our loved ones away. God knows where to. When I looked again I could not find them . . ." He choked. "The heat from the fires is appalling; it will soon be impossible to stay up here. Our only hope is the hospital. There's a landslide flaming beyond it down Camp Hill. A terrible sight with the whole hill down to the town in flames. People are attempting to get down the cliffs to the beach with the hospital's tennis nets. No way down here? No, I didn't think there would be. Quick! No time to waste."

"Nanna!" Louise called. "Come now. We've got to go."

They scrambled over what remained of the gates but they did not get far down Bluff Road, nothing like as far as the hospital. Even in the ten minutes since Kirkland had come up it as fast as he could, the situation had rapidly deteriorated. The fires from inland were blowing right across the road. Rounding the next bend, handkerchiefs to their noses, they found themselves cut off from the Naval Hospital by an impenetrable bank of swirling smoke-fires roaring over from the conflagration of villages in the folds of the valley. They watched stupefied as huge flames fanned by the gale-force wind were being thrown out and across the road like tongues of molten metal. Balls of fire rolled and leapt from one ruined house to ignite another and gust their way all along the road on either side, the voracious flames going on to lick at the cliff tops opposite.

Louise, Kirkland, and Nanna carrying Izolda, stood in the middle of the road staring aghast, horrified at the sight, their figures blasted by the heat as if standing in front of a furnace which indeed they were, their eyes stinging and watering so that they could barely see. There was no way ahead. There was no way inland. There was no way down over the cliffs. The way beyond Akamatsu had long since been evacuated by those who lived further up the heights.

They were trapped!

Chapter Three

"*Turn!*" yelled Kirkland, his voice cracking on the command. "Make for a way down by The Niche, or Jackson's Hill; after that . . ." He shrugged. Both he and Louise knew that after that there was no possible way of getting down the steep Honmoku Cliffs at the end of the Bluff by Treaty Point, the highest and sheerest of the lot, and covered at the top in a thick group of dry, inflammable pine trees. If they could not find a way down before that, they would be roasted alive on the Bluff.

Neither Louise nor Kirkland, at this stage of their lives, cared much if they were roasted as long as it was done quickly. Their whole concern was for the bewildered and frightened child and the plucky young nanny carrying her heavy burden. Nanna plodded on, not knowing the landscape, nor where they were going, nor what their chances were, but knowing that her beloved mistress, who had always treated her affectionately and informally as one of the family, was dead, and that Izolda's life was shattered. She knew that she had to follow the two elderly folk blindly, that she must not panic (she'd been brought up by her Scot parents on Kipling's '*When all about you . . .*'), and that her duty was to do her utmost to save the baby, even at the cost of her own life.

In a small clutch, as hurriedly as they were able on the uneven road, the three grownups retraced their steps past Kirkland's ruined house where Katie had been killed, and on to 'Akamatsu,' hardly giving them a glance. They went past Baldwin and Maude's old house, deserted now by the new owners, but not so badly damaged as theirs. They could have gone in to rest and shelter if it had not been for the fires chasing them. Nanna, lagging behind, faltered and staggered at one point to give her ankle a sharp twist on a rut. Izolda was whimpering and spluttering from the smoke.

"Here, give her to me." Kirkland snatched Izolda from Nanna's arms. The child screamed at the unfamiliar man. "My God, where's the Niche track gone to?" he frowned, while roughly hitching Izolda onto his hip. He looked around despairingly. "The whole bloody dog-leg of Mandarin Bluff seems to have shifted."

"Let me have a look," Louise said, stumbling over rocks and upturned tree roots to get to the edge, the flames behind all the time on the verge of catching up. "No good," she returned, "quite impossible. Try Jackson's Hill. I'll go ahead. Nanna, keep close."

They plunged on down the deserted road, Louise leading, Kirkland carrying the wailing child, Nanna limping behind, and always the fires chased them, closing the road behind them as clapboard house after clapboard house was swallowed up in shooting balls of flame. Intrepidly, knowing it was their last hope, they came to a spot where Louise groped her way from the road across a landslide of dislodged earth and boulders. And all the while the ground under her feet still grumbled and lurched.

"It's here for sure . . . somewhere. I know the track takes off from this corner," she muttered to herself. "Come on

The Order of the Star

woman, figure out where the line is even if you can't see it." She searched on, poking, prying around, looking below the cliff to get her position from the Juniten headland and bay to her right glimpsed between billows of smoke.

Behind, Nanna, her ankle rapidly swelling, relieved Kirkland of the crying child and hushed her in her arms, great sobs quivering through Izolda's small body. Kirkland looked grey with exhaustion. He had lost his wife, he had dug out Camille, and he had had a severe blow on the head which needed stitches – the blood was oozing through the bandage – and he felt, for the first time in his life, his age. He was an old man.

"I can't find the track, but it's not so sheer here and it must be near. The lie is right and we should be able to pick it up further down. What d'you think, Kirkland?"

"Have to try it . . . Nowhere else possible. Must have a go. Over the edge, Nanna."

"I can't," Nanna gasped at the drop below her.

"No, of course you can't. Your hands must be freed. Here—" Louise took the cot sheet out of the basket she was clutching as if everything depended upon it. "Kirkland, help me bind Izolda onto Nanna's back . . . Peasant fashion . . . That's right; now over and under the child. I'll tie it at the waist. You tie it round Nanna's shoulders." Their trembling fingers fumbled. "Is that comfy, Izolda? Stay in there quietly, honey, for goodness sake. See, you're having a lovely pick-a-back on Nanna! All right?"

"Yes, Mrs Winter."

"I can't cope with this basket." Louise threw it on the ground. "Pity; the milk might come in useful for Izolda . . ."

"Here. I'll take it." Kirkland undid the stud from his stiff collar and wrenched off his tie, using it to hang the basket round his waist. They took a short breather whilst eyeing the horrifying drop below. "Better get a move on," urged Kirkland apprehensively as more pine trees caught with a blistering crackle. "You go ahead, Louise; I'll help steady from behind. Nanna, face to the cliff and cling on with your hands for all you're worth to anything you can grasp."

Louise went over, slithering and sliding, earth and stones glissading with her. Nanna followed, then Kirkland on his backside.

"There's a sort of sheer bit below," Louise paused peering ahead, her heart racing and pounding, her breath coming short-windedly. "Can't go on . . . Overhang drop . . . Stumped."

"Let me see." Kirkland slithered further down beside her to look over her shoulder. He searched for a way on one side and then the other. "This way. There's a small ledge below on the left. Have to risk it. Not too bad as long as you don't lose your balance. Here," he took off his jacket and twisted it into a short rope. "Take one sleeve, Cousin Louise; I'll hold the other, and pray the goddamned thing doesn't tear. Face to the cliff. Now off you go."

Holding on for dear life, Louise lowered herself, scrabbling with her feet until the jacket was fully extended, her arms stretched above her head. She looked down. Not too far. She let go and jumped the last bit to the ledge, cutting her arm on a sharp rock as she did so and falling heavily, winding herself. She laughed feebly. Jumping down mountains at her age!

Nanna came down next with a thump on her bad ankle. Louise clutched her to steady her as she let off a yelp of pain on landing. She rested to recover and leant forwards on the ledge to get her breath as the pain dulled. A sleeve

The Order of the Star

of her uniform was torn off, the cuff on the other missing. Izolda's crying came muffled, half smothered by the sheet. No one bothered with her, their only thought was to get on and down to the sea, away from the flames already licking overhead. With nothing to hold on to, Kirkland came down in a rush to tumble at their feet, his clothes smelling of singe. Louise clung on to him to stop him from teetering over the brink of the shelf. In a heap they crouched together, holding on to each other.

They stayed there a moment or two, hearts banging and pounding, while Izolda, bewildered and frightened, sobbed quietly.

"Come on!"

They went on down slithering and sliding, the quaking earth all the time causing minor landslides. A great chunk of the Honmoku cliffs by the Point cascaded down in the distance as if in slow motion. The landslide reached the sea with a mighty splash which sent up great spindrifts of white froth.

By now they were in the lower glissade and gradually the descent became less steep. Groping ahead, Louise found the line of the Jackson's Hill track. Though it was blocked at every yard by rocks or shale, at last she could see where it was going and could pick it up on the other side. Over rocks, earth and slippage of heather roots, there was the visible track again. And now the slope became easier to manoeuvre. Louise battled on ahead of the others, following the route she knew so well foot by foot. Her long skirt was split to the knee, and the nasty cut on her arm stuck to her blouse with dried blood. She stopped to ease her straining lungs, winded by the very exertion of clambering over the debris. Then again she reached up to guide Nanna's blind steps with her living burden on her back, Kirkland behind sitting and sliding to find a foothold so that he could hold her steady for the next yard.

Thus, somehow, they finally descended the lower part of the cliff, till at last, exhausted, blackened, filthy, aching, hurt and parched with thirst, they reached the comparative safety of the foreshore.

For a long while they rested by the rocks. The child was quieter now in Nanna's arms, and Kirkland tore up the sheet into strips to bind up Louise's wound and tie a supporting bandage round Nanna's painful ankle. They looked up and saw the flames far above them belching out over the cliffs, sparks eddying up into the sky, the aromatic resinous scent of burning pines pungent on the air, and they were amazed to see the way they had come. How was it possible that they had negotiated those over-hanging tumbling heights without falling to their deaths?

Stiffly they got to their feet, and with Nanna limping but carrying Izolda again, the small battered party picked their way along the reclaimed shore that had once been Dare's Beach. They jumped or scrabbled their way across yard-wide fissured gaps in the concrete slabs, Louise all the time thinking of her three children playing there and remembering, remembering . . .

Often they had scampered along here, the wind in their hair, their excited voices shouting when they picked up mother-of-pearl shells and pieces of driftwood from some ship that had been wrecked in a typhoon on the rocks. Of the three, only Jimmy was left. Dear God, was it true Camille had been killed? Could it really be so or was it all part of this nightmare?

The Order of the Star

They passed all that was left of Eustace Dare's 'The Niche', the house he had built for his magnetic half Red Indian bride. It could still be glimpsed buried in the cliff. They stumbled on past bodies of those who had lost their footholds when escaping the fires and had plunged to their deaths. It could so easily have happened to them. The corpses, which Kirkland went over to examine to make sure none were living, lay like crumpled dummies at the base of the cliffs. Finding all were lifeless, he left them lying. Nobody at that stage had the strength to deal with the dead; every ounce of effort was needed to rescue and succour the living.

The most distressing part of Louise and Kirkland's slow progress came beneath the British Naval Hospital cliffs where a group of people stood helping those injured who had attempted to slide with ropes and tennis nets down the 200-foot drop. Many of these escapees from the fires were being attended to where they had fallen, some with broken legs and arms, others with damaged back and head injuries. A dishevelled Florrie Mendelson, seeing Louise passing, limped over with bound knee to ask for Camille. All Louise could do in the terrible emotion of the moment was to shake her head.

"Maurice Russell's up there." Florrie indicated the path she had descended, where flames now raged over the cliffs. "You know how portly he's grown in old age; not agile enough to attempt the descent. We had to leave him clinging to the top to burn. His poor daughters are hysterical." Maurice Russell, James's great pal from the old settler days . . . a horrible way to die. For the first time since James died fourteen years ago Louise was glad that he had passed on in his bed and not lived to see this horror and end of all he had built up. She stumbled on blindly, following Kirkland's lead until they reached the end of Dare's Beach. There she met another old friend, no longer the dapper man of erstwhile, but one grey with fatigue and covered with grime.

"I don't recognize you," she said, startled when he addressed her.

"I'm not surprised. I've just spent the last two hours helping to dig out the French Consul from the ruins of his house, only to see him die as we got him to the surface," he uttered grimly. "Camille?" he asked, looking at their small group enquiringly. Dumbly, Louise shook her head. They moved on.

They went right to the edge of the reclaimed land by the broken sea wall that had half subsided into the water. Others had gathered there, more coming in all the time. Scooping up water in cupped hands they bathed their faces and wetted their lips in the sea and some sipped and licked, but the salt only added to their raging thirst.

Between the blocks of the harbour breakwater they found a space where some rough grass grew, and the three adults sank down gratefully. Wearily Kirkland looked at his fob-watch. It *must* be later than that? He shook it, and putting it to his ear listened for the ticks.

"Has it stopped?" Nanna asked. She was trying to hush Izolda, who sat on her lap crying.

"No."

"What time is it?"

"Three-thirty."

"Unbelievable," Louise murmured. Only three and a half hours since the noontide gun boomed . . . Since the first colossal shock . . . Since Camille . . . Had they already

The Order of the Star

buried her? A lifetime of disasters in three hours. A city fallen and now burning out of control.

After a while Kirkland got stiffly to his feet. "Think I'll go along to Silk Street and see what's happened to the office," he said and left them. Louise nodded. The beautiful new office James had had built for the firm designed by a British architect and beautifully worked outside and in by Japanese craftsmen, to include a board-room and spacious suites for visiting businessmen. Was there anything left of that?

The refugees trickling in from the town to the harbour grew into a stream. Some were carried on substitute stretchers of torn-down doors, others, with gashed heads and terrible burns, struggled in on supportive arms. All of them, men women and children, were in various stages of exhaustion and shock. Their clothing was torn, shoes plastered with earth and clay, some with hair and eyebrows scorched off, others unrecognisable with their burnt and blackened faces. Many were unable to repress their groans and the worst cases screamed in pain. There were some doctors in the gathering crowd, but there were no bandages, no morphia.

"Oh, Mrs Winter, there you are. Have you seen Arthur? No? Have you met anyone who has heard anything about him?" Hilary, Camille's schoolfriend, enquired frantically. She was limping badly and could barely walk.

"I'm afraid not, dear," Louise replied. "Oughtn't you to sit down? You look done in."

"It's my hip. Arthur was in the town in his office. I know he's dead, I know he's dead . . ." She floundered off.

Old Dentici sat down near Louise. He clutched his arm. His white hair was filthy with smuts.

"What is it, Dentici?"

"My shoulder, Madame."

"Come here. I have a sheet." Louise ripped up the last of it and folded it into a sling. And all the time Izolda, tired, hot, dirty, went on and on whimpering. "Why is she crying, Nanna? Here, give her a biscuit," she suggested and handed over the broken packet from the basket Kirkland had dumped at her feet. Izolda took the piece handed to her but she did not eat it. She held it, sobbing, her whole body shaking.

"She needs a drink. The milk, Mrs Winter."

Louise took a tin from the basket and bashed it against a rock and went on bashing it. It only dented it. She got to her feet and moved among the crowd asking the men if they had a penknife with a tin opener on it. They looked at her as if she were demented. "I only want to open a tin of milk for my grandchild," she said crossly. "A corkscrew would do." But not in the whole of that distressed group of humanity could she find anything that could pierce a tin, let alone a can opener. She returned to their spot frustrated.

"Sshh, darling, hush, hush," soothed Nanna.

"Why are you crying?" Louise, in some exasperation asked the child.

"Doll. *Daddy doll!*" came the lament, the wails bursting forth afresh. Nanna and Louise exchanged amazed glances.

Izolda was not crying because she had lost her mother; no, she could have no knowledge of that though she had seen her lying on the ground – perhaps she thought that was some kind of game? She was inconsolable because they had forgotten to bring her rag doll – they had left it in the cot where Camille had made sure it was tucked in beside her, and Louise had dropped it without noticing what it was when she had whipped off the sheet to make a bandage for Kirkland's head. In all the anguish of that day,

The Order of the Star

the small child was suffering her own particular anguish. Daddy's doll. DD had given it to Izolda as a parting present in Shanghai, and from that day the child would not be without it.

How would Louise break the news to the father of his wife's death? Estranged though they may have become during the last few years, she knew that DD would take it desperately badly. He would be devastated, shattered, even destroyed by his young wife's death, for though Louise herself had not cared for him or believed him to be the right man for her daughter, she knew that he truly loved her – even adored her. She knew too, from letters written in the war, that whatever had happened in subsequent years when Camille had taken up her career again, DD to begin with had made his bride supremely happy. Camille had written in the war that she had *'found paradise without dying'*. And there was another factor: DD was good with children; liked to give parties for them on board his ship. He would want Izolda.

Then Joel. What about him? How deeply was *he* involved? In Paris he had asked for Camille's hand. Since then all that touring together with McLaughlan, the lady's maid, and Nanna as her chaperones? Chaperones my foot! He, too, would be shattered. But both these men had another passion beside Camille: DD had his Royal Navy; Joel his conducting. Which man would suffer most? Who would be most damaged by her death? It was the more vulnerable one who would be the most impaired and that, to Louise's mind, was undoubtedly the Commander.

The disaster-laden wind continued to blow fiercely, fanning the fires. This made it impossible for boats from the pier across the harbour to get in close enough to the breakwater to take off the hundreds of people (mostly Europeans) gathered there; Louise, Nanna and Izolda among them. They sat on where they were through the rest of that terrible day, and the wind still blew at dusk.

The holocaust continued all night with the Bluff, the Bund, the Settlement, China Town and the whole of the Japanese city in flames, shock spasms and smaller tremors continuing to tumble the remains of buildings that had not already fallen.

Some survivors of the initial quake squatted neck high all night in ponds or creeks while the fires raged round them. Others bobbed up and down in the sea, one foot on the bottom of an unsteady shore. Fuel tanks beyond the Custom House burst into huge jets of flame to redden the sky. Palls of smoke swelled upwards; cascades of burning slicks of oil spilled into the water. Ships in harbour caught fire, exploded and burnt fiercely. Every sort of craft, from sailing-boats to rowing-boats, tossing on the waters and now crammed with humanity, made out to beyond the broken lighthouse and waited throughout the night far out in the bay, for the fires to burn themselves out. Overcrowded sampans submerged, spilling their human content into the sea. Many drowned. The liner *Empress of Australia*, ready to take off on the second of September, had had her propeller damaged on the first violent earthquake strike, but remained securely tied up to the partly broken pier. Miraculously, so far she had escaped the fires in harbour.

At last, imperceptibly, the wind began to drop, and the *Empress*'s lifeboats gingerly nosed their way into the breakwater. First they took off the groups of badly injured, then the walking wounded, next the queues of women and children – Nanna and Izolda with them – then the men. But

The Order of the Star

Louise was in no hurry to go. She told Nanna she would come later. She sat on in the dark watching the nightmare, the never-to-be-forgotten sight of the Treaty Port, of which she, too, had been a founder member, burning.

The childhood remembrance of her first home burning in the Civil War was but a bonfire compared to this inferno. Why did fires dog her life? One at the beginning of it, and now one at the end. She did not believe she could survive the shock, terror and anguish of this hideous day. What she saw before her was an amazing sight; horrific but beautiful in its way as a spectacle. Endlessly, before her eyes, the town burnt, red flames dying down only to leap up again in a renewed orange frenzy of firework sparks blown by the fiendish wind.

The blazing fire-red monstrosity was magnificent in its very infamy. It took a fresh hold again and again to lick and lap and leer at the last vestiges of hotels, clubs, offices, shops, homes, until in the dark early hours of a new day, all grew silent in a blackened, stunted, stunned landscape; the fires giving up and dying away when the wind, some twenty-four hours after it had started blowing during the sudden night storm, finally died down.

On the occasion she had visited Jimmy in North China, the plague in Wei-chu had slunk off like a mass murderer without a backward glance after doing its worst for weeks, and here, as if suddenly ashamed of the devastation it had caused, the wind skulked away before daybreak could reveal the enormity of the damage it had wrought in the wake of the earthquake.

And at last, cramped and stiff after her long self-imposed vigil at the deathside of her adopted home town of fifty years, Louise made her way to a lifeboat.

Chapter Four

The women and children refugees were given cabins on board the *Empress of Australia*. The men dossed down in the saloons for what was left of the night. Someone led Louise off to have her arm dressed. Then she found a bunk and lay down. But she could not rest, could barely close her eyes for the pictures that throbbed through her brain, and in an hour or so, while Nanna and Izolda slept deeply the sleep of the exhausted young, she was up on deck to watch the stragglers arriving on the ship. She found a life-raft to sit on by the gangway.

From there scenes of sorrow and joy were enacted before her eyes. Anxious relatives fell into each others' arms, thanking God; for when the earthquake struck practically all the men were in their offices in the town while their families were in their homes on the Bluff. Friends met and clasped hands gratefully, others comforted and condoled. Many came up to Louise to express their sorrow on hearing about Camille. All knew her. Everyone had a story to tell of those killed, those hurt, and of the hundreds of miraculous escapes.

Kirkland arrived on board and informed Louise that there was nothing left of James's silk factories and ware-houses. Several of the staff had been killed on Silk Street, others

The Order of the Star

had died on the road in cars squashed like pancakes. Hilary's husband, Arthur Tait, had been engulfed in his rickshaw on the way to the United Club as the noontide gun had sounded.

Very many original settlers were killed in the famous club; Sammy, the now elderly head bar-boy being one of the few survivors. The massive granite and brick building had gone down like a stone at the first onslaught as the wall behind the long bar with its three tall, arched windows fell inwards and crushed those forgathering for the Saturday get-together.

Thus were the tidings of the dead brought in by those who had seen them die – some saved, some killed, fate relentlessly selecting young and old at random. Most grievous to Louise was the news that Dr Edwin Wheeler, loved by the whole colony, had been killed by falling masonry down Main Street, his last drink of sherry barely downed before he fled as fast as his aged legs would take him into the open. Mrs Wheeler, also in her nineties, was said to be in a state of shock, but safe and cared for by faithful servants in the outhouses of her home above Creekside.

Two young men from the Hongkong and Shanghai Bank were seen arriving up the gangway practically naked and carrying lozenge-shaped bundles between them. Evidently they had stripped off jackets, shirts, trousers, and even underwear in which to carry the contents of several safes. The odd sight raised a titter of hollow laughter from the throats of the old-timers watching – their last laugh while the treaty port writhed in its death throws.

Finally and mercifully, Louise saw her lifelong friends Commodore and Mrs Campbell arriving with their daughter and her husband Charles Poole and family of three boys, followed by Bertie and his wife. Apparently they had escaped down the cliffs with the children in dramatic manner and had then all spent a fraught night on the Commodore's yacht in the harbour amidst the explosions and patches of burning water. On seeing Louise, Bertie detached himself from his wife to stride up to her and sit cross-legged on the deck at her feet.

"One entire family saved, thank God," Louise expressed. And, with broken voice, she told him about Camille. For a long while Bertie did not speak as he struggled to regain his composure, his face showing the overwhelming sadness he felt at the news.

"Not Camille," he said at last. "It should not have been Camille, not with her brilliant future, her indestructible spirit. How I shall miss her letters. All who knew or met or even just heard of her will never forget her, dear Mrs Winter. We will always remember her, keep her in our hearts . . . That voice, those looks, that sympathy, radiance and joy. She was like a bright star in our lives, a star that will shine on in glorious memory . . ."

In the deathlike quiet of the aftermath, when the tremors had ceased, and the fires had burnt themselves out, Louise, in her torn and dirty clothes, started determinedly off on her own for her home, No. 152 The Bluff. Mrs Wheeler was living in No. 97's outhouses. 'Akamatsu' had kitchen and outhouses still standing. She would find something, find some shelter where she could live on her home ground. Telling Nanna that she would be back soon, down the Bund she went, carefully picking her way through the debris as surely as a homing pigeon.

She found the bridge over the creek badly damaged and the way opposite up Camp Hill to the Bluff impassable,

The Order of the Star

blocked as it was by the burnt-out landslide. The roof of Montague Beart's old bungalow could be seen upended below the grounds of the now non-existent French Consulate. She turned to walk along Creekside, passing where the original British and US Consulates had been in the days when she had first arrived in 1870. Across the creek she could see that the old road together with the ancient fishing village of Yukohama, upon which the treaty port had been founded, were completely obliterated, a few blackened tree trunks the only things left standing. There was no-one about. All was eerily quiet.

She went on inland, and at the turning to China Town crossed the creek by the next bridge, a rickety halfstanding one, only to find the Hundred Steps by Hegt's hill were not there – another avalanche. Noticing a man squatting by the creek, Louise went over and bent to touch his arm.

"Canst thou tell me a way up to the Bluff?" she asked in Japanese. There was no answer. Believing him to be asleep, Louise put a firmer hand on his shoulder and repeated the question only to see him topple over in the same squatting position, his face blackened, his body rigid and dead. Swallowing her nausea she picked her way back over the half-standing bridge and went on as best she could beside the creek whose brick banks had cascaded into the water. By the third bridge she saw signs opposite of the old track. She crossed over.

Bruised, stiff from the unaccustomed physical exertion of yesterday's escape down the Bluff, weary from that day of tragic loss and frightening stress followed by a night without sleep after her long vigil on the rocks while watching the town burning, Louise found that even getting thus far had taken its toll of her remaining strength. Her bandaged arm throbbed painfully, and the hill above her looked dauntingly high. The path was in places effaced by rocks and small tumbles. She knew that if she did get to the top she still had a long way to go along the Bluff. She braced herself for the climb. She would not give up; all her hopes were pinned on reaching her home. Once there she was sure she could make some sort of life for herself in the ruins.

Slowly she began to climb and found herself panting for on this Sunday there was not even a zephyr of a breeze, though the air was fresher than yesterday as if purified by the catastrophe. Drat the wretched wig which made her hotter than ever, scratched and tickled her – filthy dirty too from the previous day's rocky descent. Once home she would find a fresh one among the debris of house – and a hat. She did not like to be without a hat.

On Louise climbed in her trailing fetid clothes. Every few yards she stopped to sit down and allow her racing heart to quieten. Though not half so steep, not half as dangerous, it was like yesterday in reverse. She rose again and toiled on and up, at times on hands and knees, her face and body wet with perspiration. She came across many charred corpses lying by the way, and passed them almost indifferently. There were a few bedraggled peasants about doing much the same sort of thing as she: crawling around looking. They took no notice of one another, neither did they give her the polite greeting in the customary way. Each was absorbed in their own tragedy, each earnestly bent on following their personal ploy. To her they all seemed like animals rootling amongst the wreckage of Cherry Mount Hill . . . it used to be so pretty in blossom time. No cherry trees now. Nothing was left but the extraordinary quietness, the desolation of

The Order of the Star

an abandoned town. Had this shabby old woman with the grimed clothes, ashen face and pounding heart really once been the girl from Georgia with the raven hair, the lithe 'little black kitten' as the sailors on her ship liked to call her? They called her their lucky mascot on the sea journey across the 'all blue' route into the haven of Yokohama harbour. How could that girl and this hapless, breathless, pain-jointed individual be one and the same person?

Breasting the rise onto Bluff Road, Louise saw that Captain Owston, the Crimean War veteran's old wooden house had not caught fire though there was no garden nor any roses left.

Winn Point, where her missionary uncle, whose boarding school for Japanese girls – the first in the land – she had come to help found, had completely vanished as had their Union Church. But on the other side the circular Bluff Gardens with the Ladies Tennis Club looked untouched as if the flames had licked the perimeter and passed on leaving the bandstand James had built firmly standing. Encouraged by the sight, Louise walked on.

Though the going was easier now on the flat, Louise found Bluff Road fissured, twisted and rent at every yard. There were slabs of tarmac which made rifts of ledgered steps, while telegraph poles lay in a tangled mass of wires beside fallen electric power lines dangling ghost-like between pancaked houses. Louise knew the road so well she found it easy to recognise where she was by the landmarks: there was her sons' Victoria Public School's gatepost, the cannon by 'drunken Lewis's' drive, the weathercock askew on the skeleton of Dutch Mr Hegt's bungalow, the iron gates of the Bluff Library leading to nowhere. She knew every inch of the road she had trodden a thousand times, both as Louise Winn and Mrs James Winter.

Progressing more rapidly, Louise passed No. 89, the senior Pooles' house, which had held so many happy musical evenings and had started Camille on her career. The only thing left standing there was the scorched cedar tree on the lawn. Now came the site of the old British Camp, erected during the *shoshi* troubles (which had been the cause of James having to go into hiding with the friendly Samurai whose daughter he had married). All long before her time. Next came the Carew's house – focus of a notorious scandal when Mrs Carew, who had a lover, was found guilty of murdering her husband by arsenic poisoning, and on to where the wreck of Christ Church lay on the ground. Here great chunks of the building, where James' funeral had taken place, mingled with the blackened fence of the Foreign Cemetery opposite.

Scrabbling her way in, Louise found a gruesome sight of tossed tombstones in a macabre upheaval of coffins split apart and scattered through the broken terraces. It was as if Hatsu's demons from the depths had forced their way through the graves in a devilish volcanic debauch. To die was one thing; to be wrenched in death from a peaceful resting plot was another. To Louise this desecration seemed to be the final indignity.

"Oh Lord, Lord," she breathed, sick with revulsion and repugnance, the words torn from her, "Lord, is there no grace left upon the earth of Thy creation? Where, where, Oh Lord is Thy mercy?" In a frenzy of abhorrence, Louise looked frantically around for James's grave. She was sure she would recognise the beautiful carved oak casket that had rested surrounded by a mountain of flowers in their

The Order of the Star

drawing-room, repelled yet drawn to think she might see his skeleton. She searched vainly here and there, but in the disorder and her distress lost her bearings and could find no trace of it or of him.

Blindly now she continued on her way. Over the broken colonnades of the Gaiety Theatre she climbed, and into the grounds of the British Naval Hospital, a mass of ruined wards, its lower terraces downthrown from where so many had fallen to their deaths or been burnt as was poor old Maurice Russell's fate. She found the new humped graves by the ruptured tennis courts, one of which was Camille's, her name scratched on a rough cross. And she had nothing, no offering to place upon it. No flowers, no branch, nor even a withered leaf left in the devastation of a scorched earth.

Blinded with tears Louise stumbled on the twisting tortured road to 'Akamatsu', Pinelands; now without any pines but still home, a home on which all her hopes were centred. Here surely something could be salvaged? It was not until she turned in over the half-burnt gates and saw the totally flattened ruins of home, stables and outhouses, with nothing left but a few blocks of chimney-stacks scattered about, a few scarred trees half standing in a desolate, blasted waste which had once been a treasured garden, that the full enormity of her loss hit her with a blow that sent her reeling onto the seared grass in a near faint. For a long time she lay there, looking up at the sky, seeing nothing, too tired to make the effort to get up.

After a while her head cleared and Louise found her practical mind going methodically over the facts: Camille lay in her shallow grave; James's bones lay scattered somewhere down the cemetery hillside; her home was no more. Everything was lost: her house, her possessions, her income,

James's fortune gone. All his money had been invested in the now non-existent factories, warehouses and offices; all the painstakingly collected silk waste that had spurred his fortune on (up until James had discovered its value, the broken threads of silk waste had been discarded and thrown into a corner of the weaving rooms) was burnt, together with those quantities of valuable bales of pure silk waiting to be exported. The very silk-worms up country must be ravaged, even the mulberry bushes they fed on razed from the earth by the inferno in the countryside.

What else had James left her? Valuable properties, other houses, blocks of shops, shares galore in local firms and businesses – he had wanted to put all his riches back into the Treaty Port for the people. The petroleums she had given Camille as her marriage *dot* were the one exception. Of what good were burnt properties? What good were banks with all their deeds and records destroyed, the very businesses no more? All gone. The work of two generations erased. There was no hope of redress, no insurance against *fire through earthquake* – it was the fire, with the insurance company's refusal to insure against it, that was the ruination. Without the fires she could have rescued some of her possessions, could have lived in the outhouses, could have rebuilt her home, the silk business could have been salvaged; but not now, not after the fires, and no money with which to rebuild.

For she did not own the shattered land she lay upon: no settler owned the land which was but leased to them from the government in the old Territorial Treaties.

It was total loss spelling absolute ruin. She saw it all clearly. She had nothing left, only the ragged clothes she stood up in – no, that was not the whole truth for she

The Order of the Star

had been wearing her usual jewellery of rings, brooch, and long jade necklace ready to go out to her bridge four yesterday.

Yesterday? Surely not *yesterday*? More like aeons ago, a lifetime away . . . Nothing left of the past . . . not even James's grave to visit to place the single rose on it as she used to pin one to his buttonhole when he went off to work. No roses, no grave . . . Dear God, where would they take Camille – twice buried, she who had a horror of interment, her 'place of gloom' in her poems?

Feeling herself driven, drifting and anchorless into an unfamiliar, alien world away from her home, bereft of her own kin and her friends, lost even to who she was or where she belonged, Louise felt impelled to scratch among the relics of her house and find something to tell her that there had been a past. Forlornly she knelt in the still-warm ashes of the building. Despairingly she sifted with her fingers through the smutty residue. All she came across were slivers of glass, blobs of metal, a scrap of one of the glazed porcelain urns that had stood by the front door, the distorted frame of the Bechstein piano, and the seemingly intact laminated ashes of books which crumpled into dust in her hands when she tried to lift them.

The afternoon sunshine shone bakingly hot upon her back; the tight wig was a torment. Unable to stand it any longer, Louise tore it off and threw it petulantly onto the pyre. She might as well chuck away the darned thing with everything else in her life! Who cared now if she reappeared with short hair turned white overnight? Could well have happened after what she had gone through! But she would not reappear. She was far too tired to start again, too tired to move even. She would lie here on the pile of her house and let merciful oblivion creep over her. To be allowed to die was all she asked.

In an automatic reflex, while half-lying face down in the ashes, Louise went on scraping away with her small, practical, dirt-ridden and grime-nailed hands. One unaccustomed ring on her finger surprised her. Ah yes, Camille's engagement ring. She had taken it off that slim hand . . . for the child. *Child*? She had forgotten about Camille's . . . What was that? Something glinting that caught her eye. A gleam of silver? She prodded in the ashes to look more closely, scraping the dirt away all round. Red glowing in the silver, rays of the sun reflected; it looked alive!

And from the depths of her despair and the debris of her home, Louise drew from the ashes James's Order: *The Order of the Star of the Rising Sun* presented to James for his philanthropic work amongst the Japanese community by the late Emperor Meiji in a grand ceremony at the Imperial Palace in Tokyo. All those years ago. How she had dressed up for the occasion. How wonderful it had been and how proud she was of her tall, handsome James! A red letter day if ever there was one . . .

Kneeling up, Louise brushed the dirt off the Star, rubbed it with her fingers, polished it on her skirt. Tenderly she held its smooth surface to her hot cheek, cupped it this way and that to watch it glinting in the sun. In wonderment she gazed at it, gazed and gazed at the bright round ruby centre surrounded by the shining white and silver rays. She saw again the purple flowers on the hasp above the green enamelled Japanese characters. Tightly she held the Order, for, as Bertie had said, with it she held the memory of Camille. Camille and the Order!

The Order of the Star

The stars still shone.

They shone for her, a path of hope that would link her old life to another one. And there *was* life, new life, Izolda's life. She, Louise, was needed, badly needed; she had work to do. She must go . . . back . . . to the child.

Slowly then, for by now she was dead weary, Louise got to her feet and began to retrace her steps the way she had come. As haltingly she progressed, for the first time that day she looked out at the view of land and sea and saw how the smoke had all cleared away; how it was a perfect late summer's day, late in the day now with the westering sun shining from a cloudless blue sky.

In the peculiarly clean, clear atmosphere, she was able to see great distances inland, over the undulating hills to the far mountains even to Fujiyama – dear old Fuji that in her young days she had climbed in a party with James and he had given her the first indication of his love. When at the summit, as they waited for the sun to rise, he had taken her gloved hand and held it in his strong warm grasp. There was Fujiyama with her everlasting summit of snow standing lofty and majestically unconcerned above the tortured plains.

The vista of land was all strangely beautiful. It reminded her of a scene long lost, long forgotten. She puzzled for a while as she staggered on in her exhaustion as to what it was, and then it came to her with such clarity that her eyes lit up, a smile crossing her drawn face. Of course! It had been like this when she had first seen the Treaty Port in its early days: flat virgin land between the headlands with only the cluster of a fishing village, and no tall buildings to block the horizon.

The old, familiar, close-knit colony that had arisen in the last century was gone. The surviving residents would be taken by ship to be dispersed all over the world. This place, this colonial life, was no more. It was finished.

The famous International Treaty Port of Yokohama was dead.

Part One

The Parsonage

1924–1928

Chapter Five

The nineteenth-century church, within a stone's throw of the red-brick Parsonage, was situated in the delightful small parish of Mesbury, south of Guildford in Surrey. Mesbury was an isolated hamlet consisting of a few half-timbered cottages looking out on to a green where, on summer weekends, leisurely cricket was played. Worshippers walked, rode bicycles or drove in dog-carts and governess-carts, while the wealthy travelled in chauffeur-driven cars, through the sleepy countryside of rolling fields, green hedges and undulating farm lands, to hear the Reverend J B Forster's rousing sermons.

The congregation filled the church in serried ranks strictly in order of precedence, the 'county' to the fore, the labourers and farm hands with their families to the rear. There was a reserved box for the local squire and another for the household of the Parson. The Forsters were well liked in the district: she was a pretty woman with two mannerly sons, and the fervid Parson was admired for his strict ethics. It looked as if nothing could disturb the untrammelled tranquillity of this regimented existence of parson and family. Therefore it was unexpected, to say the least, when Mrs Forster announced to her husband that after an eight year gap she was again with child.

However, once accustomed to the idea, Mrs Forster hoped for a daughter, and Mr Forster stoically accepted the circumstances as the bountiful Lord's will. Other than baptising babies at the church's ornate font, he had little contact with small children. Their two sons had been brought up in the large nursery wing of the Parsonage with its basement and servant's quarters well away from the main part of the house. Thus, when his wife went into labour Mr Forster took himself off in the dog-cart to stay with his sister in Guildford until it was all over. He had not the slightest inkling that the happy event was to completely disrupt the unworried, even tenor of his life.

After a lengthy and difficult *accouchement*, Mrs Forster was delivered of a nine-pound son. This beautiful baby, with his peach-like complexion and tight fair hair, when put into her arms was by common consent of all present named 'Curly'. But fever took hold of Mrs Forster and any milk that she may have had, dried up. From the day of his birth the monthly maternity nurse bottle-fed and took over the care of the adorable baby, and, so that the invalid should not be disturbed by his cries – not that he ever did cry – took him off to the nursery wing where he became entirely hers. With Mrs Forster's continuing illness, Nurse stayed on permanently, and of necessity took over the housekeeping as well.

Five years passed, during which time the main part of the Parsonage was turned into a nursing home for Mrs Forster with doctors coming and going. Consultants arrived from London, and one expert on puerperal fever and the aftermath of mental illness, travelled all the way from Munich. Three nurses lived in: a day nurse, a night nurse and a 'spare' to

The Order of the Star

take over when the other two had their days off. On top of this an extra maid was installed to wait on the nurses whose demands, Cook declared, were incessant. The expense was enormous. Mr Forster's stipend was quite inadequate to pay for the daily outgoings, let alone the nurses, the chemist's bills and the extra staff. The faithful parishioners could not help noticing how careworn Mr Forster looked in the pulpit, shoulders bowed by his misfortune.

However there was some good news in the family. The two older boys were doing well at preparatory school, Curly had grown into a fine healthy lad, Nurse was indispensable and utterly reliable, and Mrs Forster's health had somewhat improved. She could, with a little help, dress herself and walk down the polished front stairs to spend the days in a *chaise-longue* in the morning room, her meals brought to her on a tray. The doctors, however, gave out little hope that she would ever fully recover. Only one nurse was retained, the extra staff were dismissed and Nurse nobly said that she could manage without her nursery maid if the Reverend would increase her wages. He could not, and he asked her into his study.

"I wish to speak to you confidentially. Please sit down," he said stiffly, while indicating a chair. "Can I rely on you to let the information I am about to impart go no further than these four walls?"

"Of course, Reverend. I would not dream of repeating . . ." Nurse sat back in a comfortable leather chair. Never before had she *sat* in his study, and now, as well, she was being taken into his confidence! She guessed it was something to do with her wages since the nursery maid had gone. She had no idea of his financial situation, but she knew medical expenses were exorbitant unless one was 'on the panel' – the doctor's list of poor patients, covered by insurance – as she was, and considered it to be a degrading position.

Fortunately she had excellent health, as had Curly. If she adored her 'ewe lamb' and spoilt him abominably despite her strict principles, she also greatly revered his father, 'the Reverend' as she called him, and would do anything for him. He was a figure to be admired, a tall, thin clergyman with a beard and deep-set fervent eyes. On Sundays she sat with fidgeting Curly in their box, and immensely enjoyed the delivery of his thunderous sermons. The telling pointed finger sent pleasant shivers up her spine. What a man! And how frustrated he must be with an invalid wife! That poor lethargic lady who every now and then, when suffering one of her turns, had to be sedated, posed no female rival in the house, and in fact had little say in anything. She, the nurse, was in an enviable position of authority.

"The truth is, Nurse," Mr Forster sat facing her from his desk, "my small private means has entirely gone on my dear wife's illness, and I find myself in debt to the bank, a position I abhor. I can in no way increase your salary unless—"

"Please do not think of it," Nurse interrupted, eager to earn his gratitude.

"Most generous of you Nurse, but neither can I pay the staff nor my wife's nurse. We have come to a crisis: the bank is foreclosing at a time when the two older boys should soon be following in my footsteps to Rugby. More expense," he sighed heavily. "I am determined that at whatever cost they shall go."

"Quite right, Reverend, if I may say so. You must not deny them public school."

The Order of the Star

"I have a plan. To put it into practice I shall need your co-operation. It all hangs upon you."

"Anything you suggest," Nurse sat forward eagerly in her chair, her plain scrubbed face glowing with pride.

"I have been informed from certain quarters that it is a paying concern to take in so-called 'lodger children', preferably ones who are at boarding school so that one can have some peace in term time. By this I mean children from the *right background*; you understand, Nurse?"

"Oh yes."

"Those for instance whose parents are in India, maybe in the Forces, some in the Colonial Services. We have space in the nursery, and enough domestic staff. It seems common sense to make use of this if it would benefit us, and of course the children in our care, and, er . . . pay off . . . But, as I said before, it all depends on whether you are willing. I thought that I would give Curly lessons in the mornings to relieve you for a few hours. I wondered too, now that my wife is better, if you would use your hospital training to look after her as well, and then we could dispense with this nurse. As you know they are always leaving, and they upset the staff. Personally I can't stand the sight of the one we have at present! It would be so much more pleasant if you, Nurse, as a trusted member of the household, could take over. Naturally we would come to a financial agreement. For the lodgers I suggest you are paid so much extra per capita."

"How many children do you suggest?" Nurse asked, slightly overwhelmed by all this. She liked the idea, though, of looking after Mrs Forster and so not being entirely relegated to the nursery wing as she had been up until now. The hospital nurse had practically nothing to do but supervise the bathing and dressing. She herself would see that there was a handbell so that she could be called if Mrs Forster needed her during the day. As for the lodger children . . . Well, only in the holidays was not too onerous, especially if Curly had lessons in the mornings so that she could get on with other work. In any case the darling would one day have to go to boarding school and she would be given notice; that would break her heart. But if she took up this new capacity she would stay on as housekeeper and supervisor and be able to see him in the holidays; she would virtually become a permanent member of the family . . .

"The numbers are entirely up to you, Nurse. I believe I can rely on your judgement to be, er – er, as frugal as necessary. By that I mean no need for extravagances, no luxuries. Wasted on children, bad for them. Plain fare is best. Well, Nurse?" He had worked it out to his own satisfaction that they could accommodate ten boys if they doubled them up into dormitories. There was also that extra maid's room in the top attic, at the moment used as a box room. Easy to clear that out. The charge of four or even five pounds a week would soon mount up and the debt to the Bank would be paid off in a year with only Nurse's fees and the extra food to be deducted from the profit. In fact if the scheme were a success they could soon be living free themselves!

"I think it worth a try, Reverend. We can start with two or three boys and see how it works." The more Nurse thought about it the more enthusiastic she became. The housekeeping was already entirely her province. Mr Forster never interfered, and he would not query the bills. She could skimp on all sorts of things for those lodger children. No one would know. She could see herself putting away quite a nest-egg for her own retirement.

The Order of the Star

"Magnificent, Nurse! I knew I could rely on you. I shall spread the project around in the district. Humm . . . Advertise only in the parish magazine . . . don't want to make it sound like an institution with a capital 'I', and I think better not mention that my wife is an invalid. What I envisage is a 'home-from-home' atmosphere for boys like ours . . ."

And so the plan, born out of duress, took off, and in no time they were fully booked with further names put down on a waiting list. The mere mention by word of mouth that the 'home' was a parsonage with a trained nurse in attendance for the children, was enough. Parents or guardians came, saw the old creeper-clad Parsonage in its lovely country setting, and liked it.

Mr Forster kept the accounts. Everything was extra to the basic fees. The parents were naturally charged for their offspring's pocket-money, for any purchases at the village or at the nearest chemist's, outings, (such as there were) and each child supplied his own linen. Two small boys arrived who were not yet at boarding school. Mr Forster gave them lessons with Curly in his study for which he charged the parents a good bit more. All the children were of an age where they could look after themselves with supervision. A weedy little boy who was an orphan arrived, brought by his guardian; there was apparently plenty of money but he had nowhere to go. Nurse said he could share Curly's room.

To start with things ticked along nicely. The money poured in, Nurse never having earned so much in her life. Nevertheless it was not long before she began to feel the strain resulting from the new permanent lodgers so that holidays or no holidays she was always at it. The tiredness caused a consequent sharpness of temper when she chivied and shouted at her unruly flock; and when that did not prevail she took the slipper to them.

It was at about this time that a distinguished-looking man arrived to view the Parsonage. That he was in some sort of exigency was apparent due to his sombre appearance. Though he told only the barest outline of his story, he left them in no doubt that the matter was urgent. His small daughter had to be housed and housed quickly.

"*Daughter?*" Mr Forster had not thought of a girl. He turned to Nurse.

"How old?" she enquired briskly as she took in the extremely good-looking, clean-shaven man, impeccably dressed in a tropical suit. She was impressed by his air of authority despite his harassed expression. She noted the grey flecks in dark hair brushed straight across his forehead. She had never seen a more handsome man.

"Izolda is about to be four."

"We are not a kindergarten. Our youngest boys are seven years of age."

"The child is only two years younger than Curly," opined Mr Forster. The father was very much the *right sort*. "Up until now we have only had boys here, several of whom are at boarding school, you understand. Who recommended us to you, may I ask?"

"Admiral and Lady Seymour. I at one time served under him." To Izolda's father, having found himself in an appalling predicament, the Seymour's suggestion of the Parsonage paying guesthouse for children, had come like a life-saver. The 'home' was far enough away from where he lived in The Manor, a grand country house in a large estate he now managed, yet not *too* far away.

The Order of the Star

"Ah yes, the Seymours," nodded Mr Forster. They were parishioners he would not wish to offend; the Admiral was generous with money for the repair of the church tower. Better to keep in with them. "What do you think, Nurse? The top bedroom would do nicely for a girl on her own. Would you take her on?"

"She's a sweet little thing." The man who was her father appealed to the nurse, looking her straight in the eye with all his considerable charm. "I'm sure you'd look after her beautifully."

"I'll manage," Nurse succumbed, wanting to please both the Reverend and the father. "She'll make a nice quiet playmate for Curly."

Not two months previously, in the stress of the moment, Izolda's father had, under great pressure from his new wife, agreed that his daughter's constant companion all over the world since her birth, the adored Nanna, must leave. Weeping bitterly, Nanna, who had once promised her mistress that whatever happened she would never leave Izolda, and consequently had offered to take the child to Scotland with her to live with her own parents, had been torn away from her charge. Izolda, when she realized what was happening, screamed hysterically and clung to her beloved Nanna who was then driven away in a limousine to London to catch a train to Edinburgh. They said afterwards that Izolda cried solidly for four days, and the doctor had to be called in. The strict governess who was installed in Nanna's place could do nothing with her. The vale of tears had started.

Now, with her name having scarcely been mentioned, Izolda's fate was sealed for the second time. Thus she was uprooted again and left by her father at the Parsonage with a strange woman in charge and not a familiar face in the place – not even another little girl to share her room and play dolls with; instead, a crowd of big boys who teased her, and one in particular who became her tormentor.

Chapter Six

"Blow your nose, Izolda!"

"I haven't got a hanky."

"Why not? I put a clean pile in your room only a few days ago. Stop that snivelling at once!" With these usual reprimands Nurse ushered the unattractive child out of the attic bedroom where she had supervised the making of her bed. No clean sheeting in under a week was her rule regardless of the state of the sheets; laundry bills had to be kept down. Yet the ensuing unpleasant dampness seemed not to have had the desired effect upon Izolda, who was continually developing more bad habits. The girl was a hopeless case. Just look at the skinny thing slinking down the linoleum-covered back stairs. "Stand up straight will you; why haven't you brushed your hair properly? And *where is your slide?*" Nurse henpecked.

"Curly took it," Izolda said sulkily. Nurse was cross with her. However hard she tried to please, Izolda could never succeed, and Nurse was the only grown-up she had any real contact with.

"How *dare* you insinuate that Curly stole it!" A hand came from the rear and gave her a slap which, had she not been holding onto the banisters in anticipation, would have caused Izolda to stumble and fall down the narrow staircase. "Curly would *never* take anything that was not his, the little angel. As for you, you cause me more trouble than all the other children put together," Nurse scolded, sucking in breath through badly fitting teeth, and then exuding air with righteous indignation. "The way I have to nanny you, no one would think you're nearly five and still haven't learnt to tie your shoelaces." The nagging monotonous voice went on and on. "Now, go and wait for me in the nursery while I fetch some scissors. Your hair is all over your face. There is nothing for it; I shall have to cut a fringe."

"But Grandma will—" wailed Izolda.

"I know your grandmother sends ribbons and books and things," interrupted Nurse. "It's your own silly fault if you keep on losing them."

It was on a high summer's day that Izolda walked, in the curious crab-like fashion she had developed, shoulders hunched, wary head sideways expecting a cuff, along the back corridor of the dark rambling Victorian parsonage and into the empty first-floor nursery to wait. Nurse, perpetually busy, was sure to be diverted by the ringing of Mrs Forster's hand bell, but she never forgot, however long the interruption, and Izolda had learnt the hard way that if she went about her own business in the interim, even going to the lavatory, she would face Nurse's wrath on return. So, obediently, Izolda sat gingerly on the edge of a hard chair and waited. The reason why she had needed a hanky to mop the tears, and why she now sat on the *edge* of the chair was because she had been beaten with the hairbrush that morning for wetting her bed again, and her bottom felt too sore to sit on.

While waiting for Nurse to come and chop her hair, Izolda read from a large book called *Josephine and Her Dolls* that

The Order of the Star

her grandmother had posted to her as well as five little books about animals, some of which also had mysteriously disappeared with her slides. In the dolls book, one coloured illustration showed 'Granny' with spectacles (not a bit like her grandmother who in any case was 'Grandma'), another, 'Quacky Jack', a yellow duck in a sailor suit who was forever cheeky. Izolda felt a great sympathy for Quacky Jack who was always being sent to Coventry for being naughty. But at least *he* knew why he was put in the corner, whilst mostly *she* did not. She was so bemused by all the things she did wrong in the terrifying Parsonage, and all the admonishments, cuffs, whacks and now beatings she got from Nurse, that she was never cheeky as Quacky Jack was. *She* wouldn't dare! When put in the corner – the boys giggling behind her – she just stood there facing the wall with a frown on her face and trying hard to think what she had done this time. As a precaution she took to saying 'sorry' whenever Nurse appeared, hoping to diffuse the next outburst, which it never did.

Curly called the doll's book cissy, but cissy or not, Izolda loved it and longed to be Josephine with her hair neatly tied in a big bow, and to own a collection of assorted dolls. She had been given toys, but they, too, had a habit of disappearing. Worst of all, the rag doll that she always took to bed with her had vanished. Her grandmother had given it to her in China to make up for the one which had burned. She could not remember that time, but there was a sort of picture in her mind from hearing people talk about it – and there was the memory of names. She tried not to think of those names, for that made her cry. When she cried the boys sang in chorus: *'Cry-baby bunting, Dadda's gone a-hunting.'* They were always calling her cry-baby, or cissy, and now smelly, and she knew she was all those things and there was no end to it . . .

So she counted. Someone in the hazy times before she came to the Parsonage had taught her to count, and she was proud of being able to do so. Somehow it was comforting to count; totting up numbers on her fingers to get the awful disgrace of the present punishment to pass. When she was waiting she counted seconds into minutes, sometimes into an hour, though she tended to get mixed up with how many sixties she had done. And she counted the days into weeks . . . months. She knew she had come to the Parsonage when she was still three because she had had her fourth birthday there, and now her fifth was coming. One of the few things she had to look forward to was this yearly event when they had a special tea in the nursery, with a linen tablecloth over the oilcloth, and a lovely sponge cake with pink icing made by Cook especially for her, with candles on it which she was required to blow out in one puff. And there were no tears that day when everyone, including Nurse, was nice to her.

Then came the day *after* her birthday when time slowed right up, and she counted even more vigorously to get it to move again. She counted the banisters on the back stairs as she climbed them, the steps, the teeth in the design round the ceiling, the pebbles in the drive and the flagstones on the pavement on the rare occasion when Nurse had enough of that devious commodity, time, to take them out for a walk.

The Parsonage was fearsomely situated right next door to the church and the graveyard with its crooked headstones. Only an ancient and ragged yew hedge divided the two, a hedge that you could see through right to the monuments.

The Order of the Star

From the tombs at night rose skeletons dressed in white grave clothes. They made a clacking noise of rattling bones as they moved – or so Curly informed her.

He was two years older than she, and ghosts seemed not to worry him, though they terrified her. Curly had become the bane of her life – an expression Izolda picked up from Nurse – with his fearsome stories of ghosts, and the way he passed on to her the blame for things *he* had done. 'She's to blame,' with a pointed finger and a cherubic smile at her was sure to be believed by Nurse. Curly, in his turn, gave Nurse fits when he climbed the tallest tree in the garden, and then got stuck at the top bawling the place down, and the fire brigade had to be called.

The trouble was that Izolda *knew* that what Curly told her was true. When she woke in the night crying for those people she had lost in the mists of 'before' like Mummy or Nanna or Grandma, she heard the rattle of the skeletons outside her room. On moonlit nights she actually *saw* the knob of her door turning, and saw a white-clad swaying figure so frightening that she had to shut her eyes tight squeezing out the tears while she screamed for Nurse.

Understandably, Nurse did not appreciate being disturbed in the nights to have to climb the cold back stairs and shut up the screaming child who threatened to wake the household and Mrs Forster in particular, who would then need another powder to get her off to sleep again. Nurse was too stubborn, too set in her ways, too stupid, or just too unimaginative to appreciate that Izolda's ensuing second bad habit was brought on by her being so scared of skeletons – or whatever nonsense she was going on about – that she could not get out of the bed in the dark and use the potty put under it expressly for use. Instead Izolda would hold on, fall deeply asleep as small children do, and wake to find herself lying in the wet warmth and horrid smell which sometimes clung about her for days on end. To save on fuel the children were allowed only two baths a week at which time they were scrubbed by Nurse from head to toe, and their hair lathered with green soap by way of shampoo.

For the first bad habit Nurse scolded. For the second she used a slipper or hairbrush – bristle side or back, it did not matter to her which though it did to the victim – whichever weapon was closer to hand. Later, taking the cue from her admired master, she used a stick. The Reverend J B Forster, who ruled his household with a rod of iron, kept a whipping cane in full view on his desk in the study lest anyone should doubt his authority.

This then was the underlying reality, as the children sent to the Parsonage quickly found out. The older ones wrote to parents abroad complaining and asking to be taken away. Letters were vetted, but, aided and abetted by the older Forster brothers in the holidays – who suffered the same corporal punishment from their sadistic father and could not grow up quickly enough to get away – they found ways and means of smuggling letters out through servants and cottagers. As a result few of the bigger boys stayed more than a year.

But for the younger children under the charge of Nurse, who was considered mild in comparison with 'Sir', there was no escape.

To Izolda life at the Parsonage was a miasma of dark terror when she constantly got lost in the twists and turns of the building. She was forever being tripped up by Curly to fall headlong, or cuffed from behind by Nurse. She was in a

The Order of the Star

perpetual rush to try and catch up with all she had to do and keep up with the routine in a daze of not understanding what was happening to her, and in a haze about what had happened before to so change the time when there were cuddles and smiles and soothing noises if she fell down and hurt herself. Guilt set in. She must have done something terrible to be sent to the prison Parsonage.

In the times before if she slept alone the door had been left open for Nanna to come to her, and a night-light had always shone in her room so that she could see the pretty shadows on the walls. And there was the vague memory of the exquisite fragrant person who had rocked and sung her to sleep in the sweetest of tones. Sometimes she woke with the snatch of a song in her ears, and once when an older boy called Hugh was trying out the crystal set he had put together, she recognised the music.

"What's that?" she had asked.

"Puccini," he said, steady fingers manipulating a tiny screwdriver.

"What's P . . . Pu . . . ccini?" she persisted.

"He wrote opera. Oh, do go away and stop asking questions."

One of the most difficult disciplines in the Parsonage was 'regular habits'. Every morning straight after breakfast, the children queued up to 'go to the throne' – the boys called it the loo – a dark cubby-hole of a place on the floor below Izolda's bedroom, with a large mahogany seat (made for giants), upon which she perched precariously, unrelaxed and nervous lest she fall into the cracked blue porcelain pit below. If there was a non-event (often the case with the boys banging on the door and telling her to hurry up), revolting-to-taste and equally hard-to-swallow corrective castor oil was administered by Nurse. The result was agonising stomach pains which necessitated flying to the cubby-hole before further disgrace overtook her. Once, with the only bathroom she was allowed to use occupied, she had in desperation gone in the yew hedge, only to be discovered by eagle-eyed Nurse who was never there when needed but always there when one did something wrong.

"Dirty little girl; go and wash!" Nurse's tones showed her disgust and she administered the first smack Izolda had ever received in her life and she was sent to bed without supper, the door locked on her. Izolda had not cried but had sat on her bed trembling from head to toe in a state of shock at the physical chastisement, which she saw, even then, as a purveyor of much worse events to come in the unsure, nightmarish goblin world she found herself in.

Another loathed discipline was 'clean plates' at mealtimes taken in the large nursery which served as the children's dining-room as well as playroom. The rule demanded that nothing should be left on plates that was not actual bone. Due to Nurse's frugality in the interest of her master and mistress, and not a little in the lining of her own pockets, the children's food was of a cheaper quality than that served in the main part of the house, and they seldom saw a roast. The money saved went on luxuries such as chickens, game, calf's-foot jelly, salmon, hothouse grapes and peaches, even oysters to tempt delicate Mrs Forster's appetite. Much of the nursery cooking was left to the kitchen-maid who produced greasy Irish stews, fatty boiled beef served with soggy cabbage (and sometimes a cooked caterpillar found in it), and, invariably burnt black-skinned rice, sago or tapioca milk puddings to follow.

The Order of the Star

"Clean plates now," Nurse would urge after saying grace, "think of the millions of starving children in China."

Izolda, to whom the word 'China' meant something because she had gone there after the earthquake, would gladly have given her plateful to them over and over again. Often she gave up only to find herself faced by the same unfinished plate served up cold at the next meal before she was allowed anything else. Stubbornly she refused even to toy with it. A battle of wits ensued which once lasted twenty-four hours before Izolda, feeling as starved as the starving millions, gobbled up the cold fat-congested meal and was promptly sick which was even more frightening as, if she could not keep the food down, she *would* starve to death. 'And good riddance,' Nurse would probably say. But fear made Izolda cunning, and she thought up the ruse of spitting the offending bits of fatty horror into her fists and stuffing the remains under the gaps between the thumb tacks that kept the oilcloth in place.

Chapter Seven

The endlessness and hopelessness of Izolda's situation was, at infrequent intervals, lifted by a visit from her father. Although these events never lived up to her expectations, she always looked forward to them. She was given a bath and dressed by Nurse in one of the pretty dresses that had come with her, the hated black overalls discarded for the day. Despite the fringe, Nurse managed to tie a bow in her hair for the occasion.

The visits were infrequent because in the winter her father and step-mother went skiing to St Moritz and cruising in the West Indies. In summer they either raced at Ascot, sailed at Cowes, or took tea with the King and Queen at a Buckingham Palace Garden Party. But when her father did come, Izolda was allowed to descend the wide, polished staircase into the hall and drawing-room with its faded chintz covers on deep chairs, and have tea alone with him brought in by a maid who never appeared in the nursery.

By then Izolda had usually lost her appetite through being nervous of spilling the tea or dropping crumbs on the carpet. Her answers to her father's questions were therefore almost non-existent.

"Are you happy here?"

"Yes, thank you." What else could she say? If she said

The Order of the Star

'no' and told him that she got beaten he would tell Mr Forster and Nurse would hit her harder. Besides she was not sure about being *un*happy there, for she could not remember a previous life clearly enough to compare with this one. Also her father might then ask *why* she had been punished. How could she say, 'because I went in the bushes', or 'I wet my bed'? It would be rude and he would be horrified and embarrassed! Girls did not talk to fathers about going to the lavatory which was private and only mentioned to mothers and nannies.

"Are you sure? You're very quiet."

"Yes," she repeated while hanging her head. That was the end of that conversation.

He chatted a bit about what he was doing and where he had been, every now and then glancing at his wrist watch with, "Mustn't stay long or there'll be merry hell to pay." She looked at him obliquely. He was very dark haired, very brown, very nice, very clean, very strange . . . He was a stranger.

"You're growing to look like your mother." He spoke in a funny gravelly voice.

"Oh, good," she said, pleased. "Can you tell me about—"

"She's a non-person in our household, name never to be mentioned, and therefore so are you, poor little brat. I'll tell you . . . But not now . . . not yet," he said abruptly and got up. "Come on. Let's go outside in the garden."

They walked silently up and down the gravelled paths, he unaware that his long strides made her trot along beside him. She looked up from her small height perplexed by his unsmiling face. How could a person be a non-person, and she too? Had she said something to displease him? What had she done wrong this time? Should she be saying 'sorry'? She was always displeasing people, first the nurse and now her own father who was a stranger with whom she had nothing to talk about, nothing in common: no memories, no knowledge of – just nothing. Yet he was the one person who came to see her. He could explain so many things that worried her as to what had happened and why. And then he was gone and she went back to the nursery wing and tried to sort it out.

No, one could not tell fathers of intimacies, but Nanna would have understood how she was trying so hard to cope with her own bodily functions and how difficult it was to dress on her own, especially in the time allotted. Nurse was always in a hurry: 'Come on now; hurry up, child; for goodness sake get on with it!' It was hard to do up the buttons at the front of her bodice which also had buttons all round for her knickers to hang on; to tie her shoelaces or use the stiff button hook to button gaiters in winter; to put on her long-sleeved black overall which had to be tied at the back where she could not reach; to brush her hair, do her teeth, go to the loo and get the buttons undone before anything happened; to eat the large meals put before her; to undress, go to bed, try to sleep, open her eyes in the pitch dark, hear noises and be too terrified to get out of bed . . . Wet . . . Get up . . . bend over, be beaten; wash perfunctorily while sobbing . . . dress, the whole cycle starting up again. All these daily tasks appeared insurmountable in that first, endless year.

But the counting helped, and a year passed and then another and she kept it up despite Nurse asking suspiciously what she was doing and saying she looked as if she had a screw loose, and to stop it at once.

After a while she no longer got lost in the rabbit warren of the secondary wing, and she began to sort out the boys.

The Order of the Star

The two eldest Forster sons she seldom saw in the holidays. They were both nearly grown-up with voices that were breaking, and sometimes they dressed up in smart suits, hair slicked with water, to have dinner with their father in the dining-room and learn how to pass the port.

Even they were not immune from a beating. No one was, presumably not even little girls if they tried Nurse too hard. If anyone fell out of step for the slightest misdemeanour, even for untidiness or slovenly appearance, the cane was administered with considerable force in the study; the culprit 'brought to heel'. The boys were all scared stiff of 'Sir' and his cane, and most frightened of all was Izolda. Whenever she saw him, even in the distance, she would scuttle away and hide in the attic, her heart beating like a captured bird's.

There were two boys Izolda came particularly to like. One was Hugh Holden, the boy with the crystal set, a big boy who was soon going to public school and came to the Parsonage for the 'hols'. His parents lived in Hong Kong which meant he seldom saw his father, and his mother only once every two years. Hugh was the first boy to speak kindly to the lost little girl with the straight lank hair who was more often than not in tears. He took notice of her because he had a baby sister not much older than she in Hong Kong.

"How cissy," said Curly. Hugh boxed him on the ears and he went off to find Nurse.

"What's her name?" asked Izolda.

"May."

Oh, what a lovely name! Oh to have a baby sister called May, all blowing bubbles and roundness and sweetness! "I wish *I* had a baby sister," she said.

"Perhaps you will."

Izolda frowned. To have a baby sister or brother you had to have a mummy, and her mummy . . . But she had a step-mother? But if it was her step-mother's she wouldn't be allowed to see the baby, would she? It was all too difficult . . .

"Don't let Curly run rings round you," Hugh advised from where he was tuning his crystal set, "he's a bloody little sneak." Nurse, coming into the room at that exact moment, heard, and reported him to Mr Forster. He was beaten for swearing.

In summer the bigger boys played tennis on the grass court overshadowed by the yew hedge into which the ball was always disappearing as the loose netting surrounding the court was full of holes.

"Be my ball-boy," invited Hugh in some exasperation one day. From then on Izolda became his shadow. She loved scampering after the ball behind the back line and soon was expert at bouncing it towards him. Occasionally he gave her three-pence in recompense so that she could buy sweets when they went to the next village, and sometimes he let her hold his racket and showed her how to hit the ball over the net. These happenings were red-letter days in her life.

The other boy Izolda liked was as unhappy as she, but unlike her was no trouble at all. He was Pip, an orphan. His father, killed in the Great War, had been posthumously awarded the VC; his mother had died of influenza soon after the Armistice. He was a shrimp of a child who spent his days sitting around as inconspicuously as possible. Sometimes he came and sat with Izolda on the low window ledge in the nursery under which she kept her few toys (those that had

The Order of the Star

not been lost), and looked at the pictures in her books while she turned the pages, though he never spoke. She knew he could *hear* because he responded to 'Pip' when called, and she made up stories about the pictures to tell him. Neither of them could read. Nurse was supposed to read to them and give them lessons, but she never did. Sometimes, when Pip had liked a story he rubbed his head on her arm to show his appreciation. She liked that. It made her feel motherly towards him.

But then things began to get worse. Izolda's third bad habit started after Hugh was caught smoking in the graveyard behind a headstone, and was thrashed in the study. He made not a sound (unlike Curly who yelled blue murder when beaten) but the whole house heard the sound of too many swishing thwacks. At tea time he stood white-faced at the nursery table unable to sit, and Izolda could not look at him for the awfulness of it and for the bleeding of her heart for him. And that day there was a burning silence in the Parsonage with the unpleasant smell of simmering resentment.

"Too bad," the pink-cheeked maid who waited on them at table said, while looking significantly at Nurse, "an 'e such a nice young gen'leman."

That night, after Hugh's thrashing, the skeletons had been especially troublesome, and Izolda had woken not only wet but to find an inexplicable hole through the wallpaper into the plaster by her beside. That day started with a furious Nurse giving her six of the best so that she should never do such a destructive thing again. But she did, again and again, and when the holes were plastered up by a man who came in, they reappeared in a new row alongside the bed. She could not stop doing it because she did not know when or how or even if it was she who did it in the haunted Parsonage. And in the mornings, without even being told, she bent over the tell-tale bed and lifted her sodden nightgown to receive the agonising red-rashed hits to add to all the other hurts.

Then, breathless with sobs and tight-chested with misery, she washed as best she could by tipping the cold water jug into the wash basin, dressed, and descended the stairs to face the taunts of Curly who held his nose and edged away from his place next to hers at the table.

There *were* some enjoyable times at the Parsonage. There were colourful postcards from her father from all over the world, and letters from her grandmother in parcels containing clothes and toys. If it were term time and the older boys were away at school, sometimes Izolda would trail Nurse for days on end with a letter in her hand, Nurse all the time getting more and more annoyed. The nice maid could not read or she would have read it for her when Nurse was busy. Cook could read, but none of them were allowed into the kitchen in the basement which was two sets of stairs down from the nursery.

She was only allowed to wear her best clothes on Sundays to church, the worst day of the week for Izolda, when she had to sit for an hour and a half listening to Mr Forster's thunderous voice. She daren't look at him. She hung her head between hunched shoulders the whole way through, tried to block her ears by swallowing, and passed the time by counting everything from the people in the pews to the tiny panes in the stained-glass windows. And she thought of her grandmother who had sent her the dress she was wearing and who had once lived in China as well as Japan, but who now lived on the Continent (wherever that was) and, after the traumas in the East, had been left with a 'bad heart'.

The Order of the Star

A bad heart meant that she could *fall down dead* at any moment which was a worry and would be the end of letters and parcels. The Continent was a long way away by boat and train and her grandmother had been too ill to make such a journey, but in her last letter she said she was better and was being pushed out for walks in a bath chair 'just like a baby'. The thought made Izolda smile – and at last she was out of the church and away from the fearsome presence of Mr Forster.

Another thing she looked forward to was going out in the dog-cart, until one day the pony fell down in the shafts spilling the children onto the road in a heap and causing Izolda to develop another phobia: one of horses in general. And there was a treat the older boys enjoyed when they were permitted to make toffee and fudge on an oil stove in the nursery while the younger children watched in anticipation of being handed pieces of the resulting delicacies.

When one day the stove, which stood on the table, caught fire, Hugh smothered it with a rug, swept it up from off the table, and flung it out of the window where it harmlessly burnt itself out on the lawn.

"Bravo!" everyone cried, "Hugh has saved the house from burning down!" But the oilcloth was ruined, and when Nurse pulled out the tacks to replace it with a new one, there, by Izolda's seat, the most revolting pieces of green, decomposing gristle, fat, and milk pudding skin were revealed. In disgrace, she was sent to bed early, without supper, and the following morning a new hole appeared next to the one that had been plastered up.

For once Nurse did not take up the hairbrush or slipper or stick or whatever. Instead, "You are beyond me, Izolda," she said throwing wide her hands in a gesture of giving up.

"Your persistent naughtiness defeats me. I can do no more. There is nothing for it but to send you to the Reverend."

"No, no, no not there. Please, please, Nurse. I'll be good; I'll never make holes again." Desperately Izolda grasped Nurse's skirt, her face as white as the starched apron.

"Yes, yes, yes. I've heard that one before. It's high time you learnt your lesson once and for all."

Ordered to make the dreaded pilgrimage to the study, Izolda knocked timidly on the door. "Come in!" boomed Mr Forster in answer to the faint tap. She opened the door, crept into the room and stood as far away from him as she could, her eyes riveted on the thin, flexible cane on his desk. She thought she was going to be sick. "Come over here!" Mr Forster ordered. Izolda advanced tentatively two steps. "Nurse tells me that you are a very naughty girl and that your behaviour is getting steadily worse; that you spit out the good nourishing food set before you; that you wake her up time and again in the night; that she has to do a great deal of extra washing on your behalf; and now the latest is that you deliberately pick holes in the wall of your bedroom. *Why?*"

"I, I don't know . . . Sir," Izolda mumbled, aping the way the boys spoke though she wondered if it should be 'Reverend' as Nurse addressed him. With horror she watched his bony hand creeping along the desk. He was reaching for the cane! He was going to whip her; he wasn't going to wait for a second, and her bottom was already sore from yesterday . . .

"What has happened to your tongue? Speak up, girl!" He thumped the desk. "Your uncooperative habits must stop immediately, understand?"

"Yes . . . Sir."

The Order of the Star

"As the only girl you ought to be a help to Nurse not a hindrance; set a good example to the boys." Mr Forster took in with distaste the small skinny child before him with her untidy straight hair cut into a fringe, wrinkled woollen stockings on thin legs, black cotton overall half off one shoulder. He wondered why she was dressed like that. But it was none of his business. Nurse knew best . . . Probably had a very good reason. Perhaps she had been teaching the younger ones to paint. She did a great job in the household. The cheques coming in were most satisfactory. Debts paid off; every comfort and care for his wife; older boys at Rugby. He appreciated that the holidays put an extra burden on Nurse. She was probably tired. "Will you try and turn over a new leaf in future?"

"Yes, sir." Her eyes were still on the cane. There was a pause when Izolda thought she was about to wet her knickers in fear.

"Off you go then." For a moment she was too paralysed to move. Then the blessed words of dismissal sank in and she bolted for the door.

"He didn't beat me, he didn't beat me!" she exclaimed, jumping up and down in relief in the nursery.

"You're such a cissy Father couldn't very well cane *you*," Curly gloated.

"If he had I'd have reported him somewhere – to the police or something." Hugh said darkly. "Now for goodness sake keep out of trouble like Pip here does."

Pip did get into trouble once. It was the day he was fiddling around with a button that had come off his house-shoe. Somehow it got up his nose, and the more he tried to fish it out the further up it went. In the nursery Izolda watched the doctor prodding Pip's nostril with a pair of surgical forceps. Eventually he produced the offending button.

"What a brave little man," he patted Pip's brown hair, "just like your soldier Daddy, eh? You won't stuff buttons up your nose again, will you?"

"NO!" said Pip very deliberately and distinctly, galvanising Izolda. So he *could* talk. It was the first time any of them had heard him say anything.

"Pip made a beautiful 'No'," she said to Hugh on the drive when his trunk was being loaded into a taxi for the autumn school term. He was not returning. His mother was coming home for the Christmas and Easter holidays. Mr Holden had, on the strength of Hugh's letters, sent in notice of his leaving.

"Pip would," Hugh replied. "He's an intelligent little boy. He only needs someone to give him a bit of individual attention and he'd soon be talking. And if you had someone to give you the same you'd soon be reading and writing instead of counting all those numbers."

"Where will you go for next year's summer holidays?" Izolda asked despondently.

"To a long-suffering aunt in Swanage. By God that'll be fun after a place run by a sadist parson and his sycophant masochistic nurse. Now come on," he saw Izolda's eyes brimming over, "why don't you get your grandmother to take you on?"

But with Hugh's departure despair overtook Izolda. No more Hugh to look forward to in the holidays. No more being his ball-boy and earning threepennies to buy sweets. The days would drag and drag with never anything to do but count the time away to try and get it to move. Then when her *Josephine and Her Dolls* book disappeared, everything

The Order of the Star

became blacker and blacker. The days were getting shorter and shorter and the dark of long winter nights closed in upon her like a heavy blanketing cloud cutting out all light and hope. She knelt up in bed on the grey towelling over the mackintosh sheet and changed her prayers from, "Please bless Mummy and Daddy, Grandma and Nanna, and make me a good girl and dry tonight and not make holes," to "Please God get Grandma to take me away like Hugh said. I'll be good for ever if you'll arrange it with her."

But God had so many prayers to cope with in His Heaven, so many starving Chinese children to rescue before He could deal with her, that really she did not expect He would ever have the time. And a great gulf of unhappiness deeper than before enveloped her, a forlorn hopelessness that in her mind was personified by the ugly black overalls she was forced to wear day after day. Izolda lived without hope because there was none for little girls who were sent to bleak parsonages where they were just a nuisance, and the only reason they were taken on was for the money they brought in. And with this despair came the next bad habit.

"Haven't you got enough habits already without having to invent a fourth?" Nurse hit her because the bed was wet and there was a new hole in the wall. Whack, whack, whack . . . "You're ripe for the loony bin, that's what you are," she panted. Whack . . . "You wretched" Whack . . . "child. You'll be the death of me . . . Phew, now let me see what you've done." She put down the weapon and examined a red patch on Izolda's forehead which was fast developing into a boil that would need lancing.

To Izolda this habit was no bad habit. It became a greater comfort than counting, and neither was she beaten for it. After saying her prayers at night kneeling up in bed with the blankets hunched over her shoulders, she clasped her hands before her and bumped her head on them gently: bump, bump, bump, so soothing and sleeping-making compared to the agony of whack, whack, whack. It disguised the noises of the dead bones rattling at her door. It bumped her into sleep.

But it did not send her to sleep quickly enough on dark haunted winter nights when the wind howled and the storms burst, the rain cascaded against her window pane and there were lightning flashes and the terrifying rumble and crash of thunder coming ever more frequently. Then the bumpings grew more violent, and she battered her forehead against the bedhead to stun her the more quickly into senseless sleep.

Chapter Eight

"Get smart! Your grandmother's coming to see you today." Nurse drew back the curtains to let the sun in. She pulled the bedclothes off Izolda's recumbent figure. "Thank the Lord you're dry. Hurry up and wash your face and do your teeth, and I'll help you to dress."

"Grandma? Wow! What shall I put on?" It was all excitement and summer again; the summer she was going to be eight. One, two, three, *four* years at the Parsonage and she had counted them all, every day of them, nearly every hour of every day. Her father seldom took her out. Had she ever been anywhere else?

"Your grandmother will be here at tea time. You can get ready now except for your dress which you'd better not put on until after lunch in case it gets dirty. Hurry now. Your forehead looks a mess. I'll put some cream on it and powder it over. Whatever will your grandmother think of a girl who bumps her head? Deary, deary me . . ."

The day dragged on. Izolda was afraid to do anything but sit still in case she soiled her best clothes. After lunch, when she had put on her dress, she waited on the garden bench facing the short rising drive. Her feet did not reach the ground, and clinging on to the bench with her hands on either side, she swung her legs clad in their white knee socks.

Evelyn Hart

She had long since grown out of her pretty party shoes, and so wore her brown lace-up ones. Her frock, loosely smocked, still fitted her. Nurse had let it down to its full length and put on a false hem. Her old petticoat trimmed with lace was far too short and felt uncomfortable underneath. Her straight hair was unadorned by bow or slide, for that would disturb the fringe and show the scar and red tell-tale bump marks on her forehead.

In agitation Izolda stared at the gate until her eyes watered. She wiped them with her now grubby hands. Would she recognise her grandmother? Would she understand the way she talked? She had boasted to the other children about having an American grandmother. That was something unusual – special. They were going to have tea on the lawn where she was not normally allowed to go because Mrs Forster could see them from her couch in the morning-room and they might disturb her. She was such a pretty lady, dressed in soft coloured gowns, so sad, languishing there and too tired to do anything for herself. Once Izolda had been invited to go in and see her, but she had felt awkward and not known what to say, and Mrs Forster had not asked for her again. None of the children knew what the trouble was, only that she had headaches.

Grandma was late. What had happened to her? Had her heart stopped, or perhaps the Blue Train with its long shiny sleeping cars had crashed? Nurse said they were always having train crashes on the Continent.

And then a taxi *did* turn in through the gates, and slowly made its way up the drive towards her. The driver got out and opened the back door and a little lady in a silk dress and straw hat descended. On seeing her Izolda felt an extraordinary rush of emotion and had to stand still and bite her lip to stop it trembling for all the scenes of the times 'before', as she called those buried moments from her past which surfaced every now and then. She *knew* her! Knew, knew, *knew* her! Even the dark green, patterned dress seemed familiar and also the small feet, not much bigger than her own, in the soft leather shoes the Chinaman had made with their dainty heels and narrow straps emphasizing her high insteps. And the hat skewed with sharp hatpins onto the silky white hair. The dark eyes under their beetling eyebrows searched round for her. The long jade necklace she remembered dangled; there was a narrow black velvet ribbon round her neck. Yes, oh yes, she knew her – knew her *exactly*!

"Why," Louise drawled in her soft Southern accent after telling the taxi man what time to return, "why, if it isn't Izolda . . . My how you've grown . . ." The child was rackabones thin, all long legs ending in those heavy shoes – quite unsuitable for a hot summer's day. Why had she not thought to bring some coloured *espadrilles* with their rope soles? And that dress? A baby dress she had sent years ago. If it had not been for Camille's eyes with the delicately marked eyebrows she would never have recognized the healthy, bouncing three-year-old she had last seen. Why did the father not buy suitable clothes? There was plenty enough money hanging around there in all conscience! The child was a shock, and she wanted no more shocks. She had had enough to last her several lifetimes. The doctor had said she would be fine in her great old age if she lived in a quiet going-along way for the rest of her life. *No more shocks.* And here was a big one. Well, what did she expect? Four years was a long time in a child's life. Louise pulled herself together and stepped forward to embrace her grandchild.

Evelyn Hart

Izolda did not respond to the embrace. She was not sure what to do. Her father always planted a kiss on her head and did not expect an answering one. Her grandmother smelt of eau-de-Cologne – she remembered that too! "I – I thought the train . . ." she managed, with an agonised look on her face.

"Why so fussed, honey? I'm not late," Louise, who never wore a watch and was always on time, said calmly. The child's flaccid lips brushed against first one proffered cheek and then the other. Where had all the sweet wet bud kisses gone? This silent child did not know how to kiss . . . They looked at one another for a while, then, "Take me to where we have tea. You are the hostess," Louise said practically.

Startled into taking the initiative, and proud to be in charge, Izolda led the way round the red-brick building, Louise taking in the oppressiveness of the heavy-leafed trees and the closeness of the graveyard which appeared to be part of the garden. Bit lugubrious wasn't that? She had had enough graves in her life as well as shocks. But the child wouldn't know about graves at her age, those many sad graves left so far away.

Under a spreading cedar in the front area facing the main bow-windowed rooms of the house, they came upon a table laid for tea.

"Come and sit down." Louise patted the seat beside her when once again the child seemed hesitant as to what to do, her sharp dark eyes at the same time taking in the moss on the lawn, the neglected herbaceous border, and the windows of the Parsonage that looked as if they could do with a lick of paint. "I've brought some books, but I've left them in the hotel as I thought it would be nice to chat on our first day.

The Order of the Star

What shall we talk about?" Louise asked as she composed herself on the cushions.

"How is your heart?" Izolda enquired politely about the instrument that had so concerned her. What if her grandmother fell down dead *now*?

"Better this year, thank you, Izarling, or I would not be here. My broken heart," she murmured to herself, and then aloud, "broken in more ways than one. The last time I came to England to deliver you and Nanna to your father, it was winter and I caught a bad cold. Didn't surprise me in the least. I dislike this country for sure. Never lived here in my life and never want to. Just look at it now, even in high summer," she gesticulated towards the overbearing yew hedge and the trees. "You can't see the sky: no upwards view." What it must be like in winter with the rain sluicing down . . .

"But, to continue with the story of my heart, the doctor explained how in a fit of coughing – and I can tell you I do not normally get colds – a valve snapped so that it was left like a motor-car running on two cylinders instead of three. Do you know about the mechanics of cars? No? No more do I. Anyway, with rest this engine of mine mended itself! I wrote that I was pushed out in a bath chair. You get my letters? I wonder why you don't answer them? It is impolite not to answer letters." Louise spoke so gently that the words could hardly be taken as a rebuke, but even so Izolda blushed. She should have answered the letters! How rude her grandmother must think her. That name 'Izarling' out of the 'before'; there had been all those 'darlings' floating around, theatrical 'darlings' someone had said – and the snatches of songs . . .

". . . made the effort to come to England once more. I

have to sign some documents in London; and, honey, I guess I wanted to see you again." Izolda heard her grandmother continuing and then felt her limp hand being taken off her lap by a warm gloved one, and squeezed.

Two years after the Yokohama catastrophe and the consequent wreck of her life, the family lawyer had told Louise that gathered from the ruins she would have a small income of about three hundred and fifty pounds a year to live on. He was investing the capital in five per cent War Loan which he declared to be 'as safe as the Bank of England'. After all she had been through Louise was quite certain that the Bank of England was no safer than anything else in this unstable world, and though after the wealthy years the amount seemed tiny, she was enormously relieved to find herself not a complete pauper. They had been poor when she had landed in Japan to live with her pioneering missionary uncle, and she could live frugally again. With no property left in the old Treaty Port to go back to, Louise had, bereft of the small child she had looked after in the interim, taken herself off to the only remaining member of her generation who had now settled in the South of France where the beautiful rocky shore resembled that of her Japanese 'Riviera'.

"Good morning, Mrs Winter. Izolda, you ought to have called me at once." Nurse bustled out to interrupt Louise's faraway thoughts, the crackle of her starched uniform showing her annoyance at having missed the taxi's arrival. "What have you done to your face? It's all grubby. Go inside and wash it this minute."

"Sorry," said Izolda and scuttled off.

The Order of the Star

"Good *afternoon*," corrected Louise in stiff tone, "I guess Izolda gave me a mighty nice welcome, thank you."

"How do you think she's looking? She's been as happy as the day's long since hearing you were coming."

"Sure, sure," Louise replied distantly. She was distracted by the very odd way the child had run off, shoulders hunched. "She's grown a lot."

"Yes, hasn't she?" rushed Nurse, "I'm always letting down hems, and never a scrap left on her plate – 'clean plates', that's my motto!"

"Grown *thinner* was what I was about to say, Nanny."

"*'Nurse'* if you please, Mrs Winter."

"That hairstyle does not suit her." Louise ignored the interruption, her down-turned lips disapproving. There was a peremptory tinkle of a handbell from the house.

"We had to cut a fringe. She's always losing her slides; such a careless child," Nurse bristled. "Excuse me a moment, that'll be Mrs Forster needing me. She has one of her bad migraines today."

"Fiddlesticks!" expressed Louise, but Nurse was already out of hearing.

"Let me see . . ." Louise began when Izolda returned with a clean face, her fringe combed down over her forehead, though Louise had noticed the red marks when grubby hands had disturbed the hair. She waited while a maid brought a tray of tea. "Do you want to pour?" Izolda shook her head. "Why not? Afraid of spilling some? Well, it doesn't matter, does it, if we spill it on the *lawn*? Some teapot spouts sure are bad pourers. I have – or rather had – a silver one which never spilled a drop." And she held a teacup over the grass and poured some tea in.

"See," she remarked merrily, "I told you it would spill! Not China tea," she sniffed into the cup, "and it's too weak for Indian. We'll have to leave the pot awhile to set. No tea cosy either. Have a sandwich while we're waitin'. Is that Nurse kind to you?"

"The trouble is . . ." Izolda hesitated.

"Well?"

"I'm so naughty she has to smack the devil out of me . . . The boys get beaten by Mr Forster," Izolda let out in a rush at the same time as giving a little involuntary shiver. "I once thought he would beat me, but he didn't . . . though he might if I go on."

"Whatever for?" asked Louise, startled.

"Making holes in walls and things like that." Izolda hung her head.

"Mercy me! Holes in walls?" repeated Louise, never having heard of such a thing. "Well, well, well." She shook her head, flummoxed. "Now, let's have our tea. How do you like yours? Plenty of milk and sugar?"

"I'm not allowed tea, just milk."

"Do you like milk?"

"No."

"Then you shall have tea." And she poured it out. "When did you last see your father?"

"Three months, one week, two days ago. I counted."

"*Three months*? Did you count on the calendar?"

"No." She was too ashamed to say that even if she had one she could not read the days and months.

"Would you like one?"

"Don't need it. I count the time."

"Isn't that rather a *waste* of time?"

". . . It, it passes it."

The Order of the Star

"What's that nasty mark on your forehead?" Louise examined it. "Did you fall down?"

"I bump it to get me to sleep," Izolda said sulkily, ashamed again.

To bump one's head to get one to sleep? What a mad idea. Was the child not quite all there, Camille's lovely bright baby? No, Louise discounted the idea. She supposed the child counted when she was doing something dull, or perhaps waiting to go out with her father – but *three* months. She could not get over that. It was not right when he lived no distance away. Instinctively she did not like the starched nurse. Nanna had never smacked – she had no need to. As for beating boys, that was a barbarous practice. She had had quite a contretemps over that in the old days with her British husband, not that he had ever beaten their sons, but he had sent the boys to boarding schools where they probably had been beaten. The child here looked to her frightened, even haunted. Certainly extremely nervous. She was obviously repressed. She should be running round the lawn turning cartwheels at her age instead of sitting beside her like a mouse, afraid of pouring the tea in case she spilled some. Camille at her age was a veritable tomboy, forever climbing trees with her older brothers.

She had only come for a few days. Maybe she would stay a few more to try and get to know the child whose appearance had given her such a shock, like a quiet fastidious little old woman with no playfulness or spark in her. It was unbelievable. Vivacious Camille's daughter, of all people! She could not stay too long for she could ill afford the hotel she had booked into in the next village and all the taxi fares. Of course coming to England was a ruse. The business documents to be signed in London could perfectly well have been sent by registered post, but she had wanted to see Izolda. The fact niggled her that the child never answered her letters or thanked her for the things she sent. She did not expect a long letter, just a few words ending with 'love from Izolda' in childish handwriting. Surely the nurse could have taken the trouble to dictate that much? Since Izolda was six she had sent money for her to have lessons. She liked to do what little she could to help, though of course the father was in charge. Even so she felt she owed it to Camille to keep an eye . . . She had been ill, very ill; she had come at the first opportunity.

"Nurse says Mrs Forster has a headache. Does she often have them?" Louise went on probing.

"I think so. Nurse looks after her as well as us."

"I hope she does not suffer from something infectious?" Louise was thinking of tuberculosis which caused many people to become permanent invalids as Mrs Forster seemed to be.

"Don't know."

The silence between them lengthened with the shadows, Louise getting nowhere with the child who appeared not to respond very much to anything, had eaten hardly any tea and sat quietly beside her swinging her legs. "Shall I read to you?" Louise asked at last. "What about the *Josephine and Her Dolls* I sent you?"

"It got lost."

"Lost? How?" Louise frowned.

"Don't know . . ." Izolda looked as if she was going to cry.

"Never mind. Go and fetch a book – any book." When Izolda returned with *Peter Rabbit*, Louise was sitting waiting with gold-rimmed spectacles on her nose. "Now, would you like to show me how well you can read, or shall I read to you?" Louise put her arm round the child to try and get some response out of her. She thought she felt the stiff little figure soften slightly to her touch and nestle into her form. That was better.

"You read please, Grandma."

"What shall we do tomorrow?" Louise asked later when it was time she left. "Would you like me to arrange for you to come to the hotel and we can have lunch together?"

"Yes, but . . . but I can't always finish my plate," Izolda gloomed.

"Of course not," Louise said smoothly. "You can order what you fancy and eat as little or as much as you like. I don't believe in Nurse's 'clean plates'."

"You *don't*?" Izolda looked up amazed.

"No I don't, and I don't believe in corporal punishment either."

"What's that?"

"Beating, or even smacking. Certainly not caning little boys. I'll come for you tomorrow, Izarling. Now run along and tell Nurse I'd like a word with her."

"*Josephine and Her Dolls* seems to be missing, along with other things I sent Izolda. It don't do for me to trouble to pack up and post playthings just for them to get lost," Louise said dourly when Nurse appeared. "I suggest you search the house until they are found."

"If the Reverend says so, Mrs Winter. I take my orders from him," Nurse replied huffily.

"Why, sure, you do just that," Louise said sweetly on her way to see Mr Forster herself. Later he saw her into the taxi and she was driven away.

Chapter Nine

Nurse was particularly cross that evening. She muttered on about being given orders from strangers, but next morning she set the servants to search, and in a built-in cupboard under the eaves in the attic, a dark place in which Curly had threatened more than once to lock Izolda, telling her that in a hundred years' time they would find her bones inside, they discovered a cache of her toys, books, hair slides, plus the beloved rag doll. Confronted by this evidence, Curly could not but confess to the crime, at the same time plainly showing his detestation for the usurper, Izolda, who had come unwanted into the Parsonage to take his rightful place as the youngest child and special pet of Nurse whose undivided attention he had had up until then.

Pained out of her usual rigid complacence that her ewe lamb could actually steal, Nurse took Curly down to his father where the story unfolded to be followed by the usual punishment. The household reverberated to Curly's howls, and Izolda stuffed her fingers into her ears, unable to bear it even for her persecutor.

A chastened Curly had lessons from his irate father, and a happy Izolda, clutching her rag doll, went off to spend the day with her grandmother. But try though she might, Louise could not get through to the child who scarcely

The Order of the Star

spoke, jumped at every sound and constantly looked over her shoulder in a twitch of nervous habit.

After lunch when they were sitting in the upstairs residents' lounge, Louise talked about her plans to return to her new home all to herself – up until then she had been staying with her sister-in-law, Maude, and her cousin, Julia – the garden she was going to make, her friends out there and the bridge parties she went to. Getting little response to all this, she opened a subject she would have preferred not to speak about. The wounds were still too raw.

"Do you remember your mother at all?" she asked inadvertently. Immediately she wished she could bite back the words for the labyrinth they might lead her into.

"No . . . but sometimes I think . . ." Izolda said uncertainly, and then, her pinched face lighting up, "but I would like . . . I mean, could you tell me about Mummy?" The unaccustomed word formed strangely on her lips. "Daddy won't talk about her."

From her chair, Louise looked across to Izolda and for the first time saw a spark of interest in the child's usually downcast face, a look of real eagerness in the large wide-set eyes so like her mother's. "Well, I guess I can tell you about her," Louise drawled. I'll veer away from the end and tell her of the early days, she thought. "Let me see, shall we start when she was a little girl like you . . . ?" And Louise began to tell her granddaughter about her mother. And in the telling she too found comfort.

Louise told Nurse that she was leaving for London on business. Nurse, as she was meant to, deduced that the trip to see Izolda was over. She also told Nurse that she had discovered that her grandchild could neither read nor write. It was absolutely disgraceful and something must be done about it and the sooner the better, as she had said to Mr Forster when she saw him yesterday, all of which left Nurse both furious and flustered because she could not very well go and complain to Mr Forster about the interfering American woman when it was assumed she had been giving Izolda lessons for the last year or so! Mercy? Where was she supposed to find the time?

Louise also said goodbye to Izolda. She told her not to fuss, and on parting rather mysteriously put a gloved finger to her lips. Izolda's life promptly reverted to the old days of black overalls, smacks and worse when Nurse lost her temper, and plates of food which were not removed until she had finished every scrap. But her life was not so dismal as it had been before her grandmother's visit for she was being taught to read, write and do figures and was fascinated by the C-A-T book of pictures, and above all she found warmth and light in the stories her grandmother had told her about her mother's childhood in Japan. She gave up counting and instead let her mind wander over those times and the people who had passed through them who all 'belonged' to her. A whole week of seven days passed with the utmost rapidity in this way. And then at the end, suddenly . . .

Although Louise had found out that Izolda's books and toys had been hidden away by the far-from-angelic Curly, had found too that she had been given neither lessons nor new clothes with the money she had sent, still she was left puzzled by her grandchild's pinched expression, nervous habits and generally unhappy appearance. On meeting the nurse she had instinctively taken a dislike to her, and became increasingly suspicious that there must be more to it all than

The Order of the Star

met the eye. The only way to find out – and Louise was not at all sure there *was* anything to find out – was to take them by surprise. Therefore, when going up to London she took only a suitcase with her, leaving the rest of her luggage at the hotel. Early (for her) on the morning after her return she stopped her taxi outside the Parsonage gates at the time she knew Izolda had breakfast. Without ringing any bells, she let herself in to the nursery wing – a wing she had not been in before. She proceeded up the back stairs.

She found the children, unsupervised, having breakfast round a large oblong table covered in an oilcloth. Izolda was not with them. Two of the children stood up politely, the others gaped. She noticed one of the smaller boys, a shrimp of a child, was wearing a black overall. "Where's Izolda?" she asked.

"Over there." One of the boys pointed.

There, facing a corner with her back to the room, sat Izolda on the edge of a hard chair. She was wearing a black overall, black wrinkled stockings on her thin legs, heavy scruffy shoes on her feet. Her hair was in a tangle, and on her lap lay a plate of cold, congealed, greasy stew obviously unfinished from last night's meal. Louise could see traces of tears on her cheeks when Izolda looked round and in astonishment saw her grandmother.

"Take me to your room," ordered Louise flint-eyed.

"But, but . . . Grandma, I am not allowed to leave until I have finished every scrap on my plate, and . . . and it makes me sick," Izolda rushed, fearful of getting into further trouble if she disobeyed. And to take her grandmother to see her room? No! The *shame* of her seeing . . .

"Do as I say *at once*," Louise said peremptorily. "*I* will take the responsibility for your leaving the nursery."

Reluctantly Izolda got to her feet, put her plate on the chair as if she expected to come back to it, and, as slowly as she could to put off the dreadful moment when her room would reveal all her bad habits, led the way up the narrow back stairs.

Louise stood at the creaking attic door. In one glance she took in the room's dark shabbiness, and the black iron-framed maid's bed with a row of holes scraped out along the wall at pillow level. The room was cold and bare except for one cupboard and a wash-stand with jug and basin. She sniffed. She knew that smell from when she had visited institutions. Approaching the bed, to Izolda's mortification, she whipped back the blankets and revealed a grey towelling covering a mackintosh sheet. The top sheet was damp and odorous.

Covering her flushed cheeks with her hands, her eyes large and dark with humiliation, Izolda tried to do a disappearing trick behind the open door. Something *awful* was about to happen! This was not the grandmother she had come to know with her soft 'honeys' and her warm cuddle on greeting, but a hard-eyed, hard-voiced Grandma who, now she knew the truth, would want to have nothing more to do with such a horrid, bed-wetting, dirty, smelly, destructive little girl as she. No one would want a person like that for a grandchild; no one could love . . . She was coming for her . . .

Izolda let out a scream as Louise turned to the cowering child, and in a swift movement pulled her towards the bed, dragged up the black overall and tugged down her knickers, tearing off a couple of buttons as she did so.

Again Izolda screamed; this time she let out a piercing shriek. She knew the routine so well, only now it was far,

The Order of the Star

far worse than it had ever been. Her grandmother was so disgusted with her that she was going to beat her! She fought, screaming, and trying to protect her bottom with her hands. "Don't smack me, Grandma. Don't, please don't. I don't do it on purpose." Helpless, hopeless and frightened she wriggled, strained and sobbed in Louise's grasp.

Heavily Louise sank down on the bed while still clutching Izolda's struggling form. She pulled the clenched little hands away, and let out a sigh that was more like a groan as she examined the weals on the child's small backside. It was a dark room under the eaves, but Louise did not need to have the electric light switched on to see that in places the skin was broken from a savage beating by a stiff brush and that from the redness and blood stains on the white knickers it must have happened that very morning judging by the welts and sore contusions. From the mauve bruises and yellow discolouration of skin all over the buttocks down to the thighs, the outrage must have been going on for a long period. Moreover, from the stale smell of the child's body, she had not taken a bath . . . Wet last night, beaten this morning – again. Black overalls. And those tell-tale holes in the walls, the reason for which she did not fully comprehend at that point . . . A whole rash of hurts. Rashes on a backside, rashes on a wall; a sobbing, terrorised child in her arms. Dear Lord, when one thought of immaculately dressed, graceful, loving Camille; that her daughter should come to this! *This*, as if there was not enough suffering in the world without an English parson's household, of all places, adding its own cruelty to defenceless children.

"Mrs Winter! So it's *you*." Nurse burst in upon them. "How dare you come in here unannounced and without letting me know!" She stood in the doorway, her face suffused with rage. Louise did not answer. She turned the trembling, hysterical child round to face her, pulled up her knickers, kissed her, and rose. She stood very upright confronting the angular nurse, an expression of pity compounded with contempt on her face.

"I dared, and I have seen what I have seen. May God forgive you for what you have done, for I reckon it is beyond me to do so. If you lift a finger to this child again, I'll have the sheriff onto you." And with that Louise drifted, drawn-faced, downstairs, out of the drive and into the waiting car and was driven away. She did not go on to confront Mr Forster because quite simply she had no breath nor stamina left to confront anyone. Just now she would lie down on her bed in the hotel and think out what to do next.

Hideously shocked, Louise's half-formed suspicions which had caused her to turn up at the Parsonage when not expected, had been confirmed far beyond anything envisaged. The truth was appalling. The child had been savagely treated by the nurse. She was terrified and neglected; and she had gotten into such a state that she had begun to wet her bed, when all that had been long left behind under Nanna's kindly and efficient training from babyhood.

It had been a cruel thing to dismiss Nanna so soon after she herself had handed Nanna and Izolda over to the Commander at his new wife's grand house, 'The Manor', after which, when still in England, she had caught the cold that had affected her heart for several years and which had put paid to a visit to see how things were going. Louise still addressed her son-in-law as *Commander* Richardson. For her to have called him DD – the soubriquet his fellow

The Order of the Star

officers bestowed on him for 'Dark Dickie' due to his black hair and pessimistic mien – was unthinkable. The ladies fell for him in a big way and in his younger days he had had the reputation of being the handsomest man in the China Fleet; also an extremely able naval officer who kept himself aloof from the goings-on in mess or bar and was adored by his men. Even to have called him 'Richard' was as unthinkable as it would have been for him to call her 'Mother'. She had continued to address him as Commander as she had in Paris when he had become engaged to her daughter; this partly out of habit, partly out of a mischievous desire to rile him. And rile him it did!

After the earthquake Louise had travelled by ship and train with Nanna and Izolda to Peking to be with her son Jimmy and his wife Toni – daughter of the Governor of Wei-chu and Camille's great friend – in their official Banking abode, which was large enough to house them all comfortably. There, Louise met in his new post, Reginald Campbell – one of Camille's beaux when Chief Magistrate in Wei-chu – and he met for the first time his goddaughter, Izolda. Shortly after, DD had arrived on compassionate leave to see his daughter. He had looked terrible. Louise had never seen a man look so shattered and haggard, and her heart had almost, but not quite, gone out to him in his loss. And just as well it had not, for within two months of Camille's death he announced his engagement and imminent marriage in Shanghai. Louise had been outraged that he could contemplate remarrying so soon, with his first wife scarcely cold in the grave. To her mind such haste was indecent. At least a year should have been allowed to elapse for propriety's sake, and she would have considered two years a more decent period of mourning. However, he had remarried, and then promptly sent in his papers and resigned from the navy just when he was on the point of being promoted Rear-Admiral. Why he resigned, she had no idea. It had seemed to her at the time a mad thing for him to have done; work, when so many others were being axed, was surely his solace and salvation after the tragedy. Now he had left himself without a career and only a small pension – but then of course this decision must be all tied up with marrying a wealthy widow. Presumably he was content to live on his wife's money; another reason for the certain regard she had once had for him plummeting.

Jimmy and Toni – who, after the birth of Winn, could have no more children – would have loved nothing better than to keep Camille's child and bring her up in China, and they had offered Louise a permanent home out there as well. The offer stayed open, but at that time Louise chose to live in the South of France to be near relations of her generation. In Peking, Reginald Campbell, shocked and saddened at Camille's death, by now a confirmed bachelor, and one devoted to children, would also have liked to adopt his goddaughter, who, of course, would bring devoted Nanna with her. There had also been a grief-stricken cable from Joel – who only knew that Camille had been killed on the day before her departure to join him in Australia – demanding to have Izolda whom, after their years together touring, he had come to think of as his own.

There were no lack of offers of loving homes for Izolda, with Louise the most loath of all to give her up. But, not unnaturally, DD wanted to have his daughter living with him, and on his remarriage, requested that Louise in Peking take Izolda to England while he and his wife went on an

The Order of the Star

extensive world honeymoon travelling home eastwards via the United States. Louise, in any case wishing to clarify what money was left to her out of the ruins, and hoping to settle her affairs with the family's London solicitors, agreed to DD's request.

All that was in the past, and now Louise concentrated on Izolda's present predicament and what her next move should be, for something had to be done and done quickly before irreparable damage took place. After nearly four years, what with holes in walls and bumpings of head, perhaps it was already too late? Whatever happened in the future she knew those years of neglect and punishment would take very many more to undo. Lying on her hotel bed after the shocking scene she had witnessed, a plan began to formulate in Louise's mind. She could see no other way out, and it was the last thing she wanted. It would upset everything she had planned for her remaining years on the Riviera, a place she had fallen in love with on a visit to Maude and Julia. It reminded her of the Bluff with its colourful gardens, pine trees and so very blue sea. Yes, this was a place where she could sit in the sun, tend her plants, and live out her last years.

Never liking to be in Maude's pocket for long, once she knew she had an income of her own, however small, and once she had recovered sufficiently from her heart condition, Louise had rented a modest villa and set out that summer to visit her grandchild. Now, if her intention came about, it would entirely disturb and disrupt the privacy and quietness she craved, and probably, in her not so robust health, kill her off into the bargain! She was not at all sure she was physically or mentally capable of carrying the idea through, but she could not, in the crisis, make excuses for herself, could not let personal considerations override desperate need in the face of what she had just seen.

Yet it was more complicated still than that. First, she would have to win over Commander Richardson to her way of thinking, and to do so would entail the most difficult, delicate, and subtle confrontation on her part between two people who actively disliked one another; he with every parental and fiscal right on his side, she with nothing to offer besides her elderly self.

Chapter Ten

DD fidgeted uneasily in his ladder-backed dining-room chair in the hotel where his mother-in-law was entertaining him to lunch. As it was near to the Parsonage he had arranged to call in and see Izolda afterwards. He was unsure of why he had been summoned urgently by wire from his mother-in-law, a call that brooked no refusal; presumably she had something of importance to discuss before she left the country. He hoped she was not going to make difficulties when all was happily resolved for Izolda with the Forster family. Though he had missed her very much to begin with, not having a small daughter at home had solved problems, not the least his wife's jealousy of the child, and also another personal matter, just as unexpected, that had since arisen.

After a few months at the Parsonage Izolda had lost much of her puppy fat, and the resultant likeness to her slim, delicately-boned mother had become more pronounced. He had begun to dread the visits for the memories of his late wife they brought back, and had spread them out as much as he felt he reasonably could. The truth was he could not bear to face the resemblance to the woman he had adored, loved even above his Royal Navy; one he had had to assiduously woo for three years before she, who had so many other beaux, had consented. Besides, he kidded himself in an attempt to salvage his conscience, life went much more smoothly the fewer the visits he made since his wife invariably threw a tantrum at each one and sulked on his return. During the Season life at The Manor was one long house-party. Izolda was far better off where she was, with other children to play with. Much more fun for her.

During the meal – an indifferent one by DD's culinary standards – the reason why he had been invited was not divulged. They talked of the weather, the political situation, the Trade Union movement that was causing unrest in the cities, and his forthcoming holiday abroad. He could see Mrs Winter thought his whole life was one long holiday, and what he needed another vacation for was beyond her! Blast it all, why would she insist on calling him Commander? It annoyed him intensely, and it was not because she had gone senile. She knew perfectly well about his promotion on appointment in Shanghai. Same old tactics of trying to denigrate him as had gone on in Paris when he had had to sit in their flat in the Rue Jacques Offenbach close to the Bois de Boulogne, and take it. Here he was sitting in the genteel private hotel and taking it again. She had not changed in that way, though in others she had changed a great deal.

With his eyes on her now, he could not imagine why she had been so imposing in China, the old Gorgon as he always thought of her, like that domineering and devilish cunning Dowager Empress Tsu Hsi! She not only looked older, she looked smaller. Gone was the elaborately waved grey head which had given her such a *grande dame* look; in its place pure white hair drawn back in what could scarcely be called a bun, under a hat that was half the size of those worn with such panache in pre-war days, its

The Order of the Star

only decoration a green Petersham ribbon bow to the fore. Truly she *was* a card!

Her long-sleeved silk dress was simply cut, low-waisted, shortish to mid calf, and flaring loosely out. He noticed pretty legs and the daintiest of ankles not revealed under the long skirts of before. Surprising how modern she looked, but then she had always been fashion conscious, he'd give her that. Funny old thing. What had *not* changed were her darting brown eyes under the dark beetling brows. He had an unpleasant feeling she was going to attempt to browbeat him; that soft voice would scathe as it had before . . .

With relief DD scraped back his chair and rose to follow his mother-in-law to the residents' lounge upstairs where a maid dumped down a tray of coffee, and on request, and with bad grace, lit the gas fire in the hearth. They had the room to themselves except for the hotel's tabby cat.

"I feel the cold in England even in summer." Louise poured out the coffee. "These red-brick houses can be mighty chilly. The Parsonage I find is a particularly draughty house," she observed, topping up the Commander's cup. My goodness he was handsome – distinguished-looking with grey at the temples. He wore a blue shirt, naval tie and a smart blazer with polished naval buttons. What in thunder was he doing being retired? For sure he should have been an admiral ruling the waves instead of which he was ruled by that wife of his . . . "Commander Richardson, had you, when you remarried, any notion that this business of turning Izolda out of the house would occur?" Louise started off on the ground she had prepared. There were some gaps in her knowledge of what had gone on before. She had not met the wife when she had handed over Izolda and Nanna to him in London, and after what subsequently happened three months later, hoped she never would.

"What do you take me for?" DD replied haughtily, his figure stiffening. Here it came. He took a sip of the dreadful coffee, which tasted of acorns. Beaumont, his batman, could make better coffee than this in a destroyer in a gale on the North Sea! He helped himself to more sugar and stirred vigorously. "One of my reasons for marrying again was to make a home for Izolda. You cannot deny, Mrs Winter, that the marriage of a widower with a small daughter to a widow, could not, on the face of it, be more eminently suitable."

"On the face of it, yes." Louise restrained herself from adding: *but it seems you were unwise to enter into a second marriage with such indecent haste.*

"I would like to emphasise that prior to my marriage there was never any question of Izolda *not* living with us," DD continued. "In fact my wife went to some lengths to equip a suite of rooms in the back premises of The Manor as a nursery—"

"*Back* premises?" echoed Louise. What was this extraordinary British custom of banning one's children from the main part of the house, banning them from family life? Her children had always used the front stairs, and the house was all the more lively for it.

"Well, er, yes, why not, Mrs Winter? My wife entertains a great deal and one cannot have . . ." DD covered up for Diamond. *He* had wanted the child around so that he could show her off to the guests, but he soon learned better.

"Had your wife met Izolda when they were in Shanghai?"

"No, of course not, why should she – then?"

"I thought if she were fond of children as Camille was . . ."

The Order of the Star

"My wife," DD cleared his throat, "was not knowledgeable about children having seldom come into close contact with them; rather averse to sticky fingers and all that. No, her interests lie in quite different areas. She is one for high society, Mayfair stuff y'know, a real socialite! How could I possibly have foreseen?" Hell. Here he was already trying to justify himself to the Gorgon. What *had* she brought him here for? Surely not to discuss his wife? If so he was not going to have any more of it.

There was a silence, except for the hissing of the gas fire, during which time the tabby cat jumped onto DD's well-pressed flannel trouser knee. It squatted there, kneading.

"*Miaouu*," he imitated, stroking its back with a firm hand which brought out a spate of pleased purrings from the animal. He liked cats; much nicer than those goddamned yip-yapping pack of pugs Diamond expected him to exercise.

"Then you don't reckon the ensuing state of affairs was predetermined?" Louise quietly persisted, eyeing the cat unfavourably. He *would* like cats! She herself did not like animals in the house. In the East they brought disease. Aunt Hattie would never allow any in the missionary bungalow on Winn's Point, and she had followed the rule in her own house.

"As I have already indicated, Mrs Winter, I do not believe the trouble over Izolda was premeditated, by that I mean I do not think my wife had any idea how extreme her reaction would be to my showing affection for my first wife's daughter." DD stroked the cat heavily as the touchy subject arose. The cat flicked her ears at him. Diamond had accused him of preferring the child's company to hers . . . He admitted that to begin with, perhaps, he had been tactless there. He was going to stick up for Diamond in front of the

Gorgon, not going to let her know how, after nearly five years of marriage, he had become convinced Diamond had conveniently side-stepped the issue of an offspring just to get her man, had hidden from him the fact that basically she actively *disliked* children.

A mutual woman friend in the East, who had first introduced DD to Diamond, had warned him that he would be in trouble if he married her. He had not believed the friend. He had believed that the woman – one of his previous mistresses or 'hers' as he preferred to call them – had expressed the view out of spite for his affair with Diamond. Too late he had found out that she, a mother, was genuinely concerned for his child, and with reason, as it turned out.

At the first opportunity, Diamond had picked a quarrel with Nanna so that she could dismiss her and sever any past connections with the Winters. Next, Izolda herself had played into Diamond's hand. She became so impossible with the new governess that the latter gave notice, but said she would stay on until she could be replaced. Diamond had no intention of replacing her. After the initial cold calculation of getting rid of Nanna, hot jealousy took over, her aim being to get Izolda out of the house as soon as possible. The rows built up every time DD went into the nursery.

The climax came on the day husband and wife were due to go to a society wedding in Town, when Diamond, ready and dressed in her best garden party finery, burst into the playroom to find Dickie (as she called him) not yet changed and having a riotous time on all fours giving Izolda a ride. In a blind rage she had let fly, literally, smashing some ornaments on the mantelpiece and frightening the child who burst into tears. There and then she had issued her

The Order of the Star

ultimatum that either his daughter leave within a few days, or they could bloody well both go and be damned to them. It was *her* house, *her* money; *she* held all the cards.

In those early days of his second marriage, it had taken DD some months to grasp that the real trouble lay not with Nanna, nor the subsequent superior governess, but simply and incontrovertibly with the presence of the small child of his loins and Camille's body. Izolda was condemned in Diamond's mind long before she met the child, for she had known that DD would never marry her as long as there was a chance of reconciliation with his wife. At that period she had drifted off from Shanghai to her in-laws in Hong Kong to try and get over her infatuation for the naval officer. News came of the earthquake, and Diamond returned post-haste to offer Dickie comfort, and not only comfort, but wealth, with a grand home and estates which she wanted him to run. That meant his retiring . . .

DD considered. His next posting had not come through. He might be passed over for promotion (he heard later that he had been selected at that time for a vice-admiral's post). He would get a slightly larger pension if he sent in his papers than if he was retired. At that vital time in his career, so soon after Camille's death, he did not care very much one way or another – and Diamond's riches were attractive. Besides, she was an attractive woman, hard as her name implied compared to all his previous flower-like 'hers', and the very opposite of Camille, his beloved, maddening 'Camule', his peerless lily, the bright star of his life . . .

His life could never be the same again, and life with Diamond to clash with for the rest of it would not be dull. With it would go plenty of sailing at Cowes, skiing in Europe and cruising in the West Indies in winter. Worth it, now Camille was no more, when all was said and done.

"Well, if Izolda's exit wasn't premeditated, what brought matters to a head?" the old lady's soft insistent voice impinged on DD's thoughts.

"Izolda's very existence. My wife will not have her name, nor Camille's, nor yours, spoken in the house. She is extremely possessive. There are sulks every time I go to see my child. I can tell you I shall be taken to account for this visit today, ha, ha, ha." DD tried to laugh it off. He took out his handkerchief and then put it back without using it.

"I'll be darned! Why not *my* name for goodness sake?"

"Pathological. Being the first wife's mother is enough to condemn you! She's an irrational woman."

"A mighty spoilt one I'd say." He'd married for money of course. She'd warned Camille as long ago as Wei-chu that he, an impecunious naval officer, was looking out for a wife with a golden egg. Well, he'd gotten one in the end.

DD refused to rise to his mother-in-law's last remark, refused to be drawn any further. He'd already said too much. He was not going to give the old Gorgon the satisfaction of knowing that he was in wholehearted agreement with her over his second wife being bloody spoilt, an only child born of wealthy parents and then married to a rich man in Jardines, much older than she, and thus on the latter's death followed by her father's, inheriting two fortunes. Suited him, and why not? He had seen what lack of money had done to his own parents. However frugally he lived in the Navy he had always been short. Now he lived in luxury, de luxe suites on trains and ships; no money worries any more. The pleasures of his life were great and made up

The Order of the Star

for his wife's jealousy if he as much as looked at another woman. Petty tantrums, he called them, and they kept him well and truly on the straight and narrow! They got on well enough together; both loved travelling and seeing the world. Never a dull moment, and he paid his way by running the estates, supervising the farm manager, etcetera. He enjoyed doing that. Funnily enough he seemed to go down well in her wealthy racing set who were slightly in awe of the much-decorated, taciturn Captain of the Silent Service. He played that up! Saved his having to make small-talk – left that to Diamond. Of course there must have been an awful lot said behind their backs when Izolda was turned out of the house, about him too no doubt, but no one had ever said anything unpleasant to Diamond to her face. An invitation to their spacious house was too valuable an asset to risk offending *her*.

"You could have left *with* Izolda." Louise went on probing in her ruthless way. "You could have found other work."

"Mrs Winter!" scorned DD with a hearty laugh. "Other work? I have no training for anything else and there is rampant unemployment throughout the country. I would also like to remind you, I had only recently married again when the ultimatum was fired at me. One cannot just walk out after a few months."

"So you . . ." began Louise. She was on the point of saying: *so you took the easy way out and sacrificed the child*, but thought better of it. The situation between them showed exacerbation enough already, and she did not want to rough him up any more before coming to the point. "Will your wife help with Izolda financially?" Louise asked instead.

"No need." Meticulously DD picked the cat's hairs off his trousers one by one. "I have my pride, Mrs Winter," he said coldly. "My pension, though ridiculously small for a *captain's*," he emphasised for her benefit "is more than enough to pay for all Izolda's needs and my modest tailor's bills. I would have you know I do not ask my wife for pin money."

"*And the child suffers*. Excuse me a moment." Louise got to her feet. "I'll be back in a minute." And she left the room before DD had time to reply.

Chapter Eleven

"*Suffers* did you say? Izolda suffer? Certainly not," DD, on his feet, attacked Louise as she reappeared through the doorway. "She could not be better off than she is at the Forsters," he said, looking at his watch impatiently, "and it's high time I went along there."

"Sit down please. I won't keep you much longer." The two resumed their seats, the cat jumping back onto DD's knee. "You always arrange a visit in advance, don't you, as you have done for today? Well," she drawled, to DD's nod, "if you believe she's well looked after at the Parsonage you'd better have another big think."

Louise took a deep breath. Here goes, she thought, and proceeded to launch into a diatribe about the nurse's cruelty, about the bad habits – though not in detail – that the child had developed since going there; about the sadistic tendencies of Mr Forster, from whom she had worked out the nurse took her cue; about the generally frugal set-up in the nursery wing; about the lack of lessons, outings or amusements; and how, to save money on clothes and washing, Izolda wore black overalls . . .

"I have never once seen Izolda in an overall." DD stopped Louise in her tracks. "She has always been in a dress." Had the Gorgon gone mad?

"No more had I until I made an unannounced call and caught them out," Louise continued, sitting very straight in her chair, one eye on the cat. She did *not* want it to jump onto her lap. "I found Izolda in the sort of clothes they wear at orphanages. Saving on your money for sure. Izolda takes the rap for every mischief the younger son they call Curly gets into. Believe me, he's far from the angelic boy Nurse makes him out to be. I found that he steals the books and playthings I send Izolda, and she gets the blame for losing them. She is cruelly beaten for things she can't help out of nerves; she has gotten thin and sulky; she is thoroughly frightened, and moreover, she shows signs of becoming mentally unstable."

"*What?*" DD sprang to his feet sending the startled cat flying. He went to the mantelpiece and stood there toying worriedly with the cheap ornaments. Phew, far too hot in the small, claustrophobic room. He bent down to turn off the gas, took out his handkerchief, and this time used it to mop his furrowed brow.

"Yes," declared Louise firmly, "that's what I said. I repeat: mentally unstable."

"What d'you you mean? What's she been doing?"

"She's been picking holes in the walls."

"Good God, what a crazy thing to do!"

"Sure. Just what I said – you could not have chosen a more apt word. Crazy. They're driving her crazy there! And that's not the end of it; if they haven't already driven her crazy, she's driving *herself* round the bend, all alone in that dark attic room, by bumping her head to stun herself to sleep at nights. If you don't believe me look under that hideous fringe Nurse cuts so badly and you'll see for yourself!"

"Did you say the nurse *beats* her?" The muscle in DD's

The Order of the Star

jaw began to work. "Spanking is surely a more accurate word?" DD was not only angry at the accusations, he was unbelieving. If things were that wrong he'd have had an inkling, smelled a rat. True, Izolda was thin-looking and had been listless the last time he saw her, but he put that down to her growing fast.

"I said beat and I mean beat. The evidence is there on her bottom for you to see."

"I wouldn't know about that." DD looked embarrassed.

"No you wouldn't. I only found out because I thought it odd she was sitting on the *edge* of a chair in a corner with a disgusting plate of cold stew left over from the previous day on her lap . . . But enough of that, I could go on and on about that iniquitous place. If I were you I would go straight there now with the local doctor, make him examine her, and have the facts put before Mr Forster so that he dismisses the nurse immediately. She is not fit to be in charge of children, and when you consider Izolda has suffered that for nearly four years . . . It doesn't bear thinking of. I declare she is a brave little girl to have survived. Four years back," Louise went on, giving no quarter, "she was a normal, happy, plump little baby. Now she is a bundle of nerves, a travesty of what she was when Camille was alive.

"You should never, never, *never* have got rid of Nanna; that was a cruel thing to have done, and I blame you for allowing that. Camille must be turning in her grave at what has happened. I only hope she can't see what's been going on. Izolda will go from bad to worse if you leave her any longer at the Parsonage. I guess she must be taken away and the sooner the better."

"Impossible! You have no idea the trouble I had in finding

a decent place in the first instance . . ." DD, white to the gills with perplexity, paced the room.

"*Decent*? She'd have been better off in an orphanage under government supervision." The scared cat rubbed itself against the door with arched back, mewing piteously. "You'd better let it out," Louise said with a frown.

"I don't know what to believe, or even what is to be done for the best." In some exasperation DD opened the door for the cat. He shut it again and went to open the window and then resumed pacing around the small room.

"The first thing you have to do is to get on to that doctor, and fix the nurse. There is another small child there, an orphan they call Pip, who looks to me thoroughly neglected as well. The least we can do is to see he—"

"Yes, yes, Mrs Winter, stick to the point if you please. The point is, if I find what you say is true and not excessively exaggerated—"

"I do not exaggerate. I have not exaggerated. I have told you but the bald truth," Louise stated with dignity.

"The point *is* . . ." resumed DD, "you must understand that I cannot have Izolda back in The Manor – murder would be done – and it is going to be extremely difficult and time-consuming to find another Home . . ."

"No, no more Homes, please God."

"What else do you suggest then?" DD glared down at Louise in her chair, his striding stilled for a moment.

"Have you any relations who could take her on?"

"I have a sister. She's ill with phthisis contracted in Africa – they call it TB these days, I believe."

"Tuberculosis? Out of the question – very infectious. Anyone else?"

"Some friends perhaps . . ." DD said vaguely.

The Order of the Star

"Would you consider leaving your wife to make a home for Izolda?"

"I'd have to get a nanny and a housekeeper and I couldn't afford both – no, it would not work. Besides, I have my duties at The Manor. I do not intend to let my wife down . . ."

"She's let *you* down badly enough. But don't let's go into that. Of course Jimmy and Toni in Peking would be the ideal answer. They wanted to adopt Izolda, but then you got married again. With hindsight—"

"With hindsight a lot of things, Mrs Winter. Peking really would mean my giving Izolda up . . . All that way away." DD laughed hollowly. "I suppose she could be sent to boarding school."

"They wouldn't take her. She doesn't even know her alphabet! No, no. What she needs is a proper home from which to go daily to nice little private school where I'm sure she would soon catch up . . ." Louise stopped and braced herself to utter the words that were going to upset her life; the words that would express the last thing she wanted to undertake at her age. "*I reckon,*" she said smoothly, "*Izolda will have to come and live with me.*"

"On the Riviera? With you? NO, certainly not!"

"Why not, pray?"

"Too far away." DD resumed his pacing. "I would hardly ever see her." He cleared his throat, desperately trying to think of some way out of the trap the blasted old Gorgon had set him. He was still not entirely convinced she was not depicting a situation at the Parsonage far worse than it actually was. Perhaps not quite as satisfactory as he had thought, but no need for all this urgency. Still, to get the doctor on to it straight away was a good idea. Clear the air. He was not going to risk having Izolda ill-treated one day longer if it were true, and if it were not, well, what did it matter if he were left feeling a bit of a fool. He was dead against his mother-in-law having Izolda, though. It was quite unsuitable for the child to live with her at her age. He wondered how she even contemplated it – and there was another pertinent reason why he did not wish Izolda to go to her grandmother's . . .

"You hardly ever see her anyway. You've got to make some sacrifice, I guess *Captain* Richardson," Louise promoted him to his correct rank. No sense in rubbing him up the wrong way further at this delicate point of discussion! "I can see no other satisfactory solution."

"I appreciate your offer, Mrs Winter," DD began. He chose his words carefully, "but no, she really cannot live with you. It is not right, nor fair on either of you. For one thing, you are not physically strong enough to cope; for another, the age gap is too great, neither should you have the burden of the extra expense . . ." he struggled on, thinking up every excuse.

"I would expect you to pay for her schooling and perhaps doctors' and dentists' bills. I can manage the rest. There is room in my villa, and I have an excellent *bonne-à-tout-faire* who comes in daily from the market and takes care of everything. I can assure you, Captain Richardson, it would cost you a good bit less than what you pay at the Forsters' to let me have Izolda; she would be in clover compared to that place."

"There are other reasons why Izolda should not live with you," DD said. He planted himself before Louise in his nautical stance, his dark eyes on her wrinkled face. He appreciated the 'Captain'!

The Order of the Star

"What now, for goodness sake?"

"For one, you will spoil her."

"Fiddle-de-dee, spoil her . . . *spoil* her?" Louise burst forth indignantly. "As if that is not exactly what she needs. She needs all the affection I can bestow on her to get some self-confidence. Masses of it, mothering, spoiling if you like, knowing she is loved – and that'll be mighty uphill work after what she's been through. I can assure you, Captain, your daughter needs lots and lots of *love!*"

DD scratched his neck with a tentative finger, his other hand clenched in his trouser pocket. The Gorgon was forcing out of him the real reason why he did not want his daughter brought up by this domineering, interfering, bloody old Dowager Empress. He was sure he disliked her every bit as much as she disliked him! But through the dislike there was the admiration. The sheer guts of the pioneering missionary harridan. There had been the earthquake and the loss of her house, possessions, her late husband's fortune – and her daughter. After all that to offer to take on the care of his and Camille's child – incredible.

"Also," he said, cross to have it dragged out of him, "also, Mrs Winter, you will *poison Izolda's mind against me.*"

The silence that this glaring statement brought was complete, a fraught silence that filled the small residents' lounge. DD stood stock still before Louise who held her breath while staring back at him. The loaded silence hung between them as Louise began to breathe again, her shock wave receding. She could see the words her son-in-law had uttered as clearly as if they had been written on the ugly hotel wallpaper. And she saw they were true. Perfectly true. What he said struck home to her very roots, to the very foundation of her Christian ethics, and he had had to say the words for she had not thought of it at all! It had simply not occurred to her. What he said was quite right; she would have spoken in disparaging terms to Izolda about her father, about his hasty remarriage, about his allowing her to be turned out of the house. And none of that was right.

"I promise you," Louise spoke at last. "I promise that I will not in any way influence Izolda against you. You are her father. During the war you served your country with bravery and distinction, and I know from Camille's letters how happy she was with you in those days. Since the tragedy of her death I know that you have been, er . . . er . . ." Louise searched in her mind for the word that Camille had once used to her in Paris when she had asked what she saw in DD, what attracted her in his character. *An unfortunate man*, she had said. Things went wrong in his life. He was indeed a dark man though she, Camille, had found her own kinder soubriquet for the name DD. She had been sorry for him and had sought to brighten his life – all the wrong reasons for marriage Louise had considered. "You have been . . . unfortunate," Louise now said, "in that your second marriage did not turn out in the way you had intended for your daughter; neither will I do more than tell Izolda the facts she already knows of what happened if she questions me when she is older. You can rest assured that I will most certainly *not* poison Izolda's mind against you."

DD looked at Louise with his melting, thickly lashed eyes, and knew she would keep her word. He knew she would be kind and gentle, caring and loving to his child as Camille would have wished.

And with Louise's promise DD had to be content.

"What if I get lost?" Izolda asked fearfully as she clutched on to her grandmother's hand for dear life in the bustle and noise of Victoria Station. For the first time since she could remember she was out in the bewildering strangeness of the big world far from the Parsonage. So many *people* in London, all those men and women! Her grandmother remained calm and unflustered in the chaos, but what if she lost *her*?

"If you get lost," Louise answered practically, "I guess all you have to do is to stay where you are and I will find you. Just remember to stand firm like the biblical Israelites!" Louise gave a pleased smile to herself. This was going to be high fun teaching her granddaughter all the old values which had stood her in such good stead throughout her long life.

"Where are we going, Grandma?" Izolda asked once they were seated on the train, opposite each other in corner seats by the window. Louise had her back to the engine so that she should not get covered in smuts, and also so that the child should see the way ahead.

"We are going to live near your Great-Aunt Maude and Cousin Julia whom I've told you about."

"Yes. I know them!" Izolda said happily. "They're my family."

"And you know about McLaughlan who is 'family' too. First thing, I shall get her to run you up some cotton dresses." Louise looked with distaste at the old smock Izolda had long grown out of. "Knickers to match with elastic tops."

"No more buttons?"

"No more beastly buttons! You shall choose the tobralco bales you fancy from the store in the old town."

"Shall I call her *Miss* McLaughlan?" *Four* old ladies in her new life, and all of them would be able to tell her stories about her mother.

123

"Plain McLaughlan, honey."

"But *where* are we going?" Izolda persisted.

And the lovely answer came: "Into the sun – where lemons grow!"

Part Two

1928–1939

'Childhood knows the human heart'

Edgar Allan Poe

Chapter Twelve

"That's ours, the Villa Micheline," Louise pointed to one of four identical villas shining whitely in the early September sun.

Each was a little distance away from the others grouped round a tall central palm tree in the middle of what had once been the garden of a large house now demolished. "Micheline," Louise went on, "is Monsieur Michelin's crippled daughter. The other villas are named after his stalwart sons. He's a property developer with a very loud voice, and he's responsible for the planting and upkeep of the communal garden. However, I've asked him to dig two patches on either side of the steps to tend myself. I've always had a garden and I'm not going to give up *yet*. As the first in I chose this one for its old well and fig tree to one side. What do you think, Izolda?"

"It's pretty; just like a doll's house." She ran ahead up the ten marbled steps which led between moulded balustrades to the front door on either side of which two long French windows opened inwards, protected on the outside by low iron grids. Above the windows were embossed friezes of brightly coloured fruit and flowers.

"My *bonne-à-tout-faire*, sometimes called *femme de ménage* in this country, doesn't seem to be here yet. I expect she is shopping in the market. I sent her a telegram to say we were arriving today." Louise took out her key to unlatch the front door which had two smoked glass windows on the inside of more iron grills. "The idea of these," she explained, "is that when the doorbell rings one can peep through the little windows to see who it is."

The cab man, who had followed them up the drive, dumped some luggage in the hall. Louise tipped him and said something in French. Her French, she had told Izolda, was enough to get by with and much better than Great-Aunt Maude's, though she tended to lapse into Japanese when lost for a word.

"I wish I could understand French."

"You will, and speak it fluently in no time at your age. Your mother spoke excellent French without a trace of accent. She learnt it at her Dame's school on the Bluff, and perfected it when we lived in Paris for her singing training. Ah, here's Monsieur Michelin to check the inventory. You go explore the layout while I'm busy."

Izolda left the large walrus-moustached landlord booming away at 'Madame' in the narrow corridor which ran the length of the house, and entered the main bedroom on her right which had a door opening through into a small side bedroom. A spare room, empty except for boxes, lay beyond. On the other side of the corridor was the drawing-room sparsely furnished with some stiff upholstered French chairs, beyond which glass doors led through to a small dining-room. It had a fireplace with mantelpiece, and an intriguing cupboard in one corner which turned out to be a hatch connected by a rope trolley to the kitchen below where Izolda could hear someone banging about downstairs – the maid? She closed the hatch and progressed to a bathroom with bath and basin

The Order of the Star

and a geyser on the wall hissing its small flame ready to pop into action. Next to this room was a steep, spiral iron staircase, surely lethal for old ladies, but fun for a child. She leapt down it to find herself in a blackened space used as a coal dump with shute in the wall in place of a window. She found the same layout below as above with three rooms on either side of a central corridor. The only difference was that here, instead of the French windows, there were small high up ones looking out at ground level, each with a substantial window-ledge. A back door opened under the outside steps. In one room she came across a peasant woman with a snowy head of white hair. She was bending over a black stove and poking at the coals to get it going. The old woman addressed her in a cackling voice. Izolda shook her head whereupon the maid pointed to herself with, "Marie," and then at her with, *"Mam'selle – la petite Mam'selle."* Izolda repeated the words then flew upstairs in search of the loo and found it right at the end of the corridor by the spiral staircase; a tiny room with a window looking out to the rear of the house where terraces rose. It had a wooden seat not too big for her. She sat there for a moment in total bliss. The villa *was* a doll's house, a perfect one, spanking new, whitewashed throughout and not a scratch or mark to be seen anywhere to spoil its prettiness. She loved it, all of it! No dark corners to frighten, no winding corridors in which to get lost, no nurse in charge to torment or boys to tease, and most of all no graveyard outside from where skeletons rose at night to haunt and terrify . . .

"Come now and help me close the shutters against the heat of day," Izolda heard her grandmother call, "after our midday meal, Marie and I have our siestas," Louise was at pains to relate the daily routine. "She is younger than I but she suffers from sciatica in her bad leg. This does not stop her from looking after everything mighty well. I let her use the hatch a lot so that she doesn't have to climb those stairs much – *I* never use them; round to the back door for me. She shops, cleans, cooks . . . though she doesn't do the washing. The *blanchisseuse* comes and takes the laundry away to wash in the *lavoir* – that's the public trough – after which the woman strings it out over the river bed to dry. The hot sun nicely bleaches the clothes laid on the stones."

"Shall I like French food?" Izolda asked doubtfully. She was feeling hungry. The train had arrived in Menton station too early for breakfast.

"I'll ask Marie to give you some *goûter*. That's the French mid-morning break of bread with something on it; no cooked breakfast in France. I shall be mightily surprised if you don't like the food here. Marie is an excellent cook. She buys the food in the market fresh every day. She has her own room in the old town. I'll point it out to you when we pass it on our way to your great-aunt's. We have our *déjeuner*, that's our midday meal, punctually at twelve o'clock, and you come directly you are called, please. It's not fair to servants to be late – I never kept my Japanese servants waiting. After the meal you can play anywhere you choose while we are resting as long as you don't make a noise. Now to close the shutters. It keeps the house cool. Should be cooling down soon this month. I do not like great heat even though I got used to it in Japan where the climate is more extreme. Here the winters are perfect, sunny and warm and bright with flowers. You'll see!"

"Oh, cuss it all," exclaimed Louise later that evening, as she tucked Izolda up in her small room where light curtains hung

The Order of the Star

over the one deep window which looked out over the garden to a high wall buttressing a steep hill. The shutters had since been thrown wide open. The room was bare except for a bed, chair and mirrored dressing-table with sheeny green top patterned in squares. "Oh fiddle it all, I shall have to have another word with Monsieur Michelin tomorrow. He has forgotten to supply us with mosquito nets, and there are plenty of those pinging nuisances here at nights. A real plague I can tell you. Now, honey, sleep tight," Louise bent to kiss her granddaughter.

Izolda snuggled down under the sheet and savoured the sweet-smelling soft flock mattress under her. The mattress was new as was the pillow and crisp unbleached sheets. "What if . . . ?" she began with a frown.

"No need to worry. I'll come in to lift you before I go to sleep, just to be sure. With these lace curtains it won't be pitch dark if you wake up in the night, and there is a potty under the bed. The landlord has actually provided us with one. Fancy that now! Now go to sleep and no bumping your head to make more horrid red marks on your forehead."

Overtired, Louise soon followed to bed, leaving the communicating door between their rooms open. She composed herself comfortably on the extra pillows she had requested from Monsieur Michelin. She was astonished at herself. Within twenty-four hours of receiving DD's consent, she had had Izolda out of the dire atmosphere of the so-called Home, and onto the train. After a night on their couchettes spent rolling down France in the Blue Train, they had awakened to another world, the one she had chosen for her old age: a world of azure skies, lazy seas, red earth, bent pine trees and a range of magnificent rocky mountains rising up steeply from the many tunnelled coastline through which the train whistled and roared and blew clouds of smoke against the darkened windows hastily shut to keep the smuts and sooty smell out. Then once more into the beautiful scenery with the blue sea calm and oily-looking in the early light. And she was arriving at her destination not alone but with a pale, thin child already battered by life's misfortunes.

The whole situation was totally unexpected. She had originally come here to stay with elderly relatives who had invited her to live with them. She too had fallen in love with the place, but as she had never seen eye-to-eye with Maude for long; had, once recovered sufficiently from the set-back of her heart trouble – during which time she had to admit Maude had been kindness and generosity itself – branched out on a place of her own. Both Maude and Julia had told her she was daft to go and live alone at her age and with her heart condition. At least, they said, she ought to have a live-in maid. But she had gone and engaged the crone Marie with her handicaps, saying something about a 'rapport' between too old women on whom life had been hard. Tosh! Tosh was Maude's favourite expression, said with a toss of her red head!

Now, Louise chuckled to herself, Maude and Julia could no longer censure her. Instead, when she turned up on her weekly visit with a granddaughter, what a surprise it would give them! She could not wait to see Maude's double chins wobbling with astonishment. Maude had last seen Izolda as a baby when Camille had visited them on one of her grand opera tours. McLaughlan had been there too.

Of course the child would cause extra expense, but she reckoned that with what remained of James's fortune invested in the War Loan, she could manage. She had budgeted in her missionary days, and she could do so again,

The Order of the Star

scrimping a bit here and there and ensuring that Marie kept to the most economical of dishes. Izolda's father would send money for the schooling. A French school, she reckoned. She couldn't get over the deplorable omission that the child had never yet had lessons.

How life repeated itself. *'Plus ça change, plus c'est la même chose'* the French said. Here she was again with a small girl in her care – the next generation, yet it seemed only yesterday it was Camille playing about another sunny house. Would Izolda take after her mother who had been a tomboy, as a child playing wild games with her brothers and loving to climb trees? Camille had grown up into a graceful woman with a glorious soprano voice. Training in Paris . . . World tours . . . 'Star of Opera' in the Treaty Port, and then – *finis* . . .

One did not exactly get *used* to disasters, but there was no doubt about it that if one survived, one could start again, however bleak the situation looked at the time. She would have no truck with those who said they were too old to start again (Louise in her mind glossed over the period in her life when after James's death it had been only with the greatest reluctance and a lot of prodding by her family that she *had* started again by going to China to make a home for her then bachelor son Jimmy.) Nonsense! As long as there was a spark of life left, there lay the challenge to pick up the pieces and get on with it.

What a challenge to take on a near eight-year-old at seventy-whatever she was. She was going to gloss over *that* one! What would Dr Pouget say? That she had been foolhardy? Rushed into it too precipitately for her health? And what of the child? Izolda had so many knots to untie, so many phobias to get rid of – so much to catch up on in education. She had discovered on the journey that the child was frightened of all sorts of things, one of them apparently horses since that time in a dog-cart at the Parsonage when the pony had fallen down in the shafts, spilling out the children. She had seen the fear in Izolda's eyes at the sight of the harmless nag after they had taken the *fiacre* at the station to drive to the villa. To divert her on the short journey up the Carie Valley, she had told her how she had once by mistake – when her French was even worse than it was now – called the *cocher* (driver) a *cochon* which stood for pig, and how the man, insulted, refused to carry her one step further! She had been rewarded by the white-faced child giving a giggle – the first time she had heard her utter the semblance of a laugh.

So, somehow she had to build up Izolda's confidence, show her how to face up to life, to unpleasant truths, and not hide from them; to banish imaginary fears, rise above tragedies. She hoped there would be no tragedies, no more wars such as she herself had been through. But in every life there were difficulties and troubles, and in this particular case, one day there would be the sadness to the child of her own death. That was one of the inevitabilities of being brought up by a grandmother as old as she. Now that she had taken this enormous step, she prayed to be spared until Izolda was old enough to stand on her own feet. Was it too much to ask for ten years, perhaps even a few more, when one had a dicky heart?

The thing that worried her most was that she had no legal rights over Izolda. There was no adoption, nor, she knew, would the child's father hear of it. If he felt so inclined, he could take Izolda away from her at any moment.

"Over my dead body," Louise mumbled to herself having

taken out her dental plate and placed it in the glass on her bedside table. Dipping her fingers into the water, she proceeded to roll her baby-fine straight white hair into pipe cleaners she had bought at the *tabac* shop. Next morning, on brushing it out, there would remain pleasing waves when the hair was drawn back into a small roll and fixed with hairpins at the nape of her neck. She had once had abundant raven hair down to her waist and perfect little even white teeth. The sprue in China had put paid to all that. She still had *some* hair, and dark eyebrows though the long black eyelashes that James had raved about seemed to have vanished . . . Ah well, 'sans teeth, sans everything . . .' It all came to the same in the end.

Switching off the light, Louise composed herself for sleep which came through drifting thoughts. Tomorrow – today – Dr Pouget was coming to check up on her and she would ask him to have a look at Izolda. What would the child grow into? So far she seemed not to have inherited either of her parents good looks, neither her father's handsome darkness, nor her mother's Titian beauty. Izolda was fair, but there was no light in her hair which was dull mouse. Same with her eyes which were neither green like her mother nor brown like her father, but flecked, and had only to her knowledge lit up once since arriving, and that was when perching on a window-sill! Her eyes were her best features, they and her delicately arched eye-brows, and her dark eyelashes. Then too she had a rather endearing overhanging top lip and a truly perfect creamy complexion . . .

Next morning, to her horror, Louise saw that Izolda's complexion had been bitten to bits by mosquitoes. Monsieur Michelin arrived with mosquito nets, and later Dr Pouget was expected. A plump pasty-faced man he raised his eyes to heaven at the unexpected addition to the household, pulled back Izolda's eyelids, glanced down her throat, suggested calamine lotion for the itchy bites, ordered malt to build up her thin form, and plenty of liquids. "The *bonne*, Madame, will make you *tisane* or fresh lemons boiled. It is dangerous not to 'ave liquids in an 'ot climate," he declared, patting Izolda on the head. He then proceeded to examine his real patient in the privacy of her bedroom.

"*Eh bien*, Madame Vintere, you 'ave done well," he said, exercising his English as he liked to do with his British patients. Spoken with a heavy accent, the sentences were punctuated with French words. Straightening up beside the bed and folding his stethoscope, he pronounced himself pleased with her progress. "Scarcely a *murmure*, Madame, after the birth of a grandchild! What about that for a miracle of science?"

"You'll have to keep me going now, Doctor!"

"There are things you must still watch: walking too fast, climbing stairs and steep hills. *Hein*, these villas 'ave dangerous spirals, 'ave they not? What foolish architects!"

"No need for me to use them. I will use the back door when I want to reach the basement."

"Slowly, slowly, Madame – I know 'ow you love to garden. Kneel when you plant out or weed, and stop before you feel fatigued."

"Thank you, Doctor. You know about children having four of your own . . ."

"Five, Madame. One more when you were away!" Dr Pouget smiled his pudgy smile. "The bumping of head? That should go when she begins school and falls tired into bed, as should the wall-picking. *Oui*, I 'ave 'eard of it before.

The Order of the Star

It augurs well that there was no trouble last night, but maybe the mackintosh precaution should be taken to begin with to ease her mind. The little one would be mortified to soil her new bedding. From what you tell me, *la petite* was innocent of many of the crimes accused of. *Mon Dieu* what *imbeciles* that lot are in *Angleterre*. She is a *mignonne* little girl with the temperament of a highly-strung filly. *Quelle chance*, Madame, to acquire *une petite fille* like that!"

"Well . . ." purred Louise, "I guess you haven't seen her at her best, not with that pock-marked face."

"Izolde," the doctor, said tossing her up onto his shoulders and prancing down the steps with her, "you 'ave to forget your 'bad 'abits' and they will forget you, *alors. Hein, n'est-ce-pas?*"

Screaming with delight – it was so high up on Dr Pouget's shoulders, higher than it would be on a horse if she ever dared – Izolda was deposited onto the drive. Adoringly she watched the funny doctor's receding form and then she turned and ran back and up the steps of her new home.

Chapter Thirteen

A few days later, Louise told Izolda that they were to visit her great-aunt, her cousin, and McLaughlan by tram. Izolda was so excited at the thought of this transport – much safer on rails than in a *fiacre* where the horse *could* bolt – and also of meeting the other three old ladies of whom she had heard so much, that she kept on waking up in the night to see if it were yet light.

The day dawned at last and grandmother and granddaughter made their way down the Carei Vallee road off which their compound lay. The river was bone dry with washing hung out on wires strung across its broad basin.

"In winter," Louise informed as she waved *en passant* to Monsieur Bienvenue, a policeman sitting on a chair outside the Gendarmerie, "the river bed becomes a roaring brown stream which goes under the railway bridge before disappearing beneath the public gardens and out to sea."

They came to the tram terminus at the top of these public gardens and sat down on a bench in the shade to wait for the tram. The garden before them was dug and tidily raked ready for grass seed and flowers to be planted once the weather had cooled. The temperature was still above ninety degrees Fahrenheit according to Louise, who on starting out had checked the thermometer hanging in the shade under the steps of the Villa Micheline.

Izolda was already more suitably dressed for the heat. She was inordinately pleased with the flowered tabralco dress of pleasant, peculiar newness of smell she was wearing that Mademoiselle Denise across the Carei had run up for her, with its matching elastic-topped knickers, all buttons discarded! She was sockless, and on her feet she wore comfortable rope-soled espadrilles purchased from a shop near the flower market. Louise had bought several of these each in a different colour to go with the other cotton dresses Mademoiselle Denise was making. Louise had told Izolda that when the soles got too ragged the shoes were thrown away. 'So simple,' she had laughed her pretty laugh, 'no buttonhooks and no cobblers!'

"To make up for the three months summer vacation that schools have in this country, they have short holidays at Christmas and Easter," Louise mused as they waited. "They start up again in mid-September so we shall have to get on with it. Dr Pouget recommends the local St Christophe School for boys and girls . . . Ah, good, here comes the tram."

Fascinated, Izolda watched a one-handed conductor, (his empty sleeve was tucked into the pocket of his jacket) her grandmother greeted as 'Monsieur Delaroux', untying the rope at the back of the trolley which was connected to the rod touching the overhead wires. He pulled the rod down, walked round with it, and then, with a skilful flick of the wrist at the other end of the tram, let it go to hit the wires in a shower of electric sparks. He then tied the rope to the tram bar. They climbed aboard.

"*Un billet-et-demi de retour pour Garavan, s'il vous*

plaît," Louise asked. Monsieur Delaroux, his legs braced in the rattling tram, neatly extracted with his one hand two tickets of a pale mauve colour from a swatch bursting out of the satchel slung across his chest. He punched the tickets, and with a flourish handed them to Izolda.

"*La petite est en visite?*" he enquired of *la vieille* whom he knew well from her journeys to inspect the progress of the new villas.

"*Petite-fille*", emphasised Louise proudly. "*Elle habite chez moi – pour toujours!*"

"*Tiens! C'est vrai, ça?*" Monsieur Delaroux's meridional tone sounded as nicely surprised as Louise had intended him to be.

"What's that?" asked Izolda.

"I was telling Monsieur Delaroux that you had come to live with me for good."

To Izolda, incomprehensible Monsieur Delaroux looked fierce in the extreme with his well waved and twirled moustachios, though she was soon to discover that he was the most indulgent of men. One arm had been lost in "*la guerre contre les sales Boches*" – as he was to tell her later. Izolda was to see many of these limbless men maimed in the same war as her father had fought in on the high seas, the terrible 'war to end all wars' that the grownups were always going on about called the Great War. The effects of this conflict, her grandmother said, were more evident in France than in England, and as the tram clattered on its way, with many stops for passengers to get off and others to climb in, she picked out several 'peg-legs' on the pavements; Monsieur Bienvenue of the Gendarmerie was also a casualty, but not, she gathered, from war. The new passengers on alighting were given different coloured

The Order of the Star

tickets, but no one, Izolda noted to her pride, were given pale mauve tickets as theirs which indicated the full whole ride from one terminus to the other.

The tram rattled on through streets lined with shops, and then into the narrow Rue Saint-Michel packed with pedestrians, from where Louise pointed out Marie's room high up in a peeling yellow building. Here, straggling the hill that lay between the Carei Vallee and the border with Italy, lay the *Vieux Caree*, the old quarter, weathered stone houses leaning huddled together thinly separated from one another by narrow arched lanes, their faded shuttered windows so close that the inhabitants could lean out when stringing up the washing and practically touch hands with those across the way. Below, every door was bead-curtained. The tiered steeple of the ancient Église de Saint-Michel rose above the old town to the level of the massive Cemetery set in deep terraces on the heights. Here, elaborate tombs, grave tablets and vast bleached monuments stood out whitely against the mourning green of the slender-taped cypress trees.

Izolda gave an involuntary shiver at the vision of graves, but to Louise they were a peaceful sight. The terraces reminded her of the Great Foreign Cemetery where James lay in Yokohama. When Baldwin – Maude's husband and James's elder brother – had died in retirement in Menton, his body had been taken home to England. Maude had also requested to be buried there, but she, Louise's wishes were to be with James in Yokohama.

As for Cousin Julia, 'poor Julia', as Izolda had learnt in a rigmarole of family history; after her non-marriage to a bigamist in the East and then the loss of her illegitimate son, Norman, at the Battle of Jutland, there had been nothing left to salvage from the Trust James had set up in Yokohama for her and her son. Maude and Baldwin, who were first cousins, were a childless couple. But loving the young as they did, they had been devoted to Julia's Norman, a most debonair young naval officer who made his base with them in Surrey after Baldwin's retirement, as had Louise and James's eldest son. This latter brilliant young man, Izolda's uncle, who had played rugger for both Scotland and England, had died before the war of meningitis in a matter of days at the age of twenty-two – the second of Maude's 'boys' to die. Now Camille, to whom Maude was equally devoted, was also no more. What with disease, war and earthquake it seemed that no family was free from tragedy during the first quarter of the twentieth century. But Jimmy was left, still out in China with the Chartered Bank. Promoted again, he was a budding tycoon with a delightful wife, Toni, Camille's great friend, and a son called Winn after Louise's maiden name. Maude had come up trumps by inviting Julia to live with her as her companion, and not only that but had housed her, Louise, when recovering from her heart trouble. As she told Izolda, if you had money you could do that sort of thing, *and* employ a ladies maid to boot!

The tram, once out of the old town area, accelerated along the Quai Bonaparte with its sixteen arches bounding the small harbour. From the windows Louise and Izolda could see the fishermen on the narrow beach smoking their pipes and mending their nets by their blue-hulled fishing vessels hauled up on the pebbles. Their bare toes held the ropes taut while their deft fingers knotted and wove the string rapidly in and out. Rounding the bay the tram came to a jangling halt at the Garavan terminus. Izolda jumped out to watch

The Order of the Star

Monsieur Delaroux doing his dexterous trick with the rope, sparks flying.

Seeing the child so intrigued, he handed her a fistful of spare tickets, climbed aboard, shouted a cheery *"à tantôt"* to her and 'Madame' and rang the bell for the return journey. Izolda stood open-mouthed looking at the tickets thrust into her hot hands.

"I expect Monsieur Delaroux wants you to start a collection; here, put them in my handbag," offered Louise. "We'll buy a *cahier* from the *tabac* shop for you to stick them into. A *cahier* is a lined exercise book. You'll have plenty of those at school."

They started slowly up the hill, Louise stopping from time to time to rest on the camp stool. They came to a level crossing barring their way, barriers down for an expected train from Ventimiglia over the border in Italy. Here was another friend of Louise's, Monsieur Ambere, the brawny young gatekeeper, uniform cap worn on the back of his head. As they approached he beckoned to them and allowed them to walk through the lynch-gate. Louise, smiling to herself, handed Izolda a five centime piece and told her to place it on the line. Monsieur Ambere looked on tolerantly while Izolda tried to fathom what it was all about.

They stood behind the bar while the engine roared past with a shriek of whistle cut off as it rumbled into a tunnel, leaving grey smoke billowing over the carriages behind. Izolda bent down to retrieve the coin. Beaming, she held it up all marvellously flattened. Monsieur Ambere nodded indulgently, and Louise looked excessively pleased. She reckoned that what with the ride on Dr Pouget's shoulders, the journey by tram, the tickets, and now the centime, Izolda had had more fun in the space of a few days than in all the years spent at the Parsonage. It augured well for the future.

On the Rue Vi Arilie, directly above the level crossing, stood the Villa Avis colour-washed in faded peach, its many green *porte-fenêtres* opened onto balconies festooned in a mass of purple bougainvillaeas. Louise, her pallid face damp with perspiration under her black straw hat, unlatched the rusty gate in the wall which opened with a protesting squeak to set off high sharp barks from a clutch of Pekinese to announce their arrival. With a smug look on her face at the surprise she was about to deliver, she led the way up the few steps to the terrace. Izolda, lagging behind, followed, her face by contrast blotched red with heat and mosquito bites.

"Gracious me," Maude exclaimed, coming out on to the terrace with the barking dogs trailing round her long skirts. She bent her ruler-stiff back to proffer a wrinkled cheek for Louise to peck first on one side and then on the other. "Gracious me," she repeated, "what on earth have you got there?" She presumed the child was some sort of waif Louise had picked up in the town. But it was not like Louise to pick up waifs. *She* was the one who visited the poor in the Vieux Caree, her special affection given to children and old men.

"Lou, how are you after the journey?" Julia sailed in from the garden in her paint-spattered kaftan smock and large straw hat. She enveloped her cousin in a sisterly embrace. "It seems odd you only visitin' and not livin' with us any more," she said in a Southern twang identical to Louise's. "It won't do, you know. You'll become ill again. I think you are crazy to—" she stopped short to stare at Izolda. "Who's that for goodness sake? Some poor little girl out of the gutter?"

The Order of the Star

"Guess!" said Louise, hugely enjoying herself. She sank into a chair on the terrace and dabbed her face with a dainty handkerchief soaked in eau-de-Cologne, while Izolda looked dumbfounded at the strange appearance of the old ladies. The tall thin one, who must be Great-Aunt Maude, was wearing a dress that swept the ground. She had a sandy fringe, a thick plait wound round her head in a flaming mass, a crop of extraordinary double chins for one so thin, and her eyes were red-rimmed. The other lady, who must be Cousin Julia since she called her grandmother 'Lou', was fat and bulgy all over. Her grey hair was cut as Eton-cropped as a boy's, which with her figure gave her a pear-shaped look. Her round face was like a rosy apple with sunken raisins for eyes, and her pinafore was dirty!

"*Quelle est ton nom, cherie?*" Maude addressed the child kindly in her execrable French. Izolda returned her look blankly.

"Where's your tongue, child; I hope those pustular spots aren't infectious?" Julia asked in English. In response to this Izolda stuck out her tongue as she was used to doing when bidden by Nurse to see if she needed another dose of castor oil. Shaking with suppressed mirth, Louise let out a gurgling laugh. Julia waved a finger before Izolda. "That for sure is *not* a pretty thing to do," she admonished.

By now the third member of the household had come bustling out of the villa. This was Maude's Scots ladies' maid, McLaughlan, who had been with the Wilson family (Maude had been a Miss Wilson) ever since anyone could remember. A sort of in-between servant who had her lunch with the family but never the evening meal, which was brought to her room on a tray by one of the maids, she made all her mistresses' lace-trimmed lawn underclothes and the

French divided knickers and bodices of a foregone age which Maude still wore. She was indispensable in the Wilson/Winter family if anyone was ill or a new baby arrived, and had many times been uprooted to go from one member to another. She had been lent to Camille to look after her wardrobe on her operatic tours. That glamorous time, when Izolda had been a baby, was the highlight of her life.

"Welcome back, Mrs James," she came up to Louise. Then seeing a child peered at her short-sightedly, her eyes focussing behind thick pince-nez glasses. "It's . . . Ach noo, it canna be?"

"Canna be *what*?" snapped Maude, aping the Scottish accent. "What's the matter with you all? It looks to me as if the child needs a good meal. McLaughlan, take her down to the kitchen and give her something to eat."

"But it *is*! I recognise you, dearie," McLaughlan knelt beside Izolda and hugged her. "What *have* they done to ma bonnie wee baby's face? Where's that peaches and cream complexion gone? Never mind, dearie, you've grown some hair at last. You were as bald as a coot as a baby. There was a time when your poor mother despaired that you'd ever grow any."

Izolda had no memory of this lady of small eyes screwed up behind her spectacles any more than she had any memory of being carried down the cliffs in the earthquake, but of the three ladies just met she liked this one the best. She unclenched her hot fist and silently showed McLaughlan the flattened centime.

"Aye," exclaimed McLaughlan still on her knees beside Izolda, "isn't that just beautiful m'bonnie wee bairn?"

"Shut up, McLaughlan," Maude frowned, "and stop putting your face into the child's; she's most probably got

The Order of the Star

impetigo or chickenpox. I've never heard anything so stupid: 'Ma bonnie wee bairn,' foresooth," she mimicked. "Take her away and give her a meal as I said."

"She's Camille's child, Mrs Baldwin, such a bonny baby; now just look at her, poor motherless bairn."

"*Izolda* . . . ?" gasped Maude, and collapsed into a chair beside Louise.

There was instant action. McLaughlan rushed for the sal volatile, Julia for a glass of water. Thoroughly alarmed, Izolda went to stand in the crook of her grandmother's arm. "It's all right, honey, your great-aunt does that rather easily. I remember her fainting in Japan once when she saw some naked gentlemen bathers. The Japanese think the Europeans are mad to put on clothes just to get wet in the sea."

"What am I? . . . What a silly thing to do, nearly passing out." Maude smiled wanly at Izolda. "Really, Louise, you're too old for playing tricks; taking us in like that indeed."

"You should have warned us, Lou," Julia said hovering anxiously over Maude, "are you sure you're all right, dear?"

"She always was a dark horse, your cousin, and apparently still is," mumbled Maude sipping at her water.

"Forgive me, Maude. It was meant as a pleasant surprise." Louise let Julia's 'dear' and her fussing, pass over her. It would be 'darling' next between those two, she wouldn't be surprised; but she could take it. No more would she resent that Julia – whom she had protected and supported all her life – had transferred her devotion from her to Maude. It no longer had the power to affect her – not now that she had Izolda.

They settled down to lunch in the shade of an awning on the

uneven terrace and were served by a maid in a black dress with starched white apron. Izolda helped herself sparingly from the dish of veal casserole, then liking the lemon flavour asked for more at which the old ladies nodded approvingly.

"What news of Jimmy?" Maude enquired.

"Fine. There was a letter waiting for me when I got back. He's doing well in the Chartered Bank; I guess they'll be moving him up again soon. They've adopted a Chinese girl as a companion for Winn, since they weren't allowed to have *you*," Louise smiled at Izolda, "your Aunt Toni couldn't have any more children after Winn."

"How public-spirited of them to adopt," Maude approved.

"Toni's a great girl," Julia addressed Izolda. "She was engaged to my son at one point but he was killed at sea, the Battle of Jutland, same battle in which your father was awarded his DSO . . ." the old ladies went on talking amongst themselves about the war, while Izolda bent down to pat the dogs, whose names she discovered were Tora, Onie, and Sato.

"I'm glad you like dogs," Maude approved, "there's nothing to beat Pekinese for intelligence. These are very highly bred from the Emperor's dogs. Pedigrees as long as my arm. Every day we give them hard-boiled eggs. No, they don't eat them, just take them into the garden and bury them; then, when a year or so later they consider they have ripened to perfection, they dig them up and have a feast! Moreover when I take them out for walks they trail along behind me and pick up the train of my dress as if I were the late Dowager Empress Tzu-hsi herself. Pure inbred instinct. You may get down now, dear child. Take some fruit from the bowl and run along and play with the pekes in the garden."

The Order of the Star

With the dogs barking excitedly, Izolda went up to the topmost terrace above the house where there was a small gate in the wall leading to the Boulevard de Garavan, along which the very rich in their big houses lived. She learnt later that there was a Hospice on the Boulevard run by the blue-veiled nuns and also a home for old men, whom her great-aunt visited with gifts of tobacco for their pipes.

Izolda sat on the steps by the gate, the dogs panting beside her, and sucked her mandarin and viewed the garden which fell away at her feet in a riot of mesembryanthemums over paths and beside fig, loquat, date, persimmon and lemon trees. The latter reminded her of the story her grandmother had related of how, when Adam and Eve were expelled from the Garden of Eden for being naughty and eating the apple, Eve had secreted on her person a lemon. After wandering round the world they found Paradise in Menton and settled there, and Eve planted the pips from her lemon.

Izolda thought it was a beautiful story and she believed it implicitly – even though she could not quite see how Eve could have secreted the lemon on her person when she was naked. She believed the story, for to her Menton (or Mentone as the old ladies called it using the Italian name) *was* Paradise.

Later that day an awful thing happened in Paradise! Izolda was still up on the terraces playing with the dogs when she saw the tram miles below crawling round the Quai Bonaparte like a green beetle, and heard her grandmother calling for her to come. Maude and Julia loaded them with presents for their new home, and Maude walked down with them carrying a heavy-framed picture of Fujiyama.

On the way, Izolda, who was walking beside her great-aunt, heard her exclaim: "Drat those tapes," while jabbing at her waist with a burdened hand as they approached the open barrier. Ambere was standing there with his cap on at its usual saucy angle. He watched the little group with the elderly Madame Vintere marching down as tall and straight-backed as usual. Then, without so much as blinking an eyelid, he saw her neatly step out of her divided knickers, which had folded about her ankles to repose on the railway line. Izolda gasped, and was immediately covered in embarrassment; but worse was to follow. Entirely ignoring the event, Maude marched on. Monsieur Ambere scooped the garment up and caught Maude over on the other side. He handed the garment to 'Madame' with a flourish and slight bow.

"Ah . . . *Merci bien*, Ambere," Maude accepted them with studied grace as if she were being handed a bouquet of flowers.

"What on earth?" exclaimed Louise in front and looking round.

"I walked out of my knickers," Maude laughed, buck-toothed. "Now, who in the whole world but a Frenchman could accomplish that with such delicate *élan*?"

But Izolda did not consider it in the least delicate. She was scarlet in the face with mortification for her great-aunt. Terribly concerned as she was with her bodily functions where things so easily got out of hand to disgrace her, she forgot all about Adam and Eve and the lemons, even about Monsieur Delaroux and the tram tickets. All she could think of for the rest of the day was the awfulness of Great-Aunt Maude having to retrace her steps over the level crossing to face Monsieur Ambere knowing that *he knew* she was not wearing any knickers at all!

Chapter Fourteen

"The Emperor Meiji awarded Grandpa the Order of the Rising Sun for his philanthropic work among the Japanese community," Louise informed on their return from Menton-Garavan as she and Izolda unpacked their house-warming presents. In the centre of the dining-room mantelshelf, over the unlit fireplace laid ready with coals for winter, she propped up the Order. "It was a great honour for a foreigner to be awarded it in those days when the accolade of chivalry was mostly reserved for princes and heads of state. Your grandfather was one of the first Europeans to be honoured. I found the Order in the ashes of our home after the earthquake; my most prized possession. I won't allow anyone to touch it and I dust it myself, but you can have a closer look at it just for once," she handed it to Izolda who gazed at the piece with its smooth ruby-red centre surrounded by golden tipped silver rays. On a hasp at the top of the Order a green and mauve enamelled link was decorated with flowers and some hieroglyphic writing.

"Once a year I thread it with narrow black ribbon and wear it to church on Armistice Day," Louise went on. "I'm proud to show it. In the Great War the Japanese were our allies. They did sterling work in China where their Fleet relieved the Royal Navy for operations in Western waters.

Now, if you fetch hammer and nails from the spare room we'll hang Fujiyama above the Order."

Izolda stood on a chair, and feeling important, hammered the nail in and then adjusted the straightness of the picture to her grandmother's instructions of 'a little bit more to the left, no that's too far; that's better, ah, just right.' They stood back to admire the picture in all its snow-capped glory.

"I climbed it with Grandpa," Louise expanded, "not in winter when it is covered in snow as in the picture but in August. We went right up to the 12,000 foot summit to view the sunrise from up there. Cousin Julia came with Cousin Kirkland and another man as well as your grandfather. We sat down in a row to wait on the rim of the crater. It had rained, and when it grew light and the mist cleared, d'you know, we found ourselves sitting in the middle of a rainbow!"

"*In* a rainbow? How could . . . ?"

"Sure. Rare phenomenon," Louise was not one to talk down to children. She expected them to get the gist of her words. "You see, there was a secondary rainbow over on the other side of the crater. Looking across at it we recognised ourselves reflected, sitting in a row. After that, at a Ball, Grandpa and I became engaged to be married," Louise related softly. "It wasn't all easy. The Winn family in the States did not in the least approve."

"Why, Grandma?"

"We were Presbyterian and Grandpa was Church of England which they regarded as 'high'; but that wasn't the only reason. Grandpa had had a Japanese wife, the daughter of a Samurai who had taken him in for safe keeping during the early 'troubles'. The children had grown up by the time I knew Grandpa. Your mother and I used to visit them at

The Order of the Star

festival times carrying presents. Now, let's get down to arranging the rest."

"But . . . were they . . . ?"

"I'll tell you more about Sumuko and her family another time, honey."

They proceeded to drape some embroidered, permanently pleated silk Japanese men's skirts over Monsieur Michelin's stiff Louis Quinze-type settee and chairs. Next came the hanging of several of Julia's watercolours. They depicted local scenes of the old town, one of the harbour with its fishing boats, another of olive groves backed by towering mountains.

"Waall," expressed Louise with a satisfied drawl when they had finished, "Cousin Julia sure is talented. She sells her pictures in the new town and thereby gains some pocket money. Yes, I figure the villa is beginning to look real homey."

The times Izolda came to think of as the most 'homey' were in this little room with its intriguing hatch when it was winter and the one fire in the villa was lit. After Marie had left, locking the downstairs back door behind her, she sat at her grandmother's side to be read aloud to before saying her prayers at her knee, and bedtime. But more often than not the book remained unread while Louise told the tales of her own childhood in the 'deep south'; of black slaves and the plantations, of the Civil War and Atlanta burning, of the journey to Yokohama by sailing ship to her missionary uncle and of the life there. She had gone to help her uncle found the first boarding school for Japanese girls, of which she became the Head. All these stories of 'Old Yokohama' were fascinating to Izolda, but best of all she liked to hear about her mother and what she had said, how she looked and dressed, and the poetry she wrote and her singing . . . Izolda could never hear enough about her mother, her eyes on the flickering fire in the grate, visualising it all. And true to her promise to DD, Louise only related the good and positive things about her father to Izolda.

By the time the next week's visit to Menton-Garavan came round, Izolda had already learned enough French words to be able to say to Monsieur Delaroux, *"Merci bien,"* when he handed her more used tickets to stick in the *cahier* bought at the Bureau de Tabac. Marie had allowed her to make a paste from flour and water stirred over the black range in the kitchen to just the right sticky thickness. Now she could ask Monsieur Ambere, *"Quelle heure est-il?"* when waiting for the next train at the level crossing, so that she could put her five centime piece on the line; and she accepted the strange old ladies in the Villa Avis with their musty smells and soft kisses, just as she accepted the quirks of Marie and her grandmother. At the rickety table on the terrace she tucked into her plate of ragout and persimmons to follow. The latter's skin was all wrinkled to ripeness; otherwise – so Great-Aunt Maude told her – they puckered the inside of one's mouth. Cousin Julia showed how to tackle them with a pointed teaspoon and McLaughlan warned her to take care not to swallow the slippery pips with their glutenous covering.

"I declare ma bonnie wee lamb's put on weight in a week," nodded McLaughlan approvingly.

"Montague died when you were away in England, Lou," Julia remembered to tell her cousin. "I'm afraid the news will be upsetting for you. Such a musical family. Oh, how I recall those concerts on the Bluff."

The Order of the Star

"Why should Louise be upset at Montague's death?" Maude enquired inquisitively.

"Never you mind, Maude," Louise grunted, "I guess all James and Baldwin's generation are dead now, either killed in the earthquake or died from natural causes. Humph. It's no good pretending. We're all pretty long in the tooth."

"There's still Mr Orange who's settled in Monte Carlo. We must resume our bridge four with him now that you're back. By the way, I heard from Cousin Kirkland in Liverpool. He's married again. His first wife, Helen, was killed in the earthquake."

"I know, Maude. You forget, I was there, next door. Her body—" Louise stopped short and looked at Izolda. She was about to say how Helen's and Camille's bodies had been laid out side by side with Shogira on the lawn at 'Akamatsu'. Instead she said abruptly: "Sit up straight, Izolda, you look all hunched, and please stop wobbling the table."

"Here, take this piece of paper and stuff it under the leg." McLaughlan tore up a bit of newspaper and folded it.

"Grownup conversation must be dull for you, dear child," Maude observed. "If you go into the drawing-room you'll find a present ready there for you and you can peep into the lacquer cabinet and look into all the little inner drawers. You can take them out as long as you put everything back in the right place."

That evening, hugging the beautiful Japanese doll her great-aunt had given her together with a scooter, Izolda asked her grandmother why the death of a man called 'Montague' would upset her.

"Because at one time in China, after your grandfather's death, I became engaged to marry him. He was a great friend of Grandpa's."

"Then why . . . ?"

"Sprue put paid to that and brought me to my senses, thank the Lord."

"Why?"

"Waal, I didn't much like the idea of living in England with its dismal climate any more than I do now. In any case I didn't *really* fancy being married again, though I wasn't about to let Maude know that just now. I bet *she's* never had an offer of marriage since your Great-Uncle Baldwin died. Now will you quit figuring things out," Louise stopped a further question forming on Izolda's lips. "I want you to go to bed real early. School tomorrow."

Izolda set forth, full of trepidation, next day with Marie. There would be boys, boys such as there were at the Parsonage to pull her hair and trip her up. There would be a sea of strange faces all gabbling away and she would not be able to understand a word. Here she was just eight and couldn't read or write – the shame of it. Worst of all, she was to be put in the lowest class with the six-year-olds.

St Christophe's turned out to be even worse than Izolda expected. The boys made the most noise. They yelled, rowed, and constantly fought one another in the echoing concrete courtyard during break time. The girls were quieter, but when they found she could not understand what they were saying they wandered off, leaving her on her own. Once again she kept on getting lost in corridors; and not only that, she was handed a black overall to put on! It was too reminiscent of the Parsonage. It all came back in great waves of shame, fear and hurt. At one point she found herself in the wrong class (they always seemed to be moving rooms), with a teacher spouting unintelligible words

The Order of the Star

at her while the children at their desks stared and sniggered. Perhaps the worst part of all was when later that morning the need became an urgent necessity and she could not find the water-closet – as her grandmother called the 'loo' nor did she know how to ask for it in French. She wet her brand new tabralco knickers, the beastliness trickling down into her white socks and new shoes.

In the Parsonage she had been whacked for such lax behaviour. In fearful anticipation she waited for it to come here. Would it be with a cane as Mr Forster used on the boys? What instruments of torture did they use on girls in France? So sure was she that she would be beaten that all through that long day she anticipated being kept back to be punished when lessons ended.

When Marie arrived to collect her Izolda was in tears. The *bonne* stood for a moment taking the weeping child in. Then, *"Té,"* she said in her nasal voice, *"té, tu à fais pipi dans tes culottes."* Though Izolda did not understand the words, Marie made them sound as if it was the most natural thing in the world to do, which of course it was. With Marie's immensely reassuring gnarled hand in hers, they ambled along together up to the public gardens and home.

Louise was sympathetic about school when it all came out, but firm. "I guess you've got to give it a month's trial, honey. By then I'm thinking you'll be feeling quite different. For one thing they don't beat little girls in French schools, as far as I know, and it was mighty careless of *me* not to think to tell you to ask for the *toilette*. No wonder no one knew what a water-closet was!" She gave her little laugh.

"But Grandma, it wasn't only that," wailed Izolda, blanching at the thought of a whole month there, "I had to wear a *black* overall . . ."

"You did? The boys too? Do you hear that, Marie? Black overalls."

"It is the custom, Madame," Marie shrugged. "It saves wear and tear on clothes."

"You have to snap out of it, Izolda." But Louise wondered to herself whether St Christophe would ever be a success psychologically for the child.

So Izolda soldiered on excessively nervously. She found out where the *toilette* was, and learnt to put up her hand to be excused. She knew which class she was in, though not which lesson she had to go to next as she was unable to read the writing on the boards. The only good part of the day was when the bell – and there were a plethora of bells – clanged for the ten o'clock break (school started at eight am), and a scrumptious *goûter* was doled out, which consisted of a slab of dark brown chocolate sandwiched into a chunk of crisp bread cut from a long *baguette*.

In her baby class, as she thought of it, even the smallest child was more advanced than she as they rattled off the words by rote. With the little ones on either side of her she sat there, licking her pencil and trying to apply herself to copy the unfamiliar words.

Worried at Izolda's downcast looks, Louise went down to the school to interview her teacher and discovered she spoke no English. Moreover the woman told her that she found her granddaughter so backward she feared, *"Izolde est un peu manquante."* Louise, outraged, vehemently denied the suggestion. Nevertheless, she returned to the Villa with an unpleasant thought niggling in her mind. Had those years of ill treatment at the Parsonage deranged the child?

The climax came when one day Izolda found herself ushered into a long queue to await she knew not what, except that, to go by the screams at the head of the line, there was some sort of torture going on up there enacted on the frightened children by a white-coated man. As she drew nearer she saw that arms were being scratched to draw blood, and she recognised what was happening. She tried to escape the queue but was roughly pulled back by a teacher. In vain she tried to explain that she had recently been vaccinated in England. Neither did the doctor take any notice of her pleas. Terrified that a second dose so soon after the first would prove fatal, she wept and struggled in the teacher's iron grip. But as other boys and girls (the former making even more noise than the latter), were howling in anticipation, no one took any notice of her struggles, and she was firmly vaccinated high up on one arm in four places.

It reacted very badly indeed. Izolda's arm became inflamed and she suffered some fever. Dr Pouget had to be called in and the whole episode left Izolda in a permanent state of fear as to what the next unexpected torture would be. She lost her appetite even for the *goûter*, and she began to have screaming nightmares all over again.

"Did you know, Lou," Julia asked, after having listened to the saga of St Christophe's on the next trip to Garavan, "that there is an English school starting up on the heights not far from you?"

"No, I haven't heard that. What sort of a school Julia?" Louise pricked up her ears.

"A girl's school, run by a Mademoiselle Blanche and her English friend Miss Sawtell, who is the Head. Apparently under French law, *étrangers* are not permitted to run schools. In this case the stumbling block has been neatly avoided by making Mademoiselle the titular Head."

"How did you know all this?"

"They'd seen some of my paintings in the shops and got in touch with me to ask if I would undertake to give drawing lessons to the pupils one day a week."

"And will you?"

"If Maude can spare me I might."

The upshot of this conversation was that Louise invited Miss Sawtell to tea. She met the proposed pupil, and within the week Izolda was removed from St Christophe's and enrolled in the new school; the fifth pupil to join. The others were a French girl (her parents wanted her to perfect her English), an American, a Hungarian and a White Russian refugee. Apart from French lessons with Mademoiselle Blanche, they were taught in English. Izolda came out of her nightmares, and a couple of months later, to her delight, suddenly found she could read the words in her precious 'Josephine and her Dolls' book. As if to make up for lost time, she became a positive bookworm who no longer wanted to be read aloud to. As for Louise, she uttered a sigh of relief, not that, she told herself, she had ever had any serious doubts that the child was *manquante*.

The establishment was known as the Villa Georgette School, VGS for short. Izolda and the French girl, Yvette, daily met by the Carei river and together climbed the Rue Colonel Herbert and on to the Chemin des Terres Chaudes on the Arbutus Ridge high up in the town. Far below the road, the trains could be seen curving their way towards the frontier.

Near the end of this Chemin stood the Villa Georgette, a tall three-storeyed house backing on to a hill and approached through a grotto of craggy limestone patterned with shells. Wetness dripped into basins where ferns and succulent plants grew in rococo shelves. Water overflowed onto the shallow steps to give a dark, dank, cool atmosphere of an underground museum.

Once through this artificial cavern lay a flat garden studded with palm trees. This was the girls' playground, and where they ate of the same mid-morning French *goûter*, although on a softer grassier surface and far less noisy area than St Christophe's. From the top storey a bridge led over a drop to connect the house with a small patch of garden and a steep track leading up to olive groves on the hill. These groves became the school's recreation grounds for rounders and the acting of outdoor plays.

Though Miss Sawtell, a woman of indeterminate age, was not exactly prepossessing to look at, she turned out to be a sound and honest Londoner whose sole purpose in starting the school was to make enough money to live abroad to escape the English winters. Her circulation was so poor that, in all reality, she appeared to be blue-blooded. She had a thin peaky face with an almost permanent drip on the end of her sharp nose. Her chilblained fingers showed red and swollen throughout the meridian winters when she piled on jumpers over thick skirts and viyella shirts. When the weather warmed up she discarded this gear for a dress with cardigan over; and for the three hottest months of the year, when the school closed, she disappeared to the family home in Holland Park. She had no qualifications for teaching, nor in those days was a teacher required to have any. She was an intelligent woman and taught her class reading, writing, literature – she had a passion for Shakespeare and for some reason, Robin Hood – history and geography. Arithmetic barely featured in the curriculum; Latin just, and higher maths or the sciences, not at all.

Not only were these two ladies unqualified to teach, they were neither temperamentally suited to do so. Miss Sawtell became so impatient with her pupils' slowness, stupidity (to her), or inattention in class, that she regularly lost her temper; spray sizzling through her badly-fitting false teeth to shower the blackboard as she let fly. Her mittened fingers stabbed at the surface in frustration and fury, the white chalk squeaking and snapping. When the spectacle first happened in front of Izolda, she watched open-mouthed, stupefied and fearsome as to what punishment would follow. None ever did. Miss Sawtell shouted and screamed, but never lifted a finger to any of them, and soon Miss Sawtell's explosions made no more impression on her pupils than did Mademoiselle's exhortations to pay attention and stop talking.

Mademoiselle Blanche, by contrast, was all sweetness and dimples. She was adored by her pupils for her pretty ways and also for the fact that, as she was quite unable to keep discipline, was easy to divert. As a result her class was more often than not in glorious uproar.

Louise, through Izolda's tales, quickly became aware of the inadequacies of these two eccentric ladies who had blithely started up a school which soon grew from its small beginnings to have twenty pupils, and in one heady year, even more. She weighed the balance of a better education for Izolda at St Christophe's as against the VGS, and came to the conclusion that atmosphere was more important to Izolda after the trauma of her early years, and hang the education. True, Izolda would not reach *baccalauréat* standard at the VGS, but she *was* rapidly learning the excellent French diction taught by Mademoiselle Blanche as a counterbalance to Marie's patois.

Chapter Fifteen

How Louise and Marie managed to communicate was a mystery to many. Perhaps it was an instinctive drawing together between two elderly women to whom life had been hard, which caused them to understand one another so well. Both were fiercely independent, both vague about their ages, Louise deliberately concealing her advancing years once she had taken on Izolda, Marie because she did not exactly know the date of her birth.

This had taken place in Tenda in the Italian mountains of the coastal area. As a small child, a boulder had fallen on her left foot crushing it cruelly. No doctor ever saw it, and for the rest of her life she walked with a heavy limp, her black leather lace-up shoe taking on the twisted shape of her foot. While working she shuffled round the house in soft *pantouffles*. She was always dressed entirely in black as was the custom for elderly peasants, with thick black stockings year round and a long-sleeved heavy cotton black dress. When she attended the Sacré Coeur Church once a week, she wore a black lace shawl over her head.

Marie suffered much pain from *la sciatique* in her bad leg, and had once made the expedition to Lourdes in the hopes of a miraculous cure, but *hélas*, the Blessed Mother of Christ failed to single her out. This disappointment did not for one instant detract from her unquestioning faith. On top of everything she had been born with a cleft palate. The resulting nasal speech was quite unintelligible to the unaccustomed ear. Although Italian was her natural language, she spoke the local Mentonnaise with her friends in the old town, and French in meridional throaty tones of singing lilt with vowels and 'g's tacked on at the end of words.

Presumably all these handicaps, with which she lived nobly and bravely, were too much to take for any young man. Marie remained a spinster. But how short-sighted of them. She was not only a delectable cook, she was extremely pretty. She had a small pointed face, smooth olive skin, lively black eyes and a beautiful froth of curling snow-white hair piled high and held in place with combs. She declared the blanched whiteness came from rinsing it in Milton, which gave her a strong antiseptic smell to drown much of the stale sweat which exuded from all who wore black. Marie was spotlessly clean in herself, but heavy black clothes could not frequently be washed; professional cleaners were beyond most people's pockets and in any case not very satisfactory, so Louise and Izolda were grateful for the overpowering Milton, and came to respect Marie's guffaws, cackling laughter and crashing ways in the kitchen as a cheerful adjunct to their home.

All her life Louise had been devoted to her servants and they to her, and Marie proved no exception though she was the very opposite of the sweet-tempered and humble Japanese servants she had trained of yore. Marie bowed to no man or woman. She was a hardy peasant, one prideful of her ancestry in the mountainous land of the Tendasques who were Niceoises and therefore French, even though they

The Order of the Star

now held Italian passports. Her working day started early. By six o'clock she was in the high-roofed market round which her friends, in their flat, colourfully embroidered straw hats, sat beside their zinc baths of massed flowers. In the covered area she loudly bargained for fish straight from the nets, tender veal, live chickens, crisp vegetables, much fruit in season and always the newly baked *ficelles* carried in a cluster under one arm. Most of her purchases were stuffed into her black shopping bag, the rest in string carriers draped about her person, and thus burdened she caught the tram by the market to the Carei terminus from where she ambled on up beside the river in time to serve breakfast from the hatch. Then came the twice weekly battle of wits.

"*Les bewas* and *kakis*, Marie, surely they cannot have cost so much?"

"*Parbleu*, Madame, what to heaven are those?"

"*Nefles alors; pardon – kaki*, I would have you know, is the Japanese for persimmon."

"*Mama mia*, am I expected to understand heathen languages as well?" Marie's straight little nose turned up disdainfully, "I would have you know, Madame, the fruit and vegetables are expensive this summer due to the crops failing in the drought."

"That does not excuse the charging of half as much again for the *salade* from last week. The price of eggs too, seems to have shot up," Louise frowned through her gold-rimmed spectacles at Marie's uneven writing in the notebook, spelt as pronounced.

"*Eh, oui, ils sont bizarres, les Anglais*," Marie expressed with considerable levity.

"The matter is *très sérieux*, I wish you to understand. I

have to watch every *sou* now I have to keep Izolde as well as myself."

Marie, who by now was heartily sick of the time being wasted when she should be getting on with preparing the midday meal, snatched the book from Louise's hand, licked her pencil, scratched out the sum total, reduced it by a few centimes, and handed the *cahier* back. "*On travaille dur ici, Madame, moi seul*," she groaned.

". . . And just look at this amount for those sardines we had yesterday," Louise ignored her.

"*Nom de Dieu, c'est la fin d'haricot!*" Marie exploded, "Fish today is hard to come by. The fishermen had a poor catch; you should have seen the empty nets they drew up on the Quai Bonaparte."

"Then why not purchase something else?"

"Madame knows we have fish on Fridays," Marie's button black eyes reproved. "You are a hard mistress, Madame. *Hélas*, the poor have to live somehow."

"There are degrees of being poor, Marie. I lost everything – well *nearly* everything – in the earthquake."

"I would be happy to be as poor as you," Marie replied, her pointed chin expressing extreme sarcasm. She shut her note book with a snap, counted the change Louise handed her, and grunted her way down the stairs.

Marie added something; Louise took something off. Honour was satisfied. It was a new form of housekeeping. In Japan, Louise had trusted the servants to be honest, and they were; in China the cook-boy added ten per cent to his purchases as was the accepted custom; here, in France, it was a battle of bargaining wits. Marie won, of course. Louise had no means of checking prices in the market where no price was fixed nor even marked, and if she shopped

The Order of the Star

there herself, the prices would automatically be raised on the spot. Marie, haggling knowingly, got her purchases far more cheaply than her mistress ever could.

But Marie had her limits. Louise knew that if she became too niggardly her Tendasque gem would shuffle off with her cleft palate, her poor twisted foot, her sage humour and her pride – and Marie's sardines *frites* were a crisp joy, her *crême brulées* a succulent dream, her *tisane* infusions guaranteed to get one quickly over any stomach upset. Even her version of milk puddings, whipped up so that there was no skin, and delicately flavoured with vanilla and lemon, were appreciated by Izolda. Milk was a problem. The few cows in the district had little grass on which to graze under the olive trees in summer, and none at all in winter when they were stabled indoors in the lower rooms of the farmhouses. As a result the milk, which was brought in metal churns and ladled into the customer's jug, was thin and expensive, and therefore only used for cooking. And that suited Izolda too.

The first winter Izolda experienced in Menton was an exceptionally cold one. Miss Sawtell declared to her girls that she might just as well have stayed in England for all the good it did her. Almost unprecedentedly it snowed one night. Though the snow vanished in the sunshine next day, it caused many eucalyptus and lemon trees to die, and havoc in the public gardens, until then blazing with flowers in their geometrically designed beds. The mimosa tree and the veronica bush which Louise had planted on either side of the Villa Micheline's steps, had to be replaced, and her thumbs became so cracked and sore from gardening that they rasped on the silk covering of her bridge table, causing Izolda to have goose pimples all over.

Winter was the time when the small dining-room came into its own with fire blazing to welcome the bridge – Auction Bridge – four who met regularly once a week in one another's house. It consisted of Louise, Maude, Julia, and Mr Orange from Monte-Carlo who had been in the earthquake, an elderly white-haired gentleman with neat Imperial beard. McLaughlan did not play bridge but came in the hired car with them and sat by the fire sewing. Izolda was brought in to 'do the honours' as her mother had in Japan before her, (*'plus ça change . . .'* Louise had sighed on the first occasion of this gathering), by passing round the scones and creamy *patisseries* of flakey *mille feuilles*, eclairs and sugary *palmes*. Tea was *'avec citron'*. Once Izolda had done her stuff, eaten several scrumptious cakes, and the old people had returned to their bridge in the drawing-room, she swung down the spiral stairs to hoist herself onto her favourite window-ledge to play with her growing collection of dolls, including the Japanese one.

Though Dr Pouget's words about Izolda forgetting her bad habits and they will forget her, proved true remarkably quickly once she had joined Miss Sawtell's school, some of her fears were less easy to eradicate. In particular her fear of horses. Then came cattle. From her high up seat in the basement, and from her bedroom window, she looked out onto the steep Rue Colonel Herbert, the way she and Yvette walked to school. On it, heavy carts laden with tar-smelling sacks of coal or heavy loads of stone, were drawn up by horses. Often, so it seemed to Izolda, the striving beasts fell. The sight of them lying, struggling to rise in their traces, was terrifying. She did not know which was worse: seeing them

The Order of the Star

slogging up the hill to the cracking of whips and curses from the drivers, or watch them slithering downhill, brakes on; in which case, when they fell, the entanglement of load, cart, shafts and beasts was sick-making to behold. Sometimes a horse had to be destroyed. Then the corpse was left where it lay until another cart and more labouring horses could be found to remove it. Marie would find Izolda huddled in a corner, white-faced and soundless, until the body was removed.

Just as terrifying were the herds of cattle regularly driven down this hill to the *abattoir* over on the other side of the river. Izolda was sure instinct told them they were nearing their end, for always at this point, with wild, staring eyes, they would panic and stampede past their drovers, bellowing as they went. Some were never found; some were rounded up miles away and sent to their fate; others, in the winters, plunged into the swollen waters of the Carei and were swept under the gardens and out to sea.

Most of the time, though, all was calm as it was on that winter day of the bridge party when Izolda went down to her perch and read aloud to the dolls from one of the children's books McLaughlan had given her. She then dreamed up a fairy story about a Prince arriving on his winged horse to rescue a maiden stuck high up in a tree. Bored with that one she lowered herself to the ground and found Marie in the kitchen up to her elbows in flour. Izolda untied the bow of her apron at the back.

"*Madre mio, tu me met en colère,*" Marie hissed under her breath so as not to disturb the bridge party upstairs. "*Je te jure*, I swear I'll tell *ta bonne-maman* what a bad girl you are. *Va-t'en enfin; je me moche de toi*!"

"*Tant-pis!*"

"*C'est pas jolie ça! Tu me donne bien de mal. J'ai de la peine aujourd'hui*," the *bonne* tried wheedling.

That having no effect, Marie managed to retie the apron and deflected Izolda by relating lurid stories of women in childbirth and the frightful agonies she would suffer when her turn came; that was if she did not cease being unkind to poor old Marie.

"What kind of agonies?"

"Since I am a spinster, I have not experienced it myself," Marie stated primly, her voice huff-huffing, "but I have attended many *accouchements*. The expectant mother screams and rolls all over the place till the baby pops out between the legs."

"*Between the legs*?" repeated Izolda, appalled at the mention of that awful place which had let her down so often in her previous life, and did so again on that first day at St Christophe's.

"Moreover," continued Marie as she got into her stride, her apron staying tied now she had the full attention of *la petite* who stood staring at her round-eyed, "moreover, every month when you grow up you will sit on the *lavabo* and do buckets of blood. One day, if you stop tormenting poor old Marie, I will tell you what *les hommes* get up to with their forks – *les salauds*. Particularly are they fond of bosoms," she pointed a finger covered in flour at Izolda's flat chest. "*Je te jure*, yours will blow up as big as mine. *Ne fais pas cette tête*," she admonished when Izolda made a facial grimace at the thought of growing breasts as pendulous as Marie's. "*Tiens*," she looked at *la petite* Mam'selle sharply, "we will try massaging your nostrils with soapy fingers in the bath; it will slim the nose down. Yours is too like a *bouton* for beauty."

The Order of the Star

"Did you massage yours?" Izolda admired Marie's chiselled features. "I wish my tooth would come out," she wobbled at a loose one.

"In my village in the Alps we have strong teeth." Marie opened her mouth to show not one filling. "Our elders yank them out before they stay too long in and weaken the new ones."

"Yank? That must hurt," Izolda goggled.

"We tie a piece of cotton round the tooth, the other end to the door latch. Then we slam the door – *v'lan*, bang! *Viens ici*," she grabbed Izolda, "Marie will show you – done in a second." She let out a guffaw of laughter as Izolda squirmed away from her grasp and returned to the safety of her window-ledge.

On the days when it was Louise's turn to go out to bridge and it grew dark, Izolda would wait anxiously at the front door to look through first one grille and then the other. No sign. Why was her grandmother late? She could fall down dead with her bad heart at any moment and once again she herself would be lost in a dark cruel world without a familiar face in it.

"*Qu'y a-t-il? Viens, mignonne*," coaxed Marie, "come and have supper in the kitchen. I have made a soufflé light as a feather. *Ça doit te faire l'eau à la bouche. Té*, if we wait much longer it will be ruined."

Even the thought of that delicacy could not distract Izolda from her worry. "*Gran'mere est si en retard, peut-être elle est morte*," she agonised, and began to bump her head on the grille.

"*Pas ça alors . . . Nom de nom de pas de Dieu*, stop banging your head at once! She is a tough one, *ta bonnemaman*, believe you me she won't die, not that one!"

"But she might, Marie; she could—"

"*Quelle bêtise!*" Marie scoffed, "bad news travels fast. If there had been an incident, Monsieur Bienvenue from the Gendarmerie would have let us know. Listen! There. Did I not tell you? *Eh bien donc. La voila!*" Before the last word was out Izolda had rushed down the steps to welcome her grandmother.

"What's all this? Don't be such a dumb-bunny," Louise soothed, "our last rubber went on rather long. It was worth it; I won five francs! You must cease being so apprehensive on my behalf, honey. I'm very much better. Dr Pouget says so." Izolda helped take off the moleskin fur her Uncle Jimmy had given his mother in Peking because she 'only had the clothes she stood up in' after the earthquake. Her low-waisted dress fell softly into folds about her form, the shorter length fashion dictated showing her pretty ankles and petite feet. She took out her hat pins, stabbed them into a cushion and adjusted her long jade necklace that doubled round her throat, touched the diamond half-moon brooch on her dress, twisted back into position the rings on her hands that the removal of gloves had disturbed, and rubbed some Icelma cream from a green jar on her sore thumbs. Izolda stood watching her, feasting her eyes on her and drinking in the perfume of eau-de-Cologne which personified her presence.

It was true that Louise was much better, and this was borne out on the day when they were late starting for the tram. They saw from a distance it was just about to start off from the top of the public gardens.

"Stop, stop!" Louise shouted, waving her umbrella and hurrying forward into a trot. Izolda dashed ahead. Monsieur

The Order of the Star

Delaroux stopped the tram and helped a panting Louise onto a seat.

"*Vraiment*, Madame," he reproved, "*vous êtes bien méchante. Restez çoi maintenant.* Keep quiet now."

"*Ça vaut la peine . . .*" puffed Louise while listening to her heart thumping strongly. It *appeared* to be going well. If she survived she would tell Dr Pouget the instrument had mended!

The sequel to this episode took place on their return. Louise and Izolda walked past the Gendarmerie where Monsieur Bienvenue was sitting in his *guichet* facing the road, taking everything in that passed.

"*Voyons!*" he exclaimed, his tubby figure stumping towards them (his trouser was folded above his knee, the stump strapped into a cumbersomely heavy harness topping his wooden leg), "I could not believe my eyes when I saw Madame sprinting past the Gendarmerie like a young 'un this morning. No ill effects, I believe? Now, Madame, I 'ave your new Carte d'Identite stamped ready for you. *La petite* will be having one of these when she is fifteen years of age."

"It was kind of you to be concerned for me, Monsieur Bienvenue. The little exercise did me no harm." Louise said, pocketing her new Carte which she was required to renew annually. "Tell *la petite* how you lost your leg," she added, seeing Izolda eyeing his peg-leg.

Without a second bidding Monsieur Bienvenue delved into his gory story of how a shark had bitten his leg off when, for a bet, he swam across the harbour from shore to pier. The encounter, he related with relish, was an experience he would not wish on his greatest enemy, not even *les sales Boches*. "*Mon Dieu non*, not all that thrashing about in one's own blood to try and frighten the beast away before the brute could take another bite. At the time the wound did not hurt at all! *Merde* though, that was made up for afterwards! I assure you Mam'selle, *ça y allait de pire en pire, figurez-vous*, my non-existent toes the worst of the torture. Let this be a lesson to you to keep close to the shore, *n'est-ce pas?*"

Izolda nodded. She had not yet learnt to swim, but when she did . . . no bets for her!

Chapter Sixteen

Though Louise was not one for poking her nose into other people's affairs, and rather prided herself that she 'kept herself to herself', Izolda noticed that her grandmother was not averse to twitching the lace curtains aside to scrutinise Monsieur and Madame Yovachitch. Marie revealed that they were refugees from Serbia when the couple arrived to take possession of the Villa Henri. In her turn Izolda was almost permanently at the window during the Easter holidays when an English family of seven rented the Villa Claude, the nearest to them.

They arrived in two cars laden with luggage. Filled with curiosity, Izolda went out to ride her scooter up and down in the compound. Round and round the central date palm she legged while obliquely taking in the father – a bronzed and handsomely moustached man – and the mother, who looked to her everything a mother should be: pretty, smartly dressed, and young-looking. There was a gangling older boy who took no notice of her, and a younger boy who did.

"I'm Christopher Paine-Talbot. Everyone calls me Chippy. What's your name?" the younger boy said, coming up to Izolda after having eyed her on her scooter for some time.

"Izolda. I live in the Villa Micheline with my grandmother."

"Izolda? What a mouthful. I'll call you 'Zol'. Come and see my baby sister." He led her over to a pram by the front steps of the Villa Claude. The fair, rosy-cheeked baby was awake, a rattle clutched in her chubby hands, and she smiled at the face appearing above her; a heavenly toothless smile that put Izolda's collection of inanimate dolls firmly into second place.

"We have an ayah to look after her," Chippy imparted. "I expect you've seen her about the place. She wears a sari. She's a Gurkha, awfully jolly. My father's in the Indian Army. He's on six month's leave, so he'll be with us for the summer hols as well."

"Here?"

"No fear. After the summer term we're going to the grandparents in Scotland. It's great up there: fishing and shooting and all that sort of thing. We're only here for the Easter hols. I expect it's going to be a bit boring."

Izolda glanced askance at him. He was nice looking, not much taller than she, with blue eyes and straight fair hair, a hunk of which fell over his forehead. She soon found out that the other man in the household was a chauffeur-cum-batman – as Chippy called him – a straight-backed man whom Izolda at first thought must be a relation until she heard him 'sirring' the Major.

"Think of having a *whole* family like that," later Izolda marvelled to her grandmother. She was bowled over by the very existence of her new neighbours. They were friendliness itself from the first day, and turned out to be every bit as nice as they looked. Mrs Paine-Talbot had invited her in to hold the baby and give her her bottle. "The children have grandparents *as well* where they go for the holidays when their parents are in India. If only Mummy hadn't been killed in the earthquake I could have had a baby sister."

"If only a lot of things," Louise commented briskly. "Now, Izolda, you'd better learn straight away that it's no use going through life envying what other people have, nor crying over spilt milk, nor thinking the grass is greener over every fence. I expect the Paine-Talbots have their problems just the same as everyone else in spite of their obvious wealth. I can't for the life of me think *how* they can all squeeze into the Villa Claude with that batman living in as well as the ayah. It don't make sense to me. From what I can see the mother's mighty familiar with the man. That wealthy set ought to be livin' out in Cap Martin. As for you, honey, I guess the only way to find satisfaction in life is to be positive and build on from what you *have* got."

An ambition was born in Izolda then and there. "As soon as I'm old enough I shall get married and have lots of children; I'm going to make my *own* family, that's positive, isn't it? And you can come and live with us," she added as an afterthought.

"Thank you very much," Louise laughed. *If* she were still alive by then, she would certainly be too old to be able to stand the racket of Izolda's hordes of children! For the present she approved of Izolda's new friend, Chippy.

With Chippy on his bicycle, and Izolda gamely following on her scooter, the two children pedalled and padded round and round the compound on imaginary world tours. For Chippy these were to India where all sorts of adventures befell them in bazaars, with ayah and baby invariably drawn in to swell the crowd. For Izolda it was to Japan where Chippy deigned to act the part of Emperor, presenting the Order of the Star of the Rising Sun to 'Zol'.

On such dangerous and rapid journeys the children quite often fell off their steeds, and Izolda in particular kept on reopening the same hole in one knee into which, ignoring her cries, Marie poured iodine. Chippy's mother painted her younger son's wounds with red Mercurochrome which did not sting and which made a gory splodge to generate sympathetic noises from the other inmates of the compound. With the Yovachitches' Alsatian puppy accompanying them on their imaginary tours, his playful bites nipping at their ankles with his sharp little teeth, keeping up with Chippy proved a fairly rough time for Izolda. But gamely she did. She followed wherever he led and revelled in the robust friendship with a boy who neither bullied, nor teased, nor found her in the least 'cissy'. Rather he praised her for 'spunk', at which she positively glowed.

All too soon the Easter holidays came to an end, and the idealised family left for England. But though the name Paine-Talbot faded for the time being from Izolda's life, the ambition born for a family of her own did not die. The husband who would father this brood did not loom largely in her mind at this stage; her only criteria was that he must be 'nice' – like Chippy!

And so, out of school hours Izolda went back to playing dolls with the cripple child Micheline who would creep in to join her in the shade under the front steps where there was a pit of sandy soil. With water from the downstairs sink they made moulds for pretend meals of patty pans. Naturally, Izolda on these occasions got herself covered in mud. At first she expected to be castigated or spanked for being in such a mess, but all her grandmother ever said was:

The Order of the Star

"Why, honey, you've got your dress all mussed up; better go and change it." All through that first winter Izolda felt nervous about getting dirty or doing something wrong. It took months before she no longer expected the reprimands followed by smacks and hits, and learnt to walk tall and free from fear.

The four villas shimmered in the summer sun. Monsieur Michelin's straight rows of colourful, soldierly zinnias, backed by brown-centred sunflowers of great height between clumps of white and yellow marguerite bushes, wilted in the heat. Izolda watered the Yovachitches' garden in the evenings for the princely sum of fifty centimes a time. With the money she bought stamps from the Bureau de Tabac to stick into the stamp book her father had sent her. Her favourite class at school became geography, where her stamps brought alive the dots she traced all over the globe. As for tram tickets, she had many scrapbooks filled with them, and Monsieur Delaroux began to collect train tickets for her as well.

Inside the villas the tap water trickled out rustily to discolour the basins. It was Izolda's duty to scrape right down to the bottom of their bath tub of preserved bath water with the can to get the last drop of sudsy liquid with which to water her grandmother's plants. The water soaked through the boxes of scented geraniums and splashed down the balustrades. In the beds on either side the new mimosa tree and veronica bush flourished. In between spread red and saffron pinks, fragrant greeny-yellow nicotiana and, as an edging, grew a mass of sweet scented mignonette – all Louise's favourite plants of sweet smells.

At nights the redeeming smell of water on dry ground,

mixed with familiar flower scents, wafted through her open window to make her dream of being back in 'Akamatsu'. From over the dry Carei bed floated the honeyed sound of a saw played with a violin bow by the war-blinded father of Mademoiselle Denise. Menton had become a sleepy place. Most villas were closed, two in the compound empty; the big hotels had shut, the fashionable shops were boarded up and the public gardens once more were dug and left bare. Streets shone in the sun dazzling the eye, and the pepper trees that lined the roads were covered in a thick coat of white dust. Trams ran infrequently. It was too hot to visit the old ladies in Garavan, or they them.

Then, joy, the man arrived on his annual visit to clean Monsieur Michelin's flock mattresses. He set up his machine under the shade of the fig tree by the covered well and proceeded to tease and card the flock through a comb instrument. The flock came out as new, all frothy, lumps gone, and was stitched back into clean, laundered covers to be neatly buttoned down with pieces of cloth. And the bliss was sleeping on them that night, all cushiony and soft and sweet-smelling.

Izolda watched the teaser working by day, and Marie, giving up bending over the hot black stove, borrowed her mistress's camp stool and went to sit under the fig tree by him and exchange news of their villages. She waited impatiently for July to come for her two months annual holiday with her family in Tenda, as impatiently as Louise and Izolda waited to meet Maude and her party in the feudal village of Gorbio, dominating the neighbouring valley from on high. The road came to an end on a square before a twelfth century chateau and an old Italian church.

From there they would take to the mountains!

The Order of the Star

* * *

"Tora! Onie! Sato! Heel. Come here at once! Stop barking at the donkeys and have a drink," Maude called. She had emerged in the dogs' wake from a hired car to join the throng assembled by Gorbio's stone fountain. "Ah, there you are Louise. I say, isn't it hot?" She went to cup her hands in the gushing water. The wetness trickled down her double chins.

The fountain, Izolda observed, had four iron spouts which poured water into basins on all sides: two small ones high up for humans, two larger ones further down for beasts of burden. Underneath there was a little one in the middle, at which the three pekes thirstily lapped.

"No one is allowed to wash anything in the basins," Julia observed on reading the *avis*. Over her bulging figure she wore a loose paisley-patterned dress with a string of amber beads hung low. Across her body was slung a canvas bag containing her sketching materials. "See," she drew Izolda's attention to the notice, "it reads: '*Défense de laver quoique çe soit, et de puiser de l'eau dans les aubreuvois*'. *Quoique çe soit* translates as: 'whatsoever it may be.' Now, isn't that just the cutest way of putting it?"

"You should not drink from there, Mrs Baldwin," McLaughlan cautioned her mistress.

"Tommy-rot. Tosh," came the usual riposte from Maude. "This is pure drinking water from the mountains; it says so. How much purer can you get than that?"

"Och, nothing is pure in France," McLaughlan would have none of it. "The municipal drains on the coast end no distance offshore with disgusting results for bathers. I wouldna' be surprised if the drains don't go straight into the drinking water here. Just look at that now," McLaughlan sniffed as a lurking village dog lifted his leg onto the stone trough. "Piffle!" Maude replied, determined to have the last word. "Don't you know that there *are* no drains up here, McLaughlan?" She walked off to supervise the loading up of the donkeys.

Louise, calm in the bustling fuss, sat on one of their straw cases by the gnarled trunk of an elm tree, while Izolda read the inscription on the large base to the effect that *l'orme* had been planted in 1713, two hundred and sixteen years previously, she calculated, counting up the years from 1913 on her fingers. How many old men had sat under that tree since then? Hundreds, perhaps thousands. They still sat there on the same rush-bottomed chairs watching with amused irony the confused scene of elderly English ladies with their dogs, one child and mounds of luggage contained in wicker panniers, all attempting to sort themselves out for the ride up to Sainte-Agnes.

"You man, you over there," Maude ordered with a point of an imperial finger, "load that basket *this* way up," she pantomined, "*voyez-vous*? Not topside-t'other-way, nincompoop!"

"*La gosse* does not understand your words, Aunt Maude," giggled Izolda. "Try '*la tête en bas*' for the other way up."

"Ha. He's got it. That's right my man. Well done! You see, dear child, he *does* understand topsy-turvy. It is the *tone* that signifies."

"Tone; get wise!" Louise observed disparagingly from her seat. "She's tone deaf; always was." Maude had been a keen partaker in amateur dramatics in Yokohama in the old days, but hopeless in musicals.

"They understand you because you are such a clever

The Order of the Star

actress, Maude dear," Julia quickly put in hoping Maude had not heard her cousin's true, if misplaced remark.

"What a fuss your great-aunt makes," Louise expressed to Izolda. "If only she'd leave the donkey men alone, I do declare they'd get it done in half the time. As for ordering them around in that dreadful French . . . Huh! She seems to think the louder she speaks the better she'll be understood. The same in Yokohama: shouting at the servants. Now she's shouting at the French peasants."

They watched the scene. While the donkeys waited patiently on the cobbled paving, heads down indulging in short naps, the donkey men were adding to the fracas by gesticulating and arguing amongst themselves as to which load should go best on which beast. These swarthy men of the mountains, faces blackened by the sun, wore voluminous shirts and baggy black cotton trousers. Flat on their heads rested navy-blue berets. Between their lips stubs of brown *caporal bleu* cigarettes bounced with every spoken word. Fascinated, Izolda watched the cigarettes, which remained stuck in place as if glued to lips.

Maude's full attention now concentrated on her pekes who were barking in unison in a very rude fashion at the large liver-coloured hound who had lifted his leg on the fountain. On his home ground by the café, the dog was in no mood to be cheeked and was growling a warning with a distinct display of yellow fangs. This obvious rudery set the pekes off into an hysterical crescendo of yaps, and with hair raised stiffly down his back, a fearsome snarl on his face, the liver-coloured dog leapt at the pekes who, with high-pitched yelps, scattered with agility.

"There's going to be a dog-fight!" Izolda moved fearfully to Louise for protection.

"For crying out loud, Maude, why can't you control your animals?" Louise put a protective arm around Izolda, raising her voice above the bedlam. "There's difficulty enough in sorting ourselves out without your pekes getting into a fight. Call them off, Maude, for goodness sake."

"*You* try controlling them," Maude cut back irritably. "Pekes have enormous pluck. They love a fight, bless the little darlings."

"Sure!" drawled Louise laconically.

With hackles up and spirits high, Tora, Onie and Sato gathered for a combined rush at the snarling enemy of snouty leer. Even as they attacked, the proprietor of the café booted his dog out of the way, cursing roundly as he did so. The dog lay whimpering against the wall.

Maude was outraged. "You shouldn't have done that, Monsieur," she flushed with anger, "I shall report you for cruelty to animals!"

"*Quelle culot*, what cheek, Madame. Your *salauds* started it, *les escrocs*!"

"In all my born days, I've never heard such a brouhaha about nothing," Louise got in quickly to check Maude from a further scathing retort. "Drop it now, Maude, and let's get goin'."

Keeping her distance from dogs and donkeys, Izolda now watched the astonishing sight of her dignified little grandmother being lifted by a brown-armed muscular donkey man into a side-saddle. She sat there, perfectly at ease, reins held high in one gloved hand, her short stature perched forward, her black straw hat held in place by a chiffon veil tied under her chin. One dainty foot lay in the stirrup, while the other leg rested over the pommel.

"You are a dumbell not to ride a donkey," Louise smiled

The Order of the Star

down at Izolda. "When I was not much older than you I used to ride along the Great Tokaido Highway with my uncle."

Izolda said nothing. Her mouth hung open. If the vision of her grandmother riding on a donkey was an astonishing one, the sight of the other three old ladies was quite amazing. She watched her great-aunt climbing onto a low wall and mounting a donkey unaided *en amazone*. Once astride, in masterly fashion she collected the tatty reins in one hand, her tall thin frame held stiffly upright, her ankle-length dress bunched about her, her long legs nearly touching the ground on either side. To shade her sore eyes from the sun she wore a large hat with trailing veil round the brim; in Izolda's eyes the perfect picture of a matador out to get her bull. "Tally-ho, halloo, halloo!" Maude cried exuberantly as if back in the days when she rode to hounds with the Chiddingfold Hunt in Surrey, immaculately attired with white stock, navy-blue habit, her face veiled under a top hat. In great form, Maude sailed ahead of her sister-in-law who, to her amusement, seemed to be having difficulty in getting her mount to move.

McLaughlan followed, grey wispy hair sticking out from under a small cuffed hat, her pince-nez trembling nervously on her nose. She clutched at the saddle before her. Like a ship in full sail Julia brought up the rear, necklace swinging. Behind her came a string of mules with panniers strapped to sides. Izolda followed on foot. She had been offered a donkey to ride, a sweet little animal with tall ears pointing inwards. But donkeys had four legs and *could* fall down, as had the pony in the trap and the horses pulling the carts up the Rue Colonel Herbert, even though her grandmother had said one could not beat a donkey for sure-footedness. She preferred to stick to her own two feet on the steep path she saw rising up the mountain before them.

Breaking into a run, the pekes at her heels, Izolda scampered past the straggling ranks of the cavalcade and took the lead.

Chapter Seventeen

'One and a quarter hours to Sainte Agnes' was written on a signpost at the start of the track above the *parvis* of Gorbio, where they had assembled. After levelling out, the path descended slightly by the small Chapel of Saint Lazare with its three arched porches shading its barred windows. The track crossed a stream on a stone bridge where the path diverged into two. Here the climb began in earnest, rising steeply upwards past terraces cultivated with vines and bounded by stone walls.

Izolda raced on, the dogs with her; one step up the curb, one stride along; up along, up along in the centre of the cobbled way, and soon she was far ahead of the cavalcade. The path narrowed into a single, unmade earth track with a drop on one side to a ravine overlooking the stream she had crossed. Already she could see Gorbio below bestraddling its own hill. Great boulders dislodged from the jagged mountain towering above had caused the landslide which made the track perilously narrow. Beyond, Izolda regained the old path and progressed through a veritable forest of shady olive trees, then out again into the hot sunshine. She came to a wayside shrine of the Virgin Mary clad in blue – Marie's 'Mary, the Mother of Christ'. Bunches of now withered wild flowers had been placed in jam jars at the base.

Sitting down on the plinth, Izolda waited for the rest to catch up. She listened in the mountain quiet to sounds the donkeys made with dislodged stones rattling down the hill. She could hear Maude's loud, county voice and her grandmother and Julia's softer answers, and she felt McLaughlan's painful silence. She buried her nose in Onie's thick, golden fur of ancient scent, one of myths and myrrh and not-quite mothballs. On glancing up she froze and clutched Onie closer to her. A snake was undulating and heaving across the track only feet away. She stared at the movement, then, seeing that it was no dangerous python, nor even a snake, she rose to investigate.

"Look," she called to the party as they approached, "look what I've come across. Hairy caterpillars head to tail on the march, masses and masses of them. The leaders have got all muddled up by a large stone and don't know where to go!"

"Well noo, I never did," McLaughlan exclaimed, peering at the sight from her perch, "that's very interesting that is; see, the surge of pressure from behind is causing them to bunch up. I mun dismount to take a closer look."

"No, McLaughlan, you're not to. We haven't the time," Maude ordered. She knew the hours McLaughlan liked to spend studying butterflies, and therefore caterpillars.

"Note what happens if you follow the lead blindly, Izolda," Louise had to have her little homily.

"For sure," echoed Julia, "you'll end up in a bunchy muddle like they have if you do. I guess it's wiser to think for yourself."

"Hua, hua, hua!" the men urged the donkeys on; "hua, hua," they encouraged, switching hind legs with branches. The donkeys were reluctant to resume the climb, and the men

The Order of the Star

leant their weight against the small beasts' flanks until they moved and began to pick their line in a clinking of hooves against stones. Steadily they zig-zagged from one side of the steep path to the other. To and fro they plodded, carefully placing dainty feet, taking their time.

"Why do they zig-zag?" Izolda asked the leading donkey man when he paused to roll and light a brown cigarette. He blew smoke from his nose. The pungent odour of the weed filled the air. He did not answer Izolda at once, but spat accurately and resoundingly onto the path. He stood looking thoughtfully at his spittle.

"*Eh, oui,*" he said at last, his black eyes shining at Izolda like polished olives, "*eh, oui, enfin. Peut-être leurs gran'mere les appris*, as yours teaches you, *té Mam'selle?*"

On and on and up and up they went until they came to the farmhouse Maude had rented on the slopes of Sainte-Agnes. There it lay, aptly names 'Les Cerisaies' for its situation by a cherry orchard, whitewashed, shuttered and cool in the freshness of the mountain air. Its ancient tiles – held down by stones against the violent winds of winter – were light terracotta in colour, bleached by centuries of sun.

Dismounting a little stiffly but exhilarated by the fun of riding again – albeit on a donkey – Louise sat on a bench on the terrace while the rest busied with the unloading and unpacking. Life, she thought, was full of marvels even when one was old. What could be more wonderful than that they four septuagenarians – she, Maude, Julia and McLaughlan – had been transported up a mountain where no road went?

Before her stretched a glorious view of hillsides patterned with mule tracks, dark olive groves, rosemary bushes and giant heather. She could see and smell the clumps of lavender and thyme. Two cedar trees stood further away, and beyond was a group of lone scrub oak. The ground before her fell steeply in terraces right down, far, far, almost giddily down to the old town of Menton with the deep blue Mediterranean sea stretching out beyond. The air was still and invigorating after the heat below, and she could pick out their own Carei Vallee though not the Villa Micheline, which was hidden from view by the curve of the Arbutus Ridge where Izolda went to school. Lengthening her gaze across the water, Louise could just see the faint coastline of Corsica on the horizon.

Calling to Izolda to come and join them for a meal in the farmhouse, Louise marvelled again when her grandchild came running towards her. Where now was the pallid, listless, dull-eyed child of under a year ago? Here was one with hair bleached by the sun into gold; face, arms and legs toast-brown, lithe body sturdy and healthy. The child's green eyes, flecked with mimosa yellow, shone with the thrill of being high up on a mountain, and her mouth was stained with cherry juice from the orchard where she had climbed the trees to indulge herself.

Louise gave herself no great credit for this transformation. She believed that as one gave, so one received, and the more generous the giving, so was the greater the reward. She saw very clearly, that if through Divine providence she had been the instrument in saving the child, so – in over-filling measure – had the child brought joy and fulfilment to her old age.

High above the village of Sainte-Agnes, which straggled the mountainside and laid claim to be the highest coastal village in Europe, lay the ruins of a Saracen castle behind

The Order of the Star

which rose a black iron cross, stark and foreboding against the vivid blue sky. Half hidden in the ruins and behind iron grids, were gun emplacements. The guns pointed down a vertical drop of thousands of feet to Garavan on the border, from where the enemy might come. This was too terrible a confrontation to contemplate when half the families in Sainte-Agnes were Italian.

"Why do they have to have guns up there?" Izolda asked.

"In case there is a war, dear," answered Maude, "but there won't be a war to worry your little head about, not since we won the last war to end all wars."

But Izolda was not so sure. McLaughlan, with her interest in butterflies and wild flowers, was a sturdy walker, and daily she set forth with Izolda and the dogs. Climbing up to the village they encountered red warning flags which barred their way and forced them to make a detour. The hills around them echoed with staccato blasts of rapid rifle fire. On several occasions they had to stand aside on the narrow paths to allow a contingent of dashing mountain troops of the Chasseur Alpins to tramp past with their gun-laden mules.

Up there the border was so ill-defined that climbers were advised to carry their passports with them. McLaughlan carried hers in her knapsack together with Louise's which had Izolda's name in it, just to be sure, especially when they climbed the Berceau Mountain, so called because it was shaped like a cradle with one peak in France, the other in Italy.

During the holiday the old ladies taught Izolda to play bridge. They said she was much better at it than McLaughlan, who had no card-sense whatsoever and constantly revoked.

Izolda felt flattered to be allowed to play, and it was a relief to McLaughlan not to have to sit there in confusion while her mistress, none too kindly, instructed her which card to play, and the other two said that was cheating.

And in the long evenings when the guns ceased their manoeuvres and the only sounds on the air were chirpings of transparent-winged cicadas and the church clock chiming out the hour – and why was it always kept at exactly twenty minutes ahead of time? – the ladies sat on the terrace of Les Cerisaies when they had finished their bridge; McLaughlan with her dressmaking and Julia in front of her easel until it was too dark to see. Izolda sat in the crutch of a cherry tree, half-listening to the murmur of Maude and Louise talking about the old days in Japan, while she picked and ate the large juicy cherries to her heart's content. The wealth of fruit was such that neither she, nor the few birds left that had not been shot out of existence for the pot by the peasants, made any impression upon their bounty.

It seemed to Izolda that the summer at Sainte-Agnes had passed in a flash on the day the cavalcade reassembled. Now the old ladies sat tipped forwards on their saddles, looking as if at any moment they would topple over their mounts' heads. McLaughlan hung on to her cantle for dear life; Maude gripped with boney knees; Louise sat back neatly; Julia looked like a sack of potatoes. Instead of making encouraging noises, the donkey men used restraining ones: soothing 'whoas' filled the air as the men leant back, acting as breaks whilst holding on to the donkeys' tails.

Running ahead, Izolda far outstripped the rest and after a while even the pekes gave up chasing her. As sure-footed in her espadrilles as the donkeys, she positively revelled in

The Order of the Star

the sensation of effortlessly flying down a mountain as if on wings. With limbs stretched out from stone to stone she sprang along the path with the instinctive balance of a child, the sun on her face, the wind in her hair. On and on she flew down to the olive forest, along the narrow landslide track two feet wide, with the steep drop on one side. She felt airborne, as detached from earth as if she were one of the gliding kites overhead.

Before her lay the stone bridge over the stream where the paths forked. Which way Gorbio? There was no signpost to indicate, and she could not recognise the path they had come by. The left or the right? She did not know, so she sat down on the parapet to wait for the others to catch up.

A great quietness surrounded her; only the bubbling of the stream below and the buzz of the bumble-bees as they collected nectar in the wild marigolds. No restraining 'whoas' from the donkey men; no pekes yapping, no old ladies' voices, no loose stones rattling downhill, no little hooves clinking. She waited and waited – and still they did not come. Now she was in the shade.

All of a sudden she felt chilled, lost and very frightened. Had she mistaken the way further back? Had they taken another path up there which she had missed in her glorious run? What if they *never* came this way? Should she retrace her steps and try and find them? But if she did and failed to meet them she would become hopelessly lost; lost on a mountain and soon it would be dark. In great hurtful sobs, Izolda wept.

Two old peasants with a donkey heavily laden with wood appeared round the left-hand track. They stopped when they saw her and spoke in Italian. She could not understand them, nor did they understand her French.

"Gorbio?" she sobbed. They pointed back to the way they had come. It did not seem right somehow, and still hoping that the cavalcade might miraculously appear round the corner, Izolda refused to budge from the bridge. The peasants indicated that she come with them, but still she would not move. They waited awhile, then, shaking their heads at the sight of a small foreigner sitting on the parapet by the stream all forlorn and alone, they left her.

When the sound of their donkey had long faded and the lonely silence was too great to bear, Izolda rose and walked up the incline beyond the bridge. And there, just round the corner, a stone's throw from where she had cried despairingly, stood the Chapel of Saint-Lazare; the rays from the setting sun turning its yellow stones to orange. Beyond, the lights from the village of Gorbio beckoned.

Louise did not see the tears on Izolda's cheeks in the twilight by the fountain in the *parvis*, and Izolda did not tell her grandmother she thought she had been lost when she was not lost at all. She learnt two important truths during that halcyon childhood summer on the mountain. She learnt that it was foolish to follow blindly as the caterpillars had, to get all bunched up in a dead end, and she learnt that it was equally foolish to give way to panic and despair in what seemed a desperate situation; for if she kept her head, around the corner she would find a light and a way.

And both these truths were to stand Izolda in good stead in the years to come when the war to end all wars proved to be a myth and she found herself swept up into the next great conflict.

Chapter Eighteen

Although Izolda still kept up with Micheline out of school hours, the landlord's daughter was too crippled to join in active games, and it was Yvette du Vivier who became her inseparable friend.

The only child of wealthy parents, Yvette was a dark-haired, rather over-dressed girl a year older than Izolda. She lived in an expensive block of flats known as the 'Palais Ausonia', recently built by an Italian landowner with the grand name of Comte Alberti della Briga. Across the way by the promenade had arisen the new Casino. The old ornate one by the gardens was now used only for official and social functions, where the two friends gathered with all the other children for the annual 'Battle of Flowers' and the Carnival Fête; for which, especially the latter which could turn into an orgy according to Louise, they were chaperoned by Madame du Vivier. She was a lively ex-tennis champion of the South of France, and had taken on Izolda's coaching with her daughter. Both girls showed promise and by now were participating in all the junior tournaments along the coast.

Yvette's father, descended from an old French protestant family, as an asthmatic had come to live in the Midi for his health, where he met his wife. Some thirty years older than she, he was an accomplished musician who taught his daughter the piano and violin, and played the organ in St John's Anglican church, situated across the way from the new Casino. Thus, tennis and church became the focal out-of-school points in Izolda's life – *and* men for the very reason of their scarcity. Every Sunday without fail Louise and Izolda walked to St John's through the public gardens. After the packed service they shook hands with the white-haired Rector, Mr Greenstreet, and chatted to the gathering before Louise made her way home, and Izolda and Yvette set off to stroll arm in arm along the Promenade du Midi to eye the chic crowd passing by. They always stopped to chat with stout Philipino, the donkey woman in her flat embroidered hat, who hired out her donkeys for small children to ride up and down the esplanade which stretched above the stacked reinforced rocks and the narrow pebbly beaches.

There were several 'sets' in Menton besides the fashionable, worldly French *mondaines* seen out with their pampered and powdered poodles. When Izolda, puzzled by the variety of inhabitants, asked her grandmother what set she was in, she was firmly told the 'church set', where she sang in the choir with Yvette and giggled over the 'ffs' instead of 'pp's in the old hymn books, dating from when the church was founded in Queen Victoria's day – not that either girl had any idea what 'f' could stand for, only that it was such a funny way of writing 'p'!

Despite getting the giggles in the choir stalls, Izolda and Yvette both approved of church and implicitly believed in its teachings. At that time, when there were six thousand British residents in Menton and Garavan, social life revolved around the church. To the locals the English were known as '*les hivernants*', the winterers, from the fact that most disappeared for the whole of the hot summers. The du Viviers

The Order of the Star

and the Winters, though, were not classed as *hivernants*. It was known that Menton was their permanent home. Even Mr Greenstreet disappeared to England for three months leaving Monsieur du Vivier 'saying' the services to the handful of congregation left, while Louise took on playing a harmonium for the hymns. During the winter season, a curate, a different one each year, came to help out and take the Sunday School and Confirmation classes. Invariably Izolda and Yvette fell in love with the young man, and inevitably they declared themselves to be broken-hearted when he left.

This passion for males stemmed from the fact that there *were* no young men in Menton – other than the town boys, with whom they were not allowed to mix – added to which there were no fathers, Yvette being the one exception, though her father was more like a grandfather, as old and as white-haired as the Rector. On her green-marbled dressing-table, in splendid naval uniform in full-rig with rows of medals, to Izolda's pride was displayed a large photograph of her father. Next to it, in a much smaller one, rested a tinted photo of her mother: slim, beautiful, laughing. Of course the other girls at school *did* have fathers, one and all, who turned out to be as shadowy as Izolda's. Louise called this lot the 'fast set', who were *hivernants*. The mothers were *mondaines* who, according to Louise, spent much of their time dancing with gigolos, drinking and gambling in the Casino. The fathers turned up at intervals bearing presents. For a short while they gave their offspring the time of their lives before vanishing once more. Some of these fathers were in the Indian Army, as Major Paine-Talbot had been, or were men from the diplomatic or colonial services. Some were rubber planters in Malaya, others 'box-wallahs', as European men in India in business or trade were known. The wives of these elusive fathers excused themselves from joining their husbands in those far-flung countries on grounds of delicate health or family commitments. Whoever the fathers were, they were all idolised by their men-starved daughters, as Izolda idolised DD, who had fast become known to her only as in the photograph. She ascribed to him every quality a man could have, plus a great many more. Sons scarcely came into the picture. Boys were banished to boarding-schools in England and only appeared occasionally in Menton for the Christmas or Easter holidays.

As well as the 'church set' and the 'fast set', there was the 'refugee set'; to Izolda the most intriguing of all. These consisted principally of White Russians, whose men in order to survive (the jewellery they had escaped with had by then run out), dug gardens and drove taxis, while their wives: princesses and countesses all, set up tea-shops and, dressed in their striking national costumes of high bead-encrusted head-dresses, ribbons and rows of jangling necklaces, waited on the impressed customers. There were also several refugee Hungarian families. One, the glamorous but poverty-stricken Countess Apponyi, who played the piano like a professional and spoke six languages fluently, as did her two daughters who joined the VGS, came to live in one of Monsieur Michelin's villas. As seemed to have become the norm with the fast set, the Countess was without a husband, though rumour had it she had married a dashing French colonel who was around somewhere. There were more Serbs to follow in the footsteps of the Yovachitches, and an ebullient hair-stylist, Monsieur Pumelic from the Balkan States, who spoke of political

The Order of the Star

turmoil and persecution in his country, where he had lost a foot. The ladies flocked to his salon, despite having to endure the gory tale of how the accident had happened.

All these *étranger* inhabitants reaped the benefit of living in a town where the exchange rate could be relied upon to stay secure at FF124 to the pound. One heady year it rose to FF244. It was then that the VGS expanded to such an extent Miss Sawtell had to get another teacher in; her outbursts in class soaring with the rise in numbers. Out of class she was a different woman, delighting in devising new entertainments for her girls. She led her pupils further and further along the Arbutus Ridge and up into the mountains in search of plants and flowers for them to press into their botany books.

The next few years flew by for Izolda in a life full of varied interests with always a new place to visit in the summers. One was to Marie's home in Tenda in the Italian mountains, where Izolda met Marie's large family of brothers and sisters, nephews and nieces, and her ancient mother of one hundred – and she had thought Marie and her grandmother old! The next summer they went to Aixles-Bains for Maude, who had been ill, to 'take the waters'. Here, Izolda watched 'Grand Guignol' puppet-shows, ate ice-cream sodas piled with fresh raspberries, and played hop-scotch with the local girls round the bandstand in the public gardens. Then back to Menton for another winter of Shakespeare plays in the olive grove terraces above the school, and another summer term of bathing in the Roché Rouge across the border, and camping out under the stars in the mountains with Miss Sawtell giving fascinating lessons in astronomy. But perhaps the most fascinating time of all was when Mademoiselle Blanche told of her prophecies.

Mademoiselle Blanche never went up into the mountains nor even as far as the olive groves. How could she with her high-heeled shoes, shiny silk stockings and pretty floating chiffon dresses? Instead she coached and coached her pupils in French verbs, regular and irregular. She made them recite the words in unison until they were blue in the face, and then write out the full verbs in verses again and again until, as Yvette said, they were *puce* in the face.

"Please Mademoiselle, I cannot write any more; my fingers have gone all funny," Izolda, fed up, would hold her hand out to show her ink-stained second finger which had developed a lump.

"That is not cramp, Izolda, that is because you dip your relief nib too far in the ink-well. You should not press so hard to make those blotches." Mademoiselle, wearing exotic scent, bent over her English pupil. The *cahier* was in a mess. She took it away and beautified it by making corrections in violet ink, her thin-nibbed slanting handwriting as elegant and dainty as she was herself.

"When did you say the cataclysm will come, Mademoiselle?" Yvette would lead after having exchanged glances with Izolda that it was time the boring verbs stopped for the day. In all innocence, she lifted her dark head from where it rested on an arm on her desk. "When, please, is the end of the world?"

"Yes, do tell us, Mademoiselle," the whole class exhorted.

"If you pay attention, I will explain." Mademoiselle Blanche put down her chalk and composed herself at her high desk, her graceful legs entwined. "We of the Society believe the fateful year to be nineteen-hundred and thirty-eight . . ."

The Order of the Star

"Oooou!" the girls echoed, pretending to be awed.

"You do not believe me?" Mademoiselle looked pained. "*Enfin*, it sounds improbable maybe but you will find when you grow up that it comes true, this I assure you. The events will be catastrophic, and then you will recall my words. It will start in Europe and spread and spread."

"How will that be?" prompted Izolda into a silence of half-belief. But to her it was true. She did not doubt it – all those guns at the ready near Sainte-Agnes; all those marching Chausseurs Alpins . . .

"The signs are there for all to read in the Egyptian pyramids. Inside the largest one there is a narrow passage which leads to the Great Chamber; a passage which measured through the centuries has faithfully pre-recorded the events of major importance in history. *Mais oui*, I assure you, *mes enfants*, this is a *sujet très sérieux*. The signs clearly indicated the Great War up to the present." Mademoiselle's large brown eyes flashed with fervent belief.

"What comes next?" the class asked breathlessly, carried away by her passion for the subject.

"The passage enters the Great Pharaoh's death chamber in the year I told you. What else can that mean, *mes cheres élèves*, than the most terrible catastrophe that has ever happened – *enfin*, the end of the world."

"It could be just another war, perhaps?" Izolda asked hopefully. That horror would be preferable to the end of the world, even though the latest curate out preached that the end of the world meant 'the Second Coming' with heaven on earth for all believers. Izolda was no waverer. She was not going to risk not being in on that one. Yvette was a waverer . . .

"It could, Izolde; and what would another war bring with

all the new tanks, guns and aeroplanes but the end of the world for us as we know it?"

Goose-pimples rose on Izolda's scalp at the thought of another war to maim more people like Monsieur Delaroux, and then, banging the desks shut, she tore out with the others into the garden under the palm trees to devour her *goûter*, while watching Yvette turn a neat cartwheel, her dress tucked out of the way into her knickers.

"I don't believe a word of it," Yvette said, looking at the sunny world upside-down in a handstand, which for a few moments she held; her slender body straight and still.

"Neither do I" Izolda lied, so as to be at one with her best friend. Anyway, 1938 was *years* away and Menton had never been more prosperous or more vibrant, and her grandmother had put Marie's wages up! Besides Mr Greenstreet would think it blasphemous to believe Egyptian pyramid forecasts.

But both Izolda and Yvette were perceptive girls, and even though 1938 seemed ages away, they could not fail to see the cracks as earthquake-like fissures appeared in the life of their home town, which the British had adopted and came to think of as their own. It started with the Germans. After not daring to show their faces in France following the Great War, and then their nation becoming bankrupt, they now reappeared prosperous and thick-skinned with it, according to Monsieur Delaroux. They were the ones to start the craze of sunbathing and were visible when the tram passed the new Lido beyond Quai Bonaparte. Large, well oiled bodies could be seen stretched out on the beaches, roasting.

"*Dégoûtant! Quelle bêtise,*" Monsieur Delaroux rasped to Louise and Izolda on their weekly tram ride. "What folly to invite the sun to lobster-boil one! Yet what care I if the

The Order of the Star

Boche is boiled alive? That they are up to their tricks again with that brash arm-saluting Monsieur Adolph Hitler is plain for every ex-*poilu* in France to recognise."

"Signor Mussolini is the one to watch, a vain and despotic man if ever there was one." Louise voiced her belief that he was the greater threat.

Tension ran high on the frontier, and Marie reported after her next holiday in Tenda, that the mountain roads were crammed with marching Carabinieri in their Napoleonic uniforms and feathered alpine caps. To counterbalance this Italian threat, the slopes of Sainte-Agnes were alive with Chasseur Alpins, the heights bristling with more defensive guns than ever; paths blasted out where a short while ago there had been only donkey tracks.

"Not at all, Madame, if you will permit me to contradict you about the Italian leader," Monsieur Delaroux politely disagreed with old Madame Vintere's views. "Benito Mussolini in my opinion is a great man. He has done much to help the poor with his reforms, *particulièrement* the Italian farmers to whom he gives free *huile de richin* for their good health."

"Pah! That revolting stuff," Izolda remembered parsonage days.

The German invasion of the beaches in search of sun did not at first affect the British residents, other than to cause them to walk past the gross sight with sunshades up and eyes averted, but when a second event occurred, the impact hit every single one of them personally, not the least Louise.

One day she returned ashen-faced from the bank after cashing a cheque which gave her only eighty-two francs to the pound. The impossible had happened: England had gone off the Gold Standard. As if that was not bad enough, her lawyer wrote from London that the five per cent War Loan into which he had put all he was able to scrape together from the ruins of the earthquake, was to be converted to three and a half per cent undated stock. He strongly advised her to adhere to Mr Neville Chamberlain's patriotic appeal to support the country in its dire need by keeping her money in the newly reduced form. Louise, who though married for over twenty years to an Englishman, had never thought of herself as anything but American, was unimpressed by the appeal of the British Prime Minister. However, she knew perfectly well that she was in no position to start speculating with her small capital on the stock market. After spending some sleepless nights, she felt she had no option but to accept her lawyer's advice.

The knowledge riled her. She was being forced into doing things she did not necessarily go along with. *Undated* stock sounded mightily to her as if the British Government was doing a con trick.

Louise approached Monsieur Michelin who, after some haggling, reduced the rent of the villa. He had his own problems. The British colony, upon whom the town was so dependent, were leaving in droves, and with anxiety he and his friends in the letting business watched the rapid exodus knowing that most would not return. The Villa Claude remained unoccupied and was likely to stay that way. He might as well hang on to the Serbs, the Hungarians and Madame Winter for what he could get out of them; all cried poverty! But still Louise's sums did not add up. She clamped down more than ever on Marie's accounts, and she wrote to DD for an extra allowance for his daughter.

'*You cannot afford to live out there any longer. You must come back to this country*', he wrote. '*Bring Izolda over.*

The Order of the Star

She should be going to boarding-school. I could find you digs or a small hotel nearby'.

'Nothing will induce me to live in England', Louise answered. *'If you arrange for Izolda to go to boarding-school, what will happen to her in the holidays? Will you pay her fare here and back three times a year, or has your wife had a change of heart?'*

Meanwhile, Louise was being forced into another matter she did not necessarily go along with. Izolda was coming up for her twelfth birthday the next summer and had expressed a wish to be confirmed in the spring before with Yvette. With her non-conformist roots Louise considered Izolda far too young to take such a step, but she had to give way after Mr Greenstreet came to see her. He explained that the Bishop of Gibraltar administered an enormous coastal parish. The diocese extended to no less than three thousand miles from west to east – from the Atlantic Ocean to the Caspian Sea – and a thousand miles from north to south across the Mediterranean from Europe to North Africa. "By the very nature of this huge district," expounded Mr Greenstreet, "it is virtually now or not until after she is grown-up before the Bishop can visit again, Mrs Winter, and I understand Izolda and Yvette would like to be confirmed together . . ."

Mademoiselle Denise ran up white dresses for the girls, who wore short veils to show the Roman Catholic element in the town that the Protestants were not as 'low church' as some supposed, and every bit as religious as they.

"How would you like to visit your father and step-mother?" Louise, with sinking heart, asked her granddaughter after the confirmation had taken place. The upshot of her correspondence with DD was a compromise that Izolda should visit her father and stepmother, to *'see how they get on. My wife can't very well refuse to have Izolda when she has not set eyes on her since she was little. Now that Izolda is growing up I hope that my wife may feel differently. Please arrange the journey for which I will send the money'*. Louise felt she was losing her granddaughter . . . They had been good years . . . would all the good be undone in England again?

"To The Manor?" Izolda looked up from where she was doing her homework on the dining-room table; a shadow crossing her eyes at the hazy memory of her step-mother having hysterics and her being turned out. "I don't know . . ." Izolda added slowly. "Would you be coming?"

"No. In any case I haven't been asked."

"Will you be all right here without me?" Izolda felt concern for Louise though she was dying to see her father again. It might be good fun staying in a posh house with lots of servants.

"I'll be all right, honey, sure I will with Marie. We are planning to go to Aix-les-Bains again. Your Aunt Maude is not well. The doctor recommends the waters. I might even have a bathe myself!" Louise laughed with a bravado she did not feel. "You can travel to England with Miss Sawtell and *back*," she emphasised. But would Izolda come back? Would she be carried away by the riches, wish to grow up in a grand country house, become a débutante in the 'fast set' who had little or no moral codes such as she had instilled into Izolda?

Louise did not know. She did not know the extent of Izolda's day-dreamings when, as a child, she sat on the basement window-sills, and how she had told her school friends that she lived with a grandmother because she had a wicked *maratre* every bit as bad as the step-mothers in

The Order of the Star

Snow White, *Hansel and Gretel*, and *Cinderella*. Neither did Louise know how Izolda fantasised about her father. He was more handsome than all the other shadowy fathers in Menton; a Naval Officer to boot, with the medals of a war hero. And he loved her! Did his letters not start with '*my darling Izolda*' and end with '*your loving Daddy*'?

Despite her excitement at the prospect of going to England, Izolda was sorry to miss the trip to Aix-les-Bains. Wherever she had gone in the summers with the old ladies it had been fun; Aix had been special. There had been that row over the French boy who had spoken to her by the bandstand, and waited for her outside the hotel until her grandmother had instructed the manager of their hotel to tell him not to shadow Mademoiselle. She had felt flattered by his attentions, sorry that he had been rebuffed when he had done nothing wrong, ashamed and cross with her grandmother who really was too hopelessly old-fashioned for words.

Yes, Izolda did want to see her father very badly. She wanted to please her step-mother and make the visit to England a huge success so that she could live permanently in a country where there must be hordes of boys of the 'right set'.

Chapter Nineteen

Miss Sawtell was such an appalling sailor that she turned green at the sight of the Channel, even on the fairly calm summer's day on which she and Izolda crossed to England. She took to a day bunk and remained there until they tied up at the Dover docks. With no chaperone in sight and spirits high with excitement and expectation, Izolda raced round the decks to show what a good sailor she was. She followed this by feeding the seagulls with buns bought at the shop, and herself munched slabs of chocolate, all of which added to the discomfiture of those watching from their deck chairs who were not feeling too good.

DD was a surprise to Izolda when he met them at Victoria Station. He was smaller than she had imagined from the photograph, and his hair was crinkly grey all over. His blue chin rasped her face when he kissed her, so different from the velvet of the old ladies' cheeks. They saw Miss Sawtell into a London taxi. Father and daughter then drove off in a highly polished Wolseley which had been left parked outside.

"It it yours?" Izolda asked tentatively. To her a ride in a car was a great treat.

"Yes; chauffeur kept. The man drives Diamond around in the Rolls. My goodness you've grown," he went on,

The Order of the Star

noticing the budding breasts under her cotton dress. Her bare legs were covered in fluffy golden hair . . . Heavens, *espadrilles* for London! "Those shoes won't be much good when it rains. I hope you've brought some sturdier ones for the country?"

"They're all right for walking in the mountains," she bristled.

"Humph. I can see we'll have to get you kitted up. You'll need to put Veet on your legs."

"Veet? What's that . . . Daddy?" The word felt as if she were being too familiar.

"Stuff which removes hair. Smells foul, but it's worth it. Girls should have smooth legs; I'm very particular about that sort of thing."

"You're hairy," she pouted. He had dark curly hair on the backs of fingers on the capable hands on the wheel. His fingernails were spotless. There was a nice clean tang about him – like the sea she had just come off.

"I suppose you must be short of funds in France?" He ignored her remark. He looked at her critically again. How badly dressed she was, but her looks; how like her mother – same dreamy eyes.

"Pretty short. Everyone's going bankrupt: shops, cafés, those sorts of places, and landlords like our Monsieur Michelin. Most English have left for good, which worries the Mayor. The municipality is arranging for sand to be carted down to the beaches for a summer season. The soles of my feet are as hard as nails from running over the stones. The school hires a fisherman with a rowing-boat for us to swim out to and jump off; it's fun."

"Listen to me carefully, darling," DD instructed putting his foot down on the accelerator when they had left the suburbs behind. "I want to put you in the picture as to what you are going into. Do you remember your step-mother?"

"Barely," Izolda gave an involuntary shiver at the thought of meeting her *marâtre*. Which one of the many wicked fairy-tale ones would she be like? She suddenly felt queasy. It was probably all those chocolates she'd had on board.

"Diamond's a difficult sort of woman; mood changes all the time. She can be absolutely charming, then perfectly b . . ., er, nasty, the next." No, he had not been about to say 'bloody' in front of the child, but 'bitchy'! How innocent was Izolda? She must have her periods by now with those sweet little breasts showing. My God, how he loved her. He had been starved of his daughter by the bloody bitch. "Promise you'll be on your best behaviour?"

"Yes . . . Only . . . Well, I expect I'll make lots of *faux pas* . . ." Nervously, Izolda bit the side of her thumb. Yvette did it. She had copied the trick and it had become a habit.

"You can rattle away in French before her friends. That'll put Diamond in her place! Musn't do that," he pulled at Izolda's hand, "that *is* babyish. You don't bite your nails I hope? No, I see you don't, but you could do with a good hair-cut and a manicure. Now, about the servants. Better not to get into conversation with them. You aren't supposed to chat, especially at table; they wouldn't understand it. Ignore them. They are there to do a job so as you don't notice."

"Marie and I chat all the time. How silly not to. Can't I even say 'good morning'?" Izolda tittered.

"Use your nous. Be polite, and particularly watch your table manners. Diamond's a stickler for that sort of thing. You know about finger-bowls?"

"Great-Aunt Maude uses them when we have fruit. Menton isn't a *complete* jungle you know." She was

The Order of the Star

sweating under her armpits. Her father would be ordering a deodorant next. He'd got her all in a twist. Dress too short, legs hairy, nails needing a manicure, stuck up servants; Diamond a stickler for this and that . . . Help!

"Most important of all is that you have to watch your behaviour towards *me*," DD cautioned. "Naturally I am devoted to you, darling, and the mistake I made when you came to live with us, was in my showing it. This time I shall behave as if I did not care a hoot. Got it? You do the same towards me, see? I shan't call you 'darling' unless we are alone, and you'd better not call me 'Daddy'."

"What shall I say then?"

"Call me 'Dick' and your step-mother 'Diamond' in the modern manner. It is the very latest thing. We won't kiss goodnight, *or* hold hands. Try not to take too much notice of me, though you'd better watch me under those long eyelashes of yours, at table with its frightful array of napery."

DD turned smoothly off the main road and onto the country lanes of Surrey. The purring Wolseley passed through open white gates by a lodge set in a tidy garden. Beyond, out of the shadows of the past, Izolda remembered the field where cattle grazed and the paddocks where horses raised their heads and came galloping up to the rails. They passed farm buildings, a small lake and a park of ancient oaks. With a sinking feeling in the pit of her stomach she saw the large, solid-stone mansion looming up before them with a conservatory on one side, a low wing on the other, and a turreted portico in the centre with massive front door, iron girded and as bold-studded as a prison. Her mouth went dry.

Izolda turned to her father for comfort. She noticed how

his hands were clenched on the wheel, his knuckles standing out whitely. Suddenly she knew that for all the brave war hero that he was, at this moment he was every bit as nervous of what was to come as she. She put out her hand to rest it on the immaculately pressed knee of his dark, pin-striped London suit.

"Dick," she said brightly, "together we'll brazen it out with your Diamond, somehow or other!"

"Wait here while I fetch your step-mother," ordered DD. He strode into an imposing hall from which, to one side, polished stairs wound up to a half-landing. On the other side double doors opened into a large drawing-room through which lay the conservatory, full of tropical flowers. A man with high, stiff collar and black suit silently appeared at her side, and with a "Good morning, Miss" and a barely-concealed curious look at her, picked up her suitcase and softly left the hall. Heavens, was he going to *unpack* it? It was borrowed from Julia and had no key. Horrors! He'd see her old pyjamas and worse, the bulky towelling 'squares' Marie had packed in case . . . Izolda blushed at the thought of a *man* seeing them. But surely a butler . . . ? She stared as a woman, who must be Diamond appeared, surrounded by pugs, from the direction of the drawing-room. Her father, following, hung back. Her step-mother was not at all like the witch-featured *maratres* of her fantasies. She was more like a fairy godmother! Dressed in a misty blue gown, the flimsy creature swayed up to Izolda, slim legs clad in the palest of sheer silk stockings, narrow feet encased in soft beige high-heeled shoes. Diamond gave her a limp handshake while her eyes flickered over her in an all-inclusive glance.

The Order of the Star

Making some reference to the damp weather, and asking pleasantly about the journey, Diamond led Izolda up the staircase to a single bedroom overlooking the drive and turreted entrance.

"If there's anything you need, ring for the house-keeper," she said, glancing round the room to see all was in order. She went over to twitch the curtains further open and adjust a rose in a bowl on the dressing-table. "I haven't planned any entertainment for the first few days of your visit. I thought it would be nice for you to have your father to yourself," she said sweetly. "At the weekend we're having a house party which I hope you will enjoy, though I'm afraid there are no young of your age coming. They're all still at boarding-school."

"We break up early because of the heat." Izolda found her tongue.

"Quite. There's always tennis, depending on the weather. I don't play but Dickie likes a game. I expect you play lawn tennis?"

"Lawn?"

"Yes, on grass." Diamond looked speculatively at the dreadfully dressed sapling, almost as tall as she, who did not seem to know the term 'lawn'.

"I've only played on hard. The tennis courts in the South of France are red," Izolda hit back.

"The gong will go for luncheon in half an hour's time," Diamond glanced at the small gold watch on her dainty wrist. "Come downstairs when you're ready." With red-nailed fingers she smoothed a wrinkle out of the counterpane and left the room.

In France, Izolda thought, her step-mother would be classed as a '*jolie-laide*'. The term described her precisely.

She was a woman in her forties, quite small; her very slimness and extreme chic together with her high heels giving her the appearance of being taller. Beautifully and expensively dressed, her complexion was smoothly tended with an oft-massaged look about the throat. Her makeup was cleverly put on to look natural, except for a splash of crimson lipstick on thin lips. Her features were small but sharp. Brown hair was parted in the centre and set in becoming waves round a narrow face; extraordinary eyes, so pale the blue was almost lost in them, completed the picture of a woman who was the acme of sophisticated *savoir-faire*.

Though the sight of her step-mother sent Izolda's confidence plunging to zero, she was at the same time filled with admiration for her. No wonder her father had married Diamond. She was *gorgeous*!

Next, on taking stock of her room, Izolda felt done out of a good thing. To think that this room, this luxurious home with its riches and servants could have been hers if things had turned out differently; still could if she were a success with Diamond. Her small, white room in the Villa Micheline with its cot bed, flock mattress, net curtains and one rug and shiny-topped dressing-table was like a cell compared with this room. Here there was a thick-piled, pink, close-carpeted floor underfoot. The glazed chintz full-length curtains at the window matched the frill round the kidney-shaped dressing-table and the valance round the deep sprung mattress. Moreover, the quilted bedspread and the bedhead were upholstered in the same pretty material. There was a cut-carafe on the bedside table and a silver box with biscuits in it. Her suitcase was nowhere to be seen. Someone in the short space of time before she had come upstairs had already unpacked. Her cotton dresses hung lost in the massive mahogany cupboard. Facing the window was an antique desk with everything laid out for writing, including stamps and the headed notepaper Izolda knew so well from her father's letters. She sat down to write:

'Darling Grandma.
It is fabulous here! My room is so pretty. The servants are frightfully grand. Daddy drove me down from London in a super car and introduced me to Diamond, who is being terribly nice to me. I hope you are all right. There goes the gong for lunch, so must dash.
Lots of love,
Izolda xxx'

She could have added a *'PS. Lunch went off all right'*. So did a game of tennis with her father, when the weather cleared that afternoon, on a manicured lawn which behaved in much the same way as the hard, red courts in Menton's Tennis Club. DD showed his pleasure and pride to find that his daughter was no rabbit at the game. For dinner that night Izolda changed into her 'best', the cream-coloured tussore dress Mademoiselle Denise had run up for her confirmation. At the meal DD was in tremendous form; her step-mother laughed and exchanged smiles with her at his jokes. Retiring early, Izolda sank luxuriantly between the slithery pink linen sheets in her bed and found a hot-water bottle at her toes. So this was how the rich lived. No wonder her father liked living with Diamond!

Even as Izolda was revelling in the linen sheets, she was being discussed downstairs:

"She's abominably dressed, Dickie."

"I agree, it's that penny-pinching grandmother of hers, though I admit with the exchange rate things must be pretty tight for the old woman now."

"She hasn't a decent thing to wear this weekend."

"Could you fix up something ready-made for her?"

"I'll do my best, though I'll be hectic preparing for the house-guests and our dance on Saturday. Somehow I'll have to make time to take her shopping."

"Very decent of you, Diamond, I must say." DD basked in the way things were going.

Step-daughter and step-mother were taken into Guildford in the chauffeur-driven Rolls and were dropped outside a department store which sported the royal coat of arms above its doors. Wasting no time and without consulting Izolda at all, Diamond selected a lightweight suit, several dresses – including a tennis one to replace her skimpy shorts, and made her try them on in a cubicle. She noticed the child had extraordinary underclothes, with a sort of cotton bodice from the last century, and promptly bought lingerie of crêpe-de-chine camiknickers and a light belt dangling long suspenders. Silk stockings and two pairs of shoes followed.

Suddenly Diamond's benign mood changed. "I'll sign for the lot on my account. Quick, pack everything up," she ordered the saleswoman. "No, I don't want them delivered. I'll take them – *now*. Hurry."

"Do you buy your clothes here?" Izolda asked, while they waited for the parcels.

"Good God no. My outfits are made in Town," Diamond said. "I wish that wretched woman would hurry up." Her manicured fingers drummed impatiently on her crocodile handbag.

The Order of the Star

"It's terribly kind of you—"

"That's all right," Diamond interrupted, brushing the words aside. The chauffeur, waiting outside for them, opened the car door, stacked the cardboard boxes on the front seat beside him, and drove smoothly off. Diamond did not utter a word on the way back to The Manor. Feeling somewhat abashed after her step-mother's brusque response to her attempt to thank her, Izolda remained silent too. Moods, her father had said. She didn't mind. There were all those lovely clothes to wear!

Later that day DD took Izolda into his study, a room Diamond, she gathered, hardly ever entered. It was sacrosanct, his domain, where he could get away from everything, he told her. Izolda found it like a museum. Framed pictures lined the walls depicting her father's boats, from his old training ship, *Britannia* to the *Kinsha* of his last command on the Yangtze, and all his many destroyers in-between. There were Chinese banners, photographs of river craft, ships at sea, Flotilla Regatta lists, framed invitations to Government House Balls, Shanghai race cards, Jockey Club badges, naval caricatures – a whole wealth of a naval past.

DD also showed Izolda snapshots of her mother which she had never seen before. She was fascinated by them, volumes of them stuck into books. One was taken in Wei-chu in China at a mammoth naval picnic, her mother wearing a marvellously elaborate hat, another taken in the Bois de Boulogne in a fur coat in the snow, others in Scotland, the wind blowing her hair. There were theatrical ones galore. One dressed up as 'Cho-cho-san' in *Madame Butterfly*.

"They're for you one day, and your mother's poems. I've typed them out myself and bound the book. Some of her later poems are the most beautiful word-music I have ever read. A singer-poetess with a string of beaux, that's what your mother was – and *I* won her . . ." DD swallowed. To Izolda's consternation he looked near to tears. "Oh darling, it's so lovely having you here," he put his arms around her and held her for a moment. "Enough for now," he pulled himself together. "Come on into the drawing-room. We must keep up the facade!"

Chapter Twenty

From her bedroom window, Izolda saw the weekend guests arriving. She went down in her new smart coat and skirt, silk stockings and leather shoes, to be introduced by Diamond to the assembly as 'Dickie's daughter'. They looked at her curiously and asked where she lived.

"The only place I know on the Riviera is the Monte Carlo Casino," laughed a retired naval officer friend of DD's. "You know it?"

"Not allowed into the gaming rooms."

"How stupid of me. You look quite grown-up."

"I've been inside the building though," Izolda smiled at the compliment. "Children are allowed into the theatre. My school did some *tableaux vivants* there for charity. That's where my mother had her début in opera."

"Oh really?" he said, "I wouldn't know about that." He quickly switched off as Diamond approached.

Meeting the visitors turned out to be not as difficult as Izolda had anticipated. This was because the guests stayed together, laughing and chatting about people she did not know, and took little notice of her. This informal tempo suited her, and soon a party led by Diamond set off for the races. Her father did not go. He entertained those who stayed behind and in the afternoon, suggested tennis, and was pleasantly surprised by his daughter.

"You play an excellent game, young lady," he praised after they had trounced the other naval officer and his partner, "who taught you?"

"She was once champion of the South, the mother of my friend Yvette."

"Wouldn't be surprised if you don't become champion yourself!" joked the other naval officer. The general *bonhomie* continued in the relaxed atmosphere of tennis and tea. The racegoing party returned in exuberant spirits in time for the dressing gong, and all retired to get ready for dinner, followed by the dance to which outside guests had been invited.

After indulging in a deep bath, into which she poured a great amount of Diamond's bath salts, Izolda dried herself with an outsize towel and was lavishing scented powder over her when she saw the stain. For a moment she panicked. Had she cut herself? If so, where? Ah, of course . . . It was what she had prepared for, what Marie had described years ago rather too vividly. It was her grandmother's monthly 'being unwell'.

Far from feeling unwell, Izolda felt thoroughly grownup and buoyant. She had caught up with Yvette, who had reached this status months ago! She felt happy and assured and perfectly at home in her step-mother's grand house with all her posh guests. She appreciated the way Diamond left her alone to find her own way. Far better than being constantly fussed over by the old ladies with their: 'Sit up Izolda, you'll get round-shouldered like that', from her grandmother, or 'don't squint into the sun, dear child, you'll get wrinkles', from her great-aunt, or from McLaughlan,

The Order of the Star

'put on a jersey, dearie, you'll catch cold in the *mistral* with those bare arms'.

Izolda had only one regret as she walked sedately down the grand staircase in her brand new, rustling, yellow evening dress to her ankles, her black patent leather shoes peeping out below, a great smile on her face. It was that her grandmother wasn't here to see her. She would not be able to believe her old eyes!

DD, watching his daughter descending, could hardly believe she was *his*. Camille . . . So very nearly . . . so sweet and young, her fair hair shining golden against the background of the yellow dress. Diamond had marvellous taste. She had already done wonders for the child.

Dinner was served round a candle-lit polished table. In a striking flame-coloured gown, the cut-on-the-cross style showing off her slim hips and flat stomach, Diamond was the perfect hostess who entertained amusingly and with assured ease.

Equally at ease that evening was Izolda in her status as daughter of the household. She sat next to her new naval friend, with a titled, rather pompous but nevertheless kindly, gentleman on her other side. It was a warm evening with a smell of dampness in the air which wafted through the open French windows as dew formed on the grass outside. Though Izolda had had several lemon squashes after her tennis sets in the afternoon, the rich food made her thirsty. She did not like to ask the white-gloved butler whom she had first met in the hall, for anything so plebeian as water, of which there was none in sight, nor any tumblers to hold it, but only a plethora of wine glasses of various sizes for the many courses. The white wine served to her in a long stemmed glass was refreshingly chilled, and each time she drank some, the glass was topped up.

Every now and then she caught her father's approving eye at the head of the table as she dealt competently with each course, tipping the plate away from her for the soup, down to using a fork for the flaccid cream sweet because it was jelly-based – so silly all these foibles of the wealthy! And she appreciated the wink he gave her when she placed the finger bowl with its little doily to one side and dipped the tips of her newly-manicured fingers into the flower scented water.

Thirstier than ever after the anchovy based savoury, she gulped down the last drop of wine which was now a red one, before leaving the table with the ladies. She went up to her room to make sure all was in place. Those bulky towels – she hoped the bulge did not show through her dress? How often should she change them? And thank goodness her stepmother had bought her a tennis dress as she couldn't possibly have disguised the bulge in her tiny shorts. What a funny business it was being grownup – good fun, really.

More people arrived for the dance. Crowds of them. Car doors banged. A gardener and the chauffeur showed the drivers where to park. A small band at one end of the long parquet-floored drawing-room struck up a catchy jazz tune, and the chattering crowd took to the floor. Izolda danced with her naval tennis friend, and then with the titled man. As soon as he could disentangle himself from his guests, DD came up to Izolda.

"I don't need to ask if you are enjoying yourself, darling," he said, while foxtrotting her expertly across the room at quite a pace. He adroitly manoeuvred her in and out of the other couples. She danced beautifully, light as a thistledown to guide. He gathered she had had dancing lessons in France.

The Order of the Star

The old Gorgon had really done her stuff with regard to his daughter.

"I am enjoying myself – hugely," Izolda answered in her father's arms. She laughed rather too loudly.

"Go easy with the booze," he said, noting she looked flushed. "How well you dance, sweetheart, just like your mother. She was a superb dancer."

"Dancing, tennis and swimming are about the only things I've learnt in France – and to speak French, of course. Lessons are a dead bore except with Mademoiselle. In Monte Carlo we are taught by an '*à la Duse*' teacher – you know, Isadora Duncan and all that with scarves and bare feet," Izolda expanded, looking up adoringly at her father. She was elated by the praise and starry-eyed about this fun life in England. "For ballroom dancing I usually have to lead . . ."

"No men in France?" DD smiled over the top of her head.

"There are the Casino gigolos whom the rich *mondaines* hire. Oh dear, that must be yours and Diamond's set! You look awfully nice in a dinner jacket, Daddy Dick-O!"

"Same one I wore many a time with your mother." And then very tenderly while holding her closer, "What I've missed not having you with me all these years."

Izolda felt near to tears at that. She felt all emotion. It must be the growing-up part. She sat out awhile, chatting animatedly with other people and drinking when anyone offered her a glass, and then took to the floor again with the nice naval officer who said she was amazing for her age the way she could dance and play tennis. "English girls at boarding-school aren't out of the egg at your age," he said. He took her into the conservatory where in a galaxy of exotic creepers and blooms of overpowering scent, he ladled out a cooling cup from a silver tureen. "Have some," he said, handing her a glass. It was well-iced, sweet and cool, and Izolda drank thirstily. She sat down on the nearest iron chair. The moist atmosphere in the conservatory was stifling. The heavy scent of the tropical flowers in the enclosed space made her feel giddy and faint, a sensation she had never experienced before. The band thumped on in the distance. the conservatory swung round; the white cascading jasmine engulfed her and the giant orchids leared at her in grotesque masks.

"Hey, steady on," the naval officer put out a hand to hold her in her chair. "I expect you're not used to the cup," he took the glass out of her hand, "rather heady stuff for little girls."

"I . . . feel . . . awful," Izolda gulped, and was promptly sick on the tiled floor. The naval officer reacted swiftly and efficiently. He mopped her up with his handkerchief and supported her out through a side door and into the study, where he left her to go in search of her father.

"Your beautiful daughter has had one over the top," he dryly informed his friend. "Poor kid, doesn't look too good. I've dumped her in the study away from this crush."

"Oh God! It's my fault. I should've . . ." DD dashed off.

"M'head's-all swimmy . . . I, I think I'm goin' to be sick again," Izolda struggled up in the study.

"Hang on," DD said, and dived for a brass bowl.

"If only I *could* beshick," she said after a while, white-faced.

"You'd best go to bed, darling; can you stand?" She attempted to, but the room turned round with her and DD

The Order of the Star

caught her as she was about to fall. He carried her in his arms to the staircase, and was a little way up when Diamond, in search of him, saw them.

"What's the trouble?" her eyes narrowed.

"She's tired, Diamond, that's all. It's time she went to bed. I'll be down in a mo."

He sat her on the bed, which had been neatly turned down by the maid, and helped her to undress. He handed her her shabby pyjamas – evidently Diamond had drawn the line at buying her a pretty nightdress. He noticed the bulky towelling pad when she pulled off the gown. It seemed all wrong for a child of her age to have to cope with the curse. Sex. Cursed sex. Divine love with Camille, his glorious, exotic white lily, an angel if ever there was one; blasted eroticism with Diamond who was as tough as old boots, spoilt and selfish and as hard as nails.

DD went into the bathroom and came back with a flannel wrung out in cold water. He sponged his daughter's face as gently as he had once sponged Camille when she had influenza.

"I feel sho ill, Daddy . . . Am I dying? Havin' a shtroke?" She not only felt more ill than she ever had in her life, she was frightened.

"No, darling, you're not dying, and for reasons that I might tell you one day, I have never felt like you do now. I don't drink, not since my father drank himself to death . . . And I don't smoke, and you shouldn't either. I blame myself for not noticing earlier and not thinking. You'll be fine tomorrow after a good sleep. I'll leave you now, darling. Just go off to sleep, there's a good girl." He bent to kiss her.

"Don't leave me, don't leave me, Daddy! Please don't go," Izolda panicked. She half sat up in the bed that swayed under her like a boat at sea. She clutched at his arm to steady herself.

"Shush, darling," he laid her back on the pillows and tucked her in again. "Try to go to sleep, sweetheart. I won't leave you." Soothingly, he stroked her forehead. He let his hand stray into her hair when she turned her hot head to one side on the pillow. His fingers lightly massaged the back of her neck as he used to do with Camille.

It was getting on for an hour before Izolda got to sleep and DD was able to creep out of her room. He had not felt so fulfilled, nor so loved, nor so loving himself since he and Camille had last been together that time in Shanghai, just before she left for Yokohama, when he had every hope of a reconciliation.

Feeling wonderfully happy, DD descended the stairs towards the noisy throng – and Diamond.

"Good morning, Miss," the maid, in a pink striped uniform, said waking Izolda and placing a tray of tea with wafer-thin slices of bread and butter on her bedside-table, "it's a lovely day, Miss." She pulled back the curtains and let the sun stream in.

Izolda sat up, poured the tea, and ate the bread and butter. She felt perfectly all right; no hangover! It was the drink. She'd watch that in future, and in the meantime this was the life for her in Diamond's posh house.

When Izolda got out of bed she saw the stain on the otherwise pristine pink sheet. Oh heck, the pad must have displaced itself in the night, soiling Diamond's linen. It brought back the horrid memory of waking at the Parsonage

The Order of the Star

and finding the bed wet. At least it was nothing like as bad as that. Who would see it? The maid, she supposed, and perhaps the stern-faced housekeeper she'd seen around the place. There was nothing she could do about it, so she pulled the bedclothes up, got dressed and went downstairs.

She felt quite at home letting herself into the dining-room. Breakfast was men only – Diamond and the lady guests had trays in their rooms – and by now she knew the ropes of helping herself from a variety of cooked egg and fish dishes kept warm on the sideboard. The men nodded to her from behind their Sunday newspapers, and then resumed their reading. DD, rather pallid looking, gave her a quick smile and remained silent.

Sunday was an odd sort of day. Nobody seemed to be going to church, whose bells she could hear ringing for the eleven o'clock service. She'd have liked to go but no one suggested it. The morning dragged by. DD was nowhere to be seen and Diamond ignored her which was off-putting. Had she been told about the sheet and was disgusted with her – once again the nasty, dirty, disgraced little girl Nurse beat regularly? A shiver from her past ran through her and with it foreboding of what was to come.

Lunch was got through, during which meal neither her father nor step-mother addressed a word to her. Afterwards the house party began to disperse, though one couple, after being shown round the estate by DD, who took the opportunity of exercising Diamond's pugs, stayed to tea. When at last these two left, DD abruptly told Izolda to go and collect her belongings.

"All of them?" she asked, eyes wide.
"Yes, all. Everything. Pack. We're leaving."
"But . . ."

"Don't argue. Do as you're told. I'll explain later."

Izolda threw as much as she could stuff into Julia's battered suitcase, which had mysteriously reappeared on a stool, and was folding her new clothes into their cardboard boxes when she heard the car being driven round to the front door. From her window she saw the chauffeur put her father's suitcase into the boot of the Wolseley. She finished packing, went to the bathroom, and came out to glance round the pretty room that could have been hers, if she had not got drunk and messed her bed to disgrace herself in her step-mother's eyes. She grabbed a padded hanger as a memento, shoved it in the suitcase and stuffed some of the headed notepaper from the desk into the pocket of her new light green summer coat.

Reluctantly, she left the room and went down stairs, carrying the suitcase which the butler took from her in the hall. She told him to go and collect the boxes from her room. She was no longer intimidated by him. What did it matter what he thought of her now?

As she waited in the hall she could not fail to hear raised voices coming from behind the closed doors of the drawing-room. Goose-pimples rose on her scalp, and the horror of long-past days came tearing back to make her heart pound, her limbs tremble, her mouth dry. A row! A terrible one was going on behind those doors. She wanted to bolt, dash back to her bedroom and put her head under the pillow; block her ears so that she could no longer hear the raised voices: her father's deep, angry one and her step-mother's shrill-pitched fury. They were shouting at one another . . . A shouting match . . . saying cruel things to each other, and all because of her. Never would she be invited here again. It was her step-mother's house. Twice was enough – too much.

The Order of the Star

She should never have wanted to come this time. She should have told her grandmother she did not *want* to come. Oh, for the serenity of her grandmother's soft Southern drawl, spoken in a tone that was never raised. But she could not block out the words that came through the shut door.

"You're bloody well going to say goodbye."

"I bloody well won't. You can't make me."

"Blast your eyes. You damn well will!"

"Try and see! I'll never have her in my house again. That's final. Why don't you go with her if you're so devoted? I dare you to. Go. Go! *I* don't care a blasted fig what the hell happens to you or what the hell you do!"

The door burst open and DD appeared, gripping his wife's wrist and propelling her into the hall. They stood there, in the hall, before Izolda, both red of face with anger and breathing heavily.

"Your step-mother wants to say goodbye," DD glowered. He released his wife's wrist, but stood at her shoulder prepared to grab her lest she should evade him. There was a fraught hush when no one said anything.

"Th . . . thank you very much for having me," Izolda stammered into the deafening silence. She swallowed. She could feel the waves of hostility in the hall, "and, and . . ." she took a step forwards and held out a hand, "and for the lovely clothes."

Izolda's hand was ignored. It remained outstretched, a child's hand stuck out there in a gesture of reconciliation, of regret, of sadness for a visit gone wrong. The hand drooped, was made to look stupid, unwanted, neglected, useless and disregarded. It looked so ridiculous there, Izolda did not know whether to laugh or cry; a foolish hand held out in front of her for no one to grasp. As if mesmerised by a snake, Izolda continued to stare into Diamond's eyes not a yard away from her. The eyes were arctic blue and ice cold. And Izolda saw the undeniable glint of contempt and intense dislike in the gaze.

Here before her was the hateful *marâtre* of the fairy tales, a woman with scarlet lips set in a thin line in the smoothness of carefully rouged and powdered faultless skin. The hand, with its red nails that would not shake, was loosely clasped in the other, unloving and uncaring. In the arctic eyes she saw real naked hatred, and slowly, like a wilting flower, Izolda's hand dropped to her side.

She was hated. In all the unhappy parsonage years when she had been neglected, ill-treated and beaten by the nurse in charge, where there had been unending crossness and continual bad temper, there had never been the chill malice she now saw in her step-mother's eyes. Izolda stood there, her lips trembling, her colour, as the insult registered, flooding back into her face.

"Damn and blast you, you bloody bitch! I'll make you sorry for this; I'll get even with you and make you recant, see if I don't," DD exploded into the fraught scene in the hall as the butler waited by the front door, eyes averted. In one swift movement DD grabbed hold of Izolda and propelled her through the open front door, and, ignoring the butler, kicked the door slam shut behind them. He bundled his daughter into the front seat of the Wolsely, leapt into the driving seat and drove off at a furious pace in a spurt of loose gravel down the drive. "Damn, damn, damn," he cursed, followed by a string of expletives unknown to Izolda. With screeching tyres he turned out from the white gates by the lodge and, with the muscles in his jaw working overtime, roared up the side roads and on to the main one, where he calmed down a little.

Izolda sniffed, unable to find a hanky. "Here," DD handed her his. Izolda blew her nose and wiped the tears off her cheeks.

"Where are we going?" she managed.

"To London. Miss Sawtell will look after you until I can arrange for you to go back."

"But how . . . ?"

"I rang her first thing this morning. She was most understanding. Diamond is a cold-blooded callous bitch; the flint-eyed iceberg of a shark's spawn . . . She was at it half the night raging on at me, accusing me of God knows what goings on because I was in your bedroom; things you wouldn't understand or know about – the dirty-minded slut. Then this morning . . . How *dare* she insult my own daughter like that on her doorstep. The enormity of the deliberate affront. I'll get my own back on her for that, sometime I will; however long it takes. I'll not forget it, you'll see. I'll make her atone for the humiliation to you, and make her do it in public too, before her smart friends. I'll make her shake hands with you in front of them all, see if I don't. *Damn* her, damn, damn!"

"I wish you wouldn't go on," Izolda said, longing for an end to all scenes. "It's no good. She hates me. Where will you be staying in London?" abruptly she changed the subject.

"At the 'In and Out'. That's the Naval and Military Club, Piccadilly."

"And then you'll go back to Diamond? Why don't you come and live with us in Menton?"

"I've a bloody good mind to."

But DD did not leave his wife. After dropping Izolda at Miss Sawtell's, he arranged for her to meet him for lunch at the Club next day in the Ladies Room upstairs. There, he spoke to her as if she were an adult. He said he only had his pension to live on which was not very much, pin money for himself the rest used for her education and allowance. He said that at his age he was too set in his ways, and perhaps too comfortable, to give everything up. He asked her not to think too badly of him but to try and understand. He had had two great loves in his life: her mother and the Navy. He said that after her mother's death he had married again in haste in what he thought would be the best interests for her, his daughter, and that Diamond had wanted him to retire so that he could run her estates. But it had not worked out like that and soon after she came to live with them as a little girl, she had been sent away from him.

Izolda refrained from asking her father why he had not left his wife that first time. In any case, with the wise eyes of childhood, she knew the answer. So she said nothing.

DD kissed Izolda goodbye very tenderly in the Piccadilly forecourt of his Club. She put her arms about his neck and rubbed her face lovingly on his blue-black chin and smelt the nice clean sea smell of him. He saw her into a taxi.

And they parted.

Chapter Twenty-One

"What *have* you done to yourself, Grandma? You look quite different." On her return to the Villa Micheline, Izolda embraced Louise boisterously. "Let's see," she said, removing her grandmother's hat and examining the tightly frizzed hair.

"I blame the result entirely upon Monsieur Pumelic," Louise answered defensively. "I took his advice to have a permanent wave which he assured would give my hair 'body' and save me from having to sleep on those pipe cleaners."

"Well, I don't like it. It makes you look sort of – ordinary."

"You'll just have to put up with it until it grows out. One thing is for sure: you won't catch me having another. The whole operation took *four* hours. He clamped me up to the ceiling on a machine that hissed and steamed, gave out a smell of rotten eggs, and scorched my scalp. I was so exhausted I had to go to bed for the rest of the day. To make matters worse, Monsieur Pumelic *would* explain in gory detail how he lost his foot under a tram."

"How did *la visite* go with *ta marâtre*?" Marie asked inquisitively on joining them in Izolda's bedroom, where her suitcase and cardboard boxes lay on the bed. She started to unpack. The handsome photograph of DD looked out at the small gathering from the shiny-topped dressing-table.

"To begin with Diamond was awfully decent and bought me these clothes. Then . . . things began to go wrong."

"What sort of things, honey?"

"Everything really. I got tiddly and Dick had to carry me to my room, and Diamond was *livid*."

"'Dick and Diamond'? I'll be danged!"

"Yes, rather. It's the very latest thing to call one's parents by their Christian names."

"And then you got inebriated and your father had to carry you to bed? That does not sound in the least circumspect to me." Louise gave her tinkling laugh and collapsed in mirth onto the bed, "That sure is the cutest thing," she chuckled away to herself in her relief that Izolda had returned to her. "But what in thunder got you into the hard liquor?"

"Not *hard*, Grandma. Wine – and some cup. I was thirsty. It can be hot in England whatever you say about the climate . . ." Grandmother and granddaughter went on talking while Marie began to put away the clothes from the suitcase. "I'd been playing tennis in the afternoon on a grass court. I could hold my own with them at tennis . . ."

"But you couldn't hold your own with the wine."

"You don't know how *ill* I felt."

"Nor do I wish to hear the details of *that*, anymore than I wanted to hear how poor Monsieur Pumelic's foot was cut off and left lying on the tram line. *La petite* drank too much wine, Marie, just fancy it! That did not please her *marâtre*, I suspect."

"*Tiens*! Not so *petite* either, Madame," Marie declared, unpacking the newly-laundered 'squares'. "*La mignonne* has used these. How fortunate I prepared in case."

The Order of the Star

"Aha. It was the shock of your step-mother's displeasure that brought on your periods, I guess."

"The drink . . . I thought I was dying. My father stayed with me until I went to sleep . . ." Izolda ignored the way Marie and her grandmother were bandying about what was to her a private affair.

"Her father stayed with her until she went to sleep," Louise repeated in French for Marie's benefit.

"She is a child still, *enfin*," Marie expressed, "*'Il fait du temps pour être femme'*," she quoted.

"Indeed Marie, it takes time to be a woman," sighed Louise. "What happened next, Izolda?"

"Next day, after the weekend guests had left, Dick abruptly told me to go and pack. I could hear a frightful row going on in the drawing-room. Dick dragged Diamond into the hall to say goodbye, but she wouldn't shake my hand. I felt such a fool . . . Standing there, hand outstretched and trying to thank her. It was pretty awful."

"What did your father do? *La marâtre* refused to shake hands goodbye, Marie. Fancy that."

"*Quelle bêtise! Une vraie catastrophe*," grunted Marie. She undid one of the parcels.

"Daddy slammed the front door in her face and drove me off hell for leather. Oh, I don't want to talk about it."

"There was a humiliating scene and a row between husband and wife, Marie. It's best forgotten, honey."

"Good riddance to that *maratre*," Marie said sourly. "Never mind, *mignonne*, you got these clothes out of her," she admired the display on the bed. "*Enfin*, it was worth it for these, *n'est-ce pas, hein*?"

Though the painful subject of her disastrous visit was closed from that day on, Izolda did tell her grandmother about her stay with Miss Sawtell, who gave her a wonderful time in London. She took her to Madame Tussaud's, to the Zoo in Regent's Park, to the Victoria and Albert Museum and, best of all, to the musical *Rose Marie*, which turned Izolda into an incurable romantic. One day she would meet a glamorous man who would sweep her off her feet and carry her up a mountain!

What with the hurtful visit to her step-mother's, the 'squares' and *Rose Marie*, Izolda had, despite Marie's well known quote, grown up in the space of a few weeks. Once back in Menton she looked at her grandmother with new eyes and noticed that in spite of the perm – or perhaps because of it – she was ageing. She knew instinctively that from now on, instead of being looked after by her grandmother, it was she who would do the looking after.

It was she who now made the decisions that had to be made, cashed the cheques at the bank, paid the bills, made sure they were living within their income and not getting into the red, which was the ultimate crime. She relished this challenge. Oh, how well she would look after her grandmother who in character and looks was the very opposite of *jolie laide* Diamond. How providential that her step-mother could *not* tolerate her, for surely the country house style of living with servants and riches and her father's affection had gone to her head. And there lay her only regret, for if she could not live in England, she would only very occasionally be able to see her father.

There were changes to be seen in Menton-Garavan too. On their weekly visits by tram Great-Aunt Maude was not quite her usual amusing self. A frown would cross her seamed face to stop the flow of words. She had a bladder infection which was painful and would not clear up despite having taken the waters again at Aix-les-Bains that summer. And there was Julia, who had developed a tremble of head and jerk of foot as she sat at her easel. She gave up teaching art at the Villa Georgette School which by now was greatly reduced in numbers. Miss Sawtell and Mademoiselle said that if things did not improve soon they would have to give up. McLaughlan seemed unchanged, though more of a jangle of nerves than ever with the strain of being constantly at the beck and call of her sick mistress. The Pekes were ageing, too. Onie had died from distemper, Sato was too old to follow Izolda to the top of the garden, and only Tora waddled up after her now.

There was another aspect of growing up which confronted Izolda during the winter after her return, and caused quite a contretemps with her grandmother, to emphasise her oft-repeated warning that 'Frenchmen are not to be trusted'. She was walking down the Avenue Felix-Faure one evening with Yvette, when a man came out of the public *pissoir* on the corner. These men's toilets were a puzzle to the girls. The middle section was screened, but the feet of the men could be seen standing apart. How did men 'do it'? Neither girl in their untutored men-starved world could imagine it. This man came out fumbling with his buttons. Seeing the girls looking in his direction he seized his chance and exposed himself. The girls hurried on with averted faces. Izolda was astonished: 'It' was flaccid and not at all like a fork as Marie had frequently told her.

"Marie called them—" Izolda stopped herself with a frown. "Can't you discover from your mother what happens?" curiosity overcame her.

"*Maman* will not divulge anything," Yvette giggled,

"she's as tight as your grandmother about such things. All I've ever been able to get out of her is that the only time she 'lived' with my father was on the night I was conceived, and that she had to 'fight to get it'. So whatever 'lived with' is, it must be pretty difficult to perform, and it can't happen very often."

"Some kind of operation, do you think?" mused Izolda. "I'm going to tell my grandmother about the man because I want to find out. I'll tell you what she says."

But instead of explaining the facts of life, Louise tore down to the Gendarmerie as fast as her little feet would carry her.

"Well, Monsieur Bienvenue," she waved the stick she had taken to using, at him. "What do you intend to do about it? Arrest the disgusting man, I trust?"

"*Parbleu*, Madame, there are plenty of these harmless *gosses* in Menton who do it to shock young girls," he shrugged eloquent shoulders.

"*Harmless*? You mean to tell me you will do *nothing*?"

"It is better so. If he is found *les mademoiselles* will have to identify him before *le Notaire*. I agree with Madame it is most improper behaviour. *Ils sont vilains, ces types*, but it does the young ladies no harm. *Voila tout. Enfin, c'est la vie!*"

"On the contrary, Monsieur, I believe it does *great* harm. They will be harmed by believing men to be vulgar beasts."

"*Bien juste*, Madame, we are beasts with the animal's natural instincts." Monsieur Bienvenue teased *la vieille*, a stickler for propriety if ever there was one, "Even I, a peg-legger like me, have my beastly moments which my dear wife suffers nobly!"

The Order of the Star

"Monsieur, *je vous en prie*, this is no joking matter. I would have thought you had more consideration . . ."

"*Vous avez raison, chére* Madame, forgive me. Yet *les jeune filles* have to learn sometime that men are men, and perhaps seeing one come out of a *pissoir* in this fashion is not such a bad way to educate."

Not long after this episode, which only made Izolda and Yvette more determined than ever to find out 'what happens', Louise had to swallow another – to her – unpalatable event; this time in relation to Julia.

Maude's condition had rapidly deteriorated and she was by now room-bound at the Villa Avis. A succession of blue-veiled nuns from the Convent above the villa on the Boulevard Garavan, came down to nurse the now skeletal figure lying on her bed. Night and day they came with the result that on Louise's visits she had Julia to herself for the first time for years.

"You haven't! You can't have!" Louise gasped at the information her cousin imparted in private. "Your dear parents must be turning in their graves . . ."

"I knew you'd be upset Lou, that is why I haven't mentioned it before, but, believe me this is no sudden conversion. For the last few years I have been having instruction from Father Sebastian."

Julia went on to explain how on her visits with Maude to the old men in the Convent, she had taken to going into the Chapel. The scene was a revelation after the austerity of her father's Union Church on the Bluff in Yokohama, which both she and Louise had attended. Here there were clusters of flickering candles against a backcloth of red and yellow draperies dimly seen through a haze of incense. There were crimson-vested thurifers swinging and swirling the censers;

the brightly painted statues; being able to pray to the Virgin Mary, a divine woman, the Mother of her Lord, who would understand the terrible tragedy of losing a son. The whole colourful setting inspired and uplifted her artistic soul into a greater, better, higher world-to-come than the one down here which had treated her so shabbily.

"Mama might well be shocked as you are, Lou, but Papa I think not. You remember how broadminded he was in the days when he welcomed all sects into his Chapel?"

"Indeed I remember," Louise sighed, thinking of those long gone days when she lived with her beloved Uncle Winn and Aunt Hattie.

"I am happy Lou, for the first time since my non-marriage – I still have nightmares about being forced . . . You cannot conceive how terribly hurt I was physically, how scarred mentally. He really was a bad man, Lou, and he broke me. My conversion has given me back what I lost all those years ago: a confidence, the certainty of His love, the revelation of glory to come with Him. I can now glimpse what I have always believed, but could not see. Despite my wretched shakes and seeing Maude lying there day after day, I am happy, Lou, truly happy."

Louise looked at her cousin's round wrinkled face and still-lovely grey eyes that were glowing with a new inner light, and saw that it was indeed so. "I guess," she stretched out her hand to pat Julia's, "I guess, dearest Juli, that I'm glad for you – real glad."

Before leaving, Louise and Izolda went into the house again to see Maude. They found her lying in the same position as before, in her bed. She lay there, her agate, red-rimmed eyes open and vacant. The long plait of her

The Order of the Star

hair was arranged neatly over one shoulder to stand out startlingly red against the pallor of her face.

"Any change?" Louise whispered to the nurse in nun's garb with blue cross embroidered on the front of her habit. The nun shook her head silently. Louise did not take the chair by the bed but bent down and kissed the cool forehead – Maude the foster-mother of her boys in England, the kindest woman she had ever known; the woman she had had so very many sparring matches with right from the day they had married the Winter brothers of Yokohama. Life would lose much of its spice without her sister-in-law to bicker with.

That night Maude died peacefully in her sleep.

"Last wishes are sacrosanct," Louise seethed in high dudgeon, "that mean old Wilson lawyer has taken it upon himself to ignore his sister's desire to be buried next to Baldwin in St Mary's churchyard in Worplesdon. Mr Heather, the grave-digger, has been tending the grave since 1915. The plot next to it is reserved for Maude. If they could take Baldwin's body there during the war, there is no possible reason why Maude shouldn't go in peace time."

Izolda squirmed. She found the whole subject ghoulish in the extreme. The thought of graves had been anathema to her ever since the ghosts had risen to haunt her at the parsonage. She was being made to wear black for the funeral, among all those ghastly tombstones on the hill. She was dreading it and had tried to get out of it, but her grandmother had insisted. "Why don't they bury her in England then if it is Aunt Maude's wish?" Izolda said hopefully, in which case she could not attend the funeral.

"Because that unspeakable brother of hers says it is the

first he's heard of it, and that it is not in her Will. I told him everyone close to Maude knows that's what she wanted. He was rude enough to throw in my face that as a non-beneficiary, I have no say in the matter. I can tell you that I'm goin' to make mighty sure about my wish to be put in your grandfather's grave, where there is an extra space made ready for me."

"All the way to Japan? How?" Izolda said, aghast at the thought of a body . . . "I don't know *how*," Louise said crossly, "it is in my Will and I guess you and your Uncle Jimmy will have to figure it out between you."

To add to Louise's upset, when Maude, without further ado, was planted in the hilltop cemetery where no Winters nor even Wilsons had been buried before, was her disappointment in the Will. Baldwin's fortune had been left in trust for his widow, Maude, during her lifetime, after which it would be divided between his several brothers and sisters, or if deceased, their heirs, and Louise expected that some of James' inheritance would come to her. What she now learnt was that James had been cut out due to his having his own fortune, which had left his widow, herself, very well off. That Baldwin had died *before* the earthquake which had left her in penury, was a hard pill to swallow. She was sure that Baldwin, if he had lived to know about the straits she found herself in, would have altered his Will to include her and her heirs. She tried to explain it to Izolda.

"Money, money, money. How boring!" Izolda exclaimed.

"Only boring if you don't have it," Louise retorted, delving once more into their lack of funds, which was fast becoming an obsession. "The only good things to come out of the whole sordid business is that Julia is going to live in the nursing wing of the Blue Nun's Convent, and

The Order of the Star

McLaughlan is going to retire to her native Scotland; both on the income Maude has left them for life out of her own funds. At last, after a lifetime's work, McLaughlan will be independent of the Wilson family, the mealy-mouthed lot. They always treated her like dirt."

"*Nom de pas du Père*, what a la-la about money, Madame," was Marie's response when Louise scrimped and scraped over the food bills, "*zut alors*, you will give yourself *une crise de nerfs* if you don't stop it."

It was not only Louise who was feeling the pinch. With the lack of British pupils in the town Miss Sawtell could no longer afford to run the Villa Georgette School. She retired to London to nurse her chilblains, and Mademoiselle went back to her home in Nice, still vowing that the end of the world would come in 1938. Mr Greenstreet left with his family, and a part-time vicar came in from Monte-Carlo. There was no longer any need for a curate. The congregation was so small – sometimes ten, sometimes less – that the winter season was like the summers had been in the days of the *hivernants*. Monsieur du Vivier still played the organ in the large structure which echoed its lonely emptiness, damp patches appearing on the walls. Izolda still went to church because it would grieve her grandmother if she refused to go, and in any case she was needed to offer an arm to steady the little steps. Yvette went with her mother to support her father, but much of the girls' fervour had gone now that there was no curate to ogle. Doubts had crept in which the girls discussed. "In England," Izolda had told Yvette on her return, "they don't believe in Jesus Christ. It's the very latest thing not to." But the girls still enjoyed their walks arm in arm along the promenade after the service.

"Business bad, Philipino?" They stopped to have a chat

with the donkey woman in her colourful garb beside her drooping donkeys.

"*Si mesdames, c'est la fin d'haricot*; the till is empty. *Hélas* the donkeys will have to go."

"Ours is empty, too," gloomed the girls. The du Viviers had had to draw in their reins and had not been away for their annual holiday, and there was no question of Louise and Izolda being able to afford a hotel without Maude there to invite them as her guest. An English tutor was hired by the du Viviers and Louise to give lessons to the girls in the flat, with better results all round in their education as both fell for the married man and wanted to please him. But no longer was there the fun of Shakespeare plays in the olive groves, and they missed Miss Sawtell's camping out expeditions into the mountains. Apart from tennis and bathing there was little for the girls to do out of lesson time.

Though the winters were quiet and dull for the young, the summers became vibrant and exciting. Louise fanned herself in the Villa Micheline, and the du Viviers grumbled about the heat and the thump-thump-thump of the jazz band at the Casino so near to them, from which noise went on far into the night. There was an influx of brilliantine-haired and perfumed gigolos with flashy ties, padded shoulders, and tight-fitting trousers emphasising narrow hips, who stood around the streets in groups and stared at the girls as they passed. More sand was ferried to the shores to extend the beaches, where half-naked bodies of every nationality lay crowded like stranded whales to offend the straight-laced Monsieur Delacroix who could see them from his tram.

It seemed to Louise that with the death of Maude, the benign, dignified Menton of before died with her. Now there was a culture alien to her, brought by people who

The Order of the Star

had no manners and gabbled away amongst themselves in unknown languages. Izolda was growing up in a loud, modern sun-seeking set with no sense of right and wrong.

She did not like the influence she saw.

Chapter Twenty-Two

One day, over two years after Izolda had returned from the disastrous visit to her step-mother, when even the English tutor had left Menton, and the girls were contemplating a typist's course so that they could earn some money, a letter came from Jimmy in Hong Kong announcing his imminent arrival en route to a banking conference in London. Though Louise did not know it, the trip was as much to see her as it was to do business in England.

Ever since the earthquake, Jimmy had been concerned about his mother's financial situation. When she had come to Peking he had hoped she would stay on with them, but in the event she had gone to Europe to hand over Izolda to her father, and then had decided to live near his Aunt Maude and Cousin Julia. Fair enough. He had sent presents, but she had always torn the cheques up saying that she had enough, and that he should keep his money for his children's education. Jimmy admired this independence. He knew her as a proud, determined and even domineering character, caring but undemonstrative as a mother, one with rigid moral rules based on her staunch faith, tempered and broadened by her great love and understanding of her adopted country, Japan, where he had been born. He and his wife Antonia – always known as 'Toni' – who had been a devoted friend of his

The Order of the Star

sister Camille, had talked it over and come to a decision. Letters weren't good enough. Anyway, it was time he saw his mother again.

Excitement ran high at the Villa Micheline with turning out of the boxes in the spare room and preparing it for Jimmy; Marie, too, entered into the spirit of the visit with her quips of: "Now, Madame, will you leave off worrying", and *"Eh, quelle chance* to have a son to depend upon in one's old age!"

Into this atmosphere of 'crabbed age and youth', as Louise called it, though she had proved the 'cannot live together' part untrue, Jimmy arrived like a blast of breezy goodwill to sweep all problems away. He gave Louise renewed verve and direction, and Izolda a second father figure; the opposite of DD's inward, complex, tortured character. Her uncle was not only an extrovert, but the dead spit of Monsieur Michelin!

Always a big man, in middle age Jimmy had become thickset and pot-bellied with it. He was very much a Winter in figure, but his bushy, black, over-hanging brows and brown eyes were pure distaff. He looked, and was, wealthy. Like his father before him, he had, through his own efforts, worked his way up to become a tycoon. He was now manager of the Chartered Bank in Hong Kong, and he lived in a mansion he had bought up the Peak.

It did not take Jimmy long to sum up the situation in the Villa Micheline after seeing his mother, much aged, and his gangling sixteen-year-old niece who was fast becoming a beauty. What was she doing in a society-less place like Menton living with a couple of ancients?

"Mother," he said in the drawing-room after an excellent lunch served from the hatch, "Toni and I want you and

Izolda to come and live with us in Hong Kong. You will have a household of people to bully to your heart's content, and Izolda can go to school to finish her education. I can assure you she'll have a great time there."

"I've never bullied anyone in my life, you ought to know that, Jimmy," Louise reproved.

"Tell everybody what to do, then," Jimmy laughed loudly, so that to Izolda, pouring the coffee, he sounded more like Monsieur Michelin than ever. "What do you think of the plan, Mother?"

"Waal," drawled Louise, cautious as ever but inwardly delighted, "we'd have to square DD first. Izolda's underage."

"That should be no problem. From what you've told me, Izolda's last visit was a fiasco." He had never liked DD; not a man's man. Not good enough for Camille – not even musical.

"What do you say to going to Hong Kong, honey?" Louise turned to Izolda. As for herself it was the answer to everything. Dear old Jimmy. Always the reliable one. She had had enough of scrimping and worrying about Izolda, who had got out of hand. She never knew where she was or what she was up to. Maude was dead and Julia was happy in her Convent. She had come to Menton to be near them. There was nothing to keep her here anymore. Besides, she would like to spend her last years with her only surviving child. Yes, she wanted very much to live with Jimmy and dear Toni, who would take over the responsibility of Izolda; and perhaps most of all she wanted to go back to the Far East. "Well, honey?"

"Sounds great. What fun!" In Hong Kong it would be *family*: uncle, aunt and cousins. And not only that, there would be loads of young English males!

The Order of the Star

"We're agreed," enthused Louise gently, her brown eyes sparkling.

"Good, that's settled then, the sooner the better now that Hitler is stirring up trouble in Europe. Could mean another conflict."

"Not *again*, surely? There are masses of Germans here," Izolda protested at the idea. She and Yvette did not take much interest in politics. They took more notice of boys, but Monsieur du Vivier was always going on about Hitler and his Black Shirts.

"There's trouble in your part of the world too, Jimmy," Louise retorted. "I read in today's *Le Matin* that the Japanese Kempeitai are infiltrating down the coast from Manchukuo. The old Samurai martial tradition seems to have got out of hand there, not for the first time in their history."

"Maybe trouble in China, Mother, but Hong Kong is not China. It seems to me the far greater danger is here, with Hitler threatening to take over Czechoslovakia's Sudetenland. The Germans are hot to revenge the Treaty of Versailles . . ."

The rest of Jimmy's visit flew by. He hired a car which he drove himself and took them to see old Mr Orange in Monte Carlo, and along the Grand Cornich to Eze with its spectacular views; to Nice to shop, and in the other direction into Italy as far as Bordighera. He entertained them to meals in smart restaurants, unheard-of extravagance for Louise and Izolda. He left with instructions to arrange a date when it suited them. He would pay their passage the other end and see they got the tickets through a travel agent. With expectations high all round he departed, leaving his mother a substantial cheque which Louise, for once, graciously accepted. She thought it unnecessary to tell him that it was to add to what she had been saving for a pension for Marie.

* * *

Neither Louise nor Izolda expected any opposition from DD. Letter writing was their only contact. It looked to Louise as if, apart from the allowance he sent, DD had washed his hands of his daughter. His reply to Louise's letter telling of their plans was therefore as unexpected as it was obstructive. Without mincing words, he forbad Louise to take Izolda to Hong Kong.

'*If*', he wrote, '*she herself insisted on the brain-crazed idea of going all that way at her age, that was no business of his, but in that case Izolda must come to England and live in a hostel and do secretarial training so that she could earn her living.*'

"Why don't we catch a boat and just disappear," Izolda stood by her grandmother. It would be horribly disappointing not to go. Think of the voyage with all those glamorous ship's officers! Yvette would die of envy!

"It wouldn't work." Louise sank back into gloom. "You are underage and will be until you are twenty-one. I know what your father is like when he's thwarted. He'd take me to court to get you back. You were taken away from me once when he made that disastrous re-marriage. I'm sure not goin' to risk letting somethin' like that happen again. I reckon you'd better go to London and do some training. He's got a point there," Louise said, as usual her Southern drawl exaggerated when she was upset.

"And you'll go out to Uncle Jimmy?" Izolda's face fell.

"I don't fancy goin' all that way by myself. I'll just stay here, I guess. Your father's got us properly stuck between the rock and the hard place."

"Me, leave you here alone? Not likely!"

"There's Marie."

The Order of the Star

"You know she's waiting on us to leave so she can retire."

"I might go join Cousin Julia," Louise grunted.

"At the Convent? All that mumbo-jumbo as you call it. You know you'd hate it."

"Of course I wouldn't *like* it, or leaving my home, but I reckon I've got to live somewhere now I've outlived my usefulness and don't seem to be able to die."

"Come off it, Grandma. We'll get to Uncle Jimmy's some way. I'll ask Yvette. She's full of ideas."

Yvette was certainly full of ideas, but they did not encompass how Izolda could get to Hong Kong without her father immediately hauling her back, or even stopping her getting onto a ship. Her ideas were fully concentrated on *men*. Her rounded figure and merry, roving eye spelt out that she had an abundance of that much vaunted 'it' of which Izolda had decided she must be lacking. Instead, Izolda buckled down to some typing lessons. After a three month course, this enabled her to get a dreary job in a shop, for which she was paid pin-money. That helped to pass the winter and into the next summer. By this time Louise had become resigned to the idea that they would have to wait another four years before they could go to Hong Kong. Louise also became convinced she would not live that long.

That summer, in the hot evenings, the girls went to see old black and white silent films shown in the open air by the Casino; Charlie Chaplin and Valentino being favourites. More often than not, Izolda found herself making her way home on her own because Yvette had picked up a *gosse* at the bioscope to go walking with afterwards, while she had not.

"How do you manage it?" Izolda asked, when yet again she had been discarded as *de trop*, "Anyway what do you do after I've left you?" she persevered. She was determined to find out what went on, and not a little anxious for her friend.

"We kiss and . . ."

"Well, go on. You've found out what happens presumably?"

"Er . . . yes . . ."

"Why so reticent? Remember, we promised to tell, whoever discovered first. Is it super?"

"I didn't like it to begin with . . . It, it sort of grows on you. The French boys'll do anything to get it."

"Have you done it with a gigolo?"

"One. Mostly that lot are only interested in women from the rich set. He was nice . . ." Yvette's voice trailed away.

"Where do you do it?"

"Oh . . . we find places," Yvette said vaguely.

"In the flat?"

"Good God, no. What do you take me for?"

"You haven't told me *exactly* what happens," Izolda exclaimed in some exasperation.

"I can't, Zol. Truly."

"Why not?"

"You're, well, you're . . . so naïve, and it's sort of private. I mean – intimate."

It was extraordinary, Izolda thought, how anyone who had done it would not talk about it, but shut up like a clam, even her bosom friend, Yvette. As for her grandmother, she was a hopeless source. She had told her in detail how babies were born, which sounded pretty near agony as Marie had once related, but never a word on how

The Order of the Star

they were *started*, which was apparently so enormously enjoyable that people eloped to achieve it. Her grandmother ruled that you did not live with a man before marriage, not even if you were engaged, and here was Yvette already going 'the whole hog'. She was so *brave*. Even if she herself had a boyfriend, she would never live with him for fear of having a baby – the ultimate disgrace out of marriage. She supposed Yvette must know a way of taking care of that. "Do you use something . . . ?" she began.

"Oh for God's sake, Zol, stop pestering me," Yvette cut her off. She looked at her friend's downcast face. "Boys aren't everyone's cup of tea, you know. Why don't you go and get yourself a more interesting job?"

"Where?"

"Anywhere. Try the Casino."

It was one of Yvette's brilliant ideas. Without telling her grandmother, Izolda went to see the new manager of the summer Casino by the raised bandstand on the promenade. The manager looked her up and down and asked her if she could ballroom dance. She certainly could, Izolda put on her most charming smile.

"How old are you, if you permit, Mademoiselle?"

"Seventeen," Izolda replied, adding on a few months.

"Not permitted to enter the gaming rooms, Mademoiselle."

"*Bien sûr*, Monsieur. But one does not dance in the gaming rooms."

"True, Mademoiselle. You look *le type* for hostessing. You 'ave permission from your parents?"

"I can get permission," Izolda answered boldly, though she knew it would be a tussle.

"Hostesses are required to attend the *Thé dansants* in the afternoons, to dance with the Latin gentlemen. Also the Saturday night Balls. At your age, Mademoiselle, the management would see you were sent home by taxi *à minuit – comme La Cendrillon*! You should understand that we run the Casino on strict lines of correct behaviour. Any client who expects more will be turned out. We pay well for the tall blonde ladies of grace such as Mademoiselle for our clients to dance with."

That evening Izolda waited until her grandmother was in bed before putting it to her. She sat down at the dressing-table and wondered how to do so tactfully, for to Izolda, who loved ballroom dancing anyway, it seemed like money for jam. She'd have to invest in some suitable dresses, both afternoon and evening. She fiddled with the empty green Icelma jar half-filled with eau-de-Cologne in which her grandmother soaked her rings to make them sparkle – the rings she had been wearing in the earthquake. Where were they? Izolda looked suspiciously over at her grandmother who was composing herself in bed, a white shawl about her shoulders. She watched her put on her spectacles and start to read the *Menton News*.

"'Second Sino-Japanese war after over forty years of truce'," Louise read out the headline. "How well I remember the first; one of Sumuko and Grandpa's sons was killed at Pyongyang. 'Tiensin has fallen to the Japanese. They are advancing on Peking'. That'll unite the Kuomintangs and the Communist Party."

"Why should it?"

"Against the common enemy, of course. I told your Uncle Jimmy war would follow the infiltration." Louise looked over her spectacles at her granddaughter sitting at

The Order of the Star

the dressing-table; her eyes became wary. "Time you went to bed, honey," she suggested.

"Where are they?" Izolda demanded.

"The Kempeitai?" Louise attempted to deliberately misunderstand.

"You know perfectly well I'm not talking about the Japanese Intelligence. Where are your rings? Your diamond brooch, too, for that matter?"

"It's got nothing to do with you."

"It's got everything to do with me. Where are they?"

"I sold them," Louise said, like a naughty child found out.

"You WHAT?!"

"There's no need to shout. I'm not deaf – yet."

"*All* your jewellery? You should have asked me. I wouldn't have let you."

"I know you wouldn't. That's why I didn't tell you. To pay the rent. Monsieur Michelin has, after reducing it, now put it up twice this year."

"Didn't Uncle Jimmy give you something?"

"That's for Marie. Her need is greater than mine."

"How much did you sell them for?"

"Not telling."

"I insist; I shall go on all night until you do."

"If you *must* know, a thousand francs."

"Is that *all*?" Izolda did a quick calculation. Barely ten pounds. "Oh, Grandma. Where?"

"At that jeweller's shop in Monte Carlo. I called in on my way to see Mr Orange."

"Your sapphire engagement ring? The diamond-shaped ring Grandpa gave you for your first-born? The half-moon brooch; the jade bead necklace with the sweet carvings of birds and flowers – they must have been worth thousands and thousands of francs. They are part of your life. I can't bear it." She was near to tears. To herself she thought: Grandma's changed, and it's all because Daddy won't let me go to Hong Kong. And why should he stop me when I never see him? Two years back her grandmother would have died rather than part from her precious jewellery which held such sentimental value. She's worn down, really old, becoming senile, worried all the time about money. I *must* get that job . . .

"I didn't sell the jade necklace," Louise said defensively, "it's in the drawer with your mother's engagement ring. You can have them now. They are for you."

"Thank the Lord for small mercies. Oh no! Oh Grandma, you didn't sell Grandpa's Order of the Star?" Izolda jumped to her feet.

"Sit down, child. I'm not that lunatic. I wouldn't sell Grandpa's Order for all the tea in China . . . I may be losing my faculties, but not entirely. The Order is for Uncle Jimmy, and that's where I ought to be right now."

"I know. I've been offered a job in the Casino as a dancing hostess, and I'm going to take it. It'll pay the rent."

"Working in that den of iniquity? Dancing with strange men? I won't hear of it!"

"The manager will introduce me and keep an eye out to see all is proper."

"What sort of a man is he?" Louise asked suspiciously.

"Ask Monsieur Bienvenue. He knows him."

"Is Yvette permitted to do this?"

"She hasn't been asked. They only want fair, tall girls, and she's dark and dumpy. Fair to contrast with the Latin Americans. Something like that."

The Order of the Star

"How odd . . ."

Louise made enquiries next day. Monsieur Bienvenue at the Gendarmerie vouched that the manager was a respected member of the community who was strict on rules. If he broke them the place would be closed and he would be heavily fined. Mademoiselle would come to no harm in the Casino.

Louise gave way, but made plain that Izolda was to come straight back by taxi after the evening sessions. On arriving home she was always to come into her room to say goodnight. She herself would stay awake until she did.

"Don't worry, Grandma," Izolda said blithely, "I can look after myself."

"So *you* think . . ." Louise expressed dourly.

Chapter Twenty-Three

Despite Europe being in political turmoil, all was pleasant and peaceful in Menton during the following sunny winter and the next summer season. Izolda's job in the Casino was a success. Now she really had turned seventeen and no longer had to fib about her age. She was proud of the fact that she earned enough to pay the rent and contribute to other expenses, and thus stifle some of her grandmother's money worries.

Mademoiselle Denise had made her a whole wardrobe of pretty afternoon dresses and shiny long evening gowns with dipping bare backs, all of which she wore with a flat pair of gold shoes bought in Monte Carlo, so as not to dwarf the Latin gentlemen further. She had to admit that they were excellent dancers, though she found little pleasure in dancing with them. Indeed she treated them as a bit of a joke with their prize-fighter padded shoulders and funny bow-ties buttoned under their collars. However, under the eagle eye of the manager, who was always hovering about, they behaved with perfect propriety, even during the tango when they led her with sweaty palms, but refrained from holding her uncomfortably close.

The manager was pleased with her and put up her salary. Mademoiselle Izolde with her cloud of golden hair

The Order of the Star

– reshaped in a page-boy turned-under style by Monsieur Pumelic – her greeny eyes in an oval face lightly tanned by the sun, attracted the Latins to the Casino. She was exactly the type of willowy, light-on-her-feet English society girl in demand from this particular wealthy clientele.

It was after Izolda had been working in the Casino for over a year, that an urgent request came from DD to visit him in London. An old friend, Lady Buchanon-Jardine, whom he had known in the East, and with whom he and Diamond annually stayed in Ascot for the Royal race week, had invited her to visit. The urgency was that, due to the tense situation with German troops now in Austria and likely to threaten Poland next, DD, in his fifties, had been placed on standby to be called up out of the Reserve. He declared himself to be as 'pleased as punch' at the prospect of going to sea again, but before he became involved he wanted to see his daughter. He also hinted that with the situation in Europe now so serious, it might be advisable for her to 'go to a safer clime'. He would be writing about that to her grandmother.

"At *last* he's coming round to it," Louise exclaimed in astonishment and delight. "Better go see him quickly, honey; strike when the iron's hot and get it fixed!"

So Izolda applied to the manager of the Casino to take a holiday, and, wearing a lightweight grey suit with pink blouse and small felt hat suitable for travelling, Yvette saw her friend off on a through train. Izolda slept fitfully, enjoyed the crossing as before and arrived at Victoria late-afternoon, feeling sweaty and longing for a bath. She looked forward to seeing her father again and meeting Lady Buchanon-Jardine who lived in a posh house in Grosvenor Square and had wanted to give her a Season and present her at Court. To her father's disappointment, she had turned the offer down.

There was no way she could leave her grandmother for a whole season.

"How nice of you to meet me," she said politely as she descended from the train and saw her father. She kissed him shyly. He hurried her along the platform.

"I'm taking you to a party," he explained, "we don't want to be late." She noticed he was dressed in a morning-suit and carrying a black top hat.

"Oh, what party? How nice. I need a bath and change first."

"No time for that," he said, bustling her through the barrier and into a taxi.

"What's this all about? I really must tidy up first," she protested.

"You'll see," DD checked his watch. "Your train was behind time. Party'll be in full swing. We've been to a Garden Party in Buck Palace; you know, royalty and all that."

"Well, I must certainly be allowed to change if I'm to meet royalty!" Izolda laughed. "Who's 'we'?" It couldn't be Diamond after that ghastly meeting, could it? Surely not. She was the last person she wanted to meet and vice versa!

"Lady Buchanon-Jardine, who's putting you up. She's giving the cocktail-party for a whole lot of us friends who've been to the Palace. It seemed a marvellous opportunity . . . Too good a one to miss."

"Miss what?" Izolda was thoroughly puzzled. Her father was talking in riddles. All she wanted to do at that moment was to change out of her crumpled clothes, brush her hair . . .

"Don't ask questions. You'll see. It doesn't matter what

The Order of the Star

you're wearing. Everyone will understand that you have just come off a train."

"Well *I* mind," Izolda said, fumbling in her handbag for lipstick and compact. She had got used to looking smart for her job. Why such a rush? Why that anxious frown on his face?

"You look very nice," he patted her hand in an abstracted way. They drew up outside a porticoed entrance in Grosvenor Street. The door was on the latch and DD led Izolda up a wide, circular staircase from where she could hear the hubbub of loud talk and laughter coming from the party. They entered a room full of men sporting buttonholes as her father was. The women were all in long party dresses down to the floor, gaily coloured summer hats, the brims swathed in chiffon and flowers, long white gloves to elbow, the right-hand one folded back at the wrist to enable them to handle rich eats of salmon and caviare being passed round. The smart scene made Izolda feel a complete frump in her little grey suit and hat. And in her suitcase she had a couple of dresses that could easily have matched theirs!

"Wait here," DD ordered by the door, "I'll fetch Katherine." A footman came up to Izolda with a glass of champagne on a silver tray which she accepted. She sipped some while watching the scene. This was the *milieu* she'd have entered for a Season. The thought did not seduce her. She was going to take her grandmother to Hong Kong. Much more fun than London and all these posh people! She eyed her father making his way towards her with a pleasant-looking grey-haired lady. She put her glass down ready to be introduced.

"Delighted to meet you at last, my dear," Lady Buchanon said, pecking Izolda on her cheek. "I was so sorry you couldn't come and stay before. I always bring several gels out for the Season. You'd have been an asset, my dear. Your father is such a very old friend, right from Eastern days. I hope you had a good journey?" But before Izolda could reply, Lady Buchanon rushed on. "Now come along, I want you to meet everyone." She took Izolda by the elbow and with DD following looking smug, introduced her to a spate of guests.

"This is Izolda, Dickie's daughter, just come off the train from the Riviera. So sweet of her to come along straight away when she must be tired . . . This is Dickie's daughter; you *must* meet her. So charming. Dickie's daughter . . . lovely girl . . . lives with her grandmother near Monte Carlo."

"Delighted," the guests murmured politely. The women stared. The men looked at her with admiration. Well, Dickie's daughter would be good-looking. Diamond might well be jealous . . . The latter was a strange character . . . worth knowing, though – marvellous hostess . . .

In this manner Izolda slowly progressed across the room, meeting everyone and having a few words with each, polite and rather amused by all the 'floss', as her grandmother would have called it. She caught sight of a distantly familiar thin figure ahead and her heart missed a beat, then thumped on. *This* was no fun. The woman was dressed in cornflower blue with a large fine-strawed hat on smooth, dark hair. The thin slash of red lipstick was unmistakable.

As she approached, now closely followed by her father who had quickened his step to be at her side, an extraordinary hush descended on the crowd in the elegant room with its large, curtain-draped windows looking over the square; a hush that reminded Izolda of Armistice Day in Menton when

The Order of the Star

the busy noise of daily life slowly ebbed away. Suddenly she saw that this was all premeditated, that everyone in the room knew what was about to happen. In the silence that had fallen Lady Buchanon-Jardine drew Izolda up to her step-mother.

"Diamond," she said, firm-voiced for all to hear, "come and shake hands with your step-daughter."

They shook hands. It was the same limp hand Izolda had shaken on arrival at The Manor when she was twelve years old, nearly six years ago, the hand that had refused to shake hers on leaving. Was there a flicker of understanding in those icy blue eyes? Diamond must have known that Izolda was as innocent as she of this plot devised by DD and the hostess to force her to redress the insult she had once played on a child. For six years it must have rankled with her father for him to have plotted this. The hushed crowd watching the forced meeting certainly knew what was afoot. Men watched with raised eyebrows, and exchanged chuckles with one another. The women smiled knowingly and nodded to each other. Some whispered: "DD's got his revenge at last. My God, there'll be an earful if not murder at The Manor tonight!"

Conversation started up again. The guests began to leave, DD and his wife with them. No words passed between Izolda and Diamond during the handshake or after, but on leaving DD kissed his daughter, a glint of satisfaction in his eye. He said he was driving his wife home but would be up on the morrow to stay at the Club for a few days and would take her out. There was much to discuss about their going to Hong Kong. Next year would be crucial unless Hitler backed down. She and her grandmother would be safe in Hong Kong, well away from a European war.

* * *

There was a tired, end-of-season feel when Izolda got back to resume her job in Menton. She found Yvette unwell.

"What's the matter?" Izolda asked when she and her friend were walking along the Promenade as usual on a Sunday; Yvette had rushed to the beach below. Solicitously, Izolda put her arm about her. "Here, sit on the rocks, you look pea-green."

"I feel pea-green. Oh my God, what am I going to do?" Yvette groaned, wiping her mouth with the back of her hand. "*Maman* will murder me and it'll kill my father. Poor old Papa, who only did it once in a lifetime and got landed with me."

"Can't you get rid of it?" Izolda, aghast, cottoned on.

"That would kill me. A crone in a filthy hovel in the *vieux quartier* sticks up a knitting needle."

"Which gigolo?" Izolda asked, knowing there had been several.

"René. The nice one. We got so carried away he forgot to put it on."

"Put what on?"

"Oh for heaven's sake, Zol, it's not funny. Can't you grow up?"

"I wasn't being funny. Do you love him?"

"Love? What's love? It's all feelings, exciting, bloody marvellous feelings. I can go on and on."

"I don't know what you are talking about because you never TOLD me. On and on – surely it can't take *that* long? Anyway, I'm jolly glad I haven't had a chance to do it and get in such a mess. One thing I do know is that if you don't have an abortion you'll have to marry him."

The Order of the Star

"René won't marry me. He'll marry some woman dripping with jewels whom he'll hate going to bed with. Gigolos all have their price."

"Then your father will have to make it worth René's while, even if it bleeds him white," Izolda reflected with wisdom.

"Oh God, I'm going to be sick again. It'll kill Papa, poor old Papa!"

The banns were read out on three consecutive Sundays to the half-dozen congregation at St John's, and the following Saturday, in late afternoon on a blustery day, Yvette, in a short white dress and veil, came down the aisle on her father's arm. Izolda, in a pretty sequined evening dress which had a bolero hiding its *decolleté*, brought up the rear. The groom was dressed in a smart well-waisted dark blue suit. The brilliantine on his jet black hair was overpowering, eclipsing Madame du Vivier's scent.

They all walked back to the Palais Ausonia where a small reception was held on the balcony of the apartment looking across to the Casino. Madame du Vivier put on a great act of happy, festive gaiety, gushing round her guests. As the storm gusted and the wind tore at the Venetian blind, Monsieur du Vivier appeared stricken and mumbling. Louise did not help the situation either. She remained quiet and as discreet as always, but she looked on sad-eyed, tight-lipped and knowing.

At last it was over and the party descended to see the couple off on honeymoon. "Have a lovely on-and-on ride!" Izolda whispered, as she kissed the bride goodbye.

"Zol! You really are the most terrible innocent," Yvette, relieved and flushed with champagne, laughed. She waved hard out of the window as René drove her off in the du Vivier's car.

Feeling happy that that was successfully over, Izolda pressed her way into the wind to the brightly-lit Casino, her flimsy dress billowing about her slender figure. The booming of the waves on the beach were loud that night, pounding away at the rocks beneath the promenade. This was a *mistral* blowing up, the *sacré vent* which could gust for days on end.

Once in the Casino, Izolda went to the cloakroom to put a comb through her hair before making her way to her table, where her clients were already seated for their evening meal. She smiled at them and they rose politely to greet her. She slipped her bolero over the back of her chair before taking to the floor with one of them for the dinner dance. The band played on in a desultory fashion with a bored end-of-season air, only a few of the tables round the floor occupied. To Izolda, who was longing to get home to chat to her grandmother about the wedding, the evening seemed to drag more than usual.

She noticed that a comparative newcomer, a heavily fleshed Argentinian from Buenos Aires, appeared particularly restive that evening. His small, close-set eyes kept swivelling around the room, and he continually crossed and recrossed his legs as he sat opposite her, puffing at a large cigar, almost blowing it in her face. She waved the smoke aside hoping he'd take the hint. He looked askance at her, never directly, and shifted his chair. Neither did he ask her to dance with him, and she spent the evening alternatively dancing with the other two men at her table. They finished their meal, drink flowed, Izolda ordered her favourite ice-cream soda and sat on toying with her wine and

The Order of the Star

smiling sweetly at them – it was her job to look pleasant – while the three rattled on to one another in rapid Spanish, only a few words of which she knew.

When it was time for her to leave, instead of following the other men to the gaming room, the Argentinian offered to escort her home. This was an old trick to which Izolda was used.

"Thank you, Monsieur, but no; I have my car waiting," she replied in her stock phrase, polite, distant and unconcerned.

"I will see you down the steps in this wind, Mademoiselle," he insisted. He helped her on with her bolero, and took her arm by the elbow. With a jerk, that was by no means polite, Izolda shrugged off the hot, plump hand as the Casino clock chimed the midnight hour into the deserted street. Izolda knew all the regular taxi men in the rank on the side street by the Casino, but, as sometimes happened, this time there was a taxi already drawn up in front of the building. Descending the steps she went towards it to make sure it was one of the drivers she knew. She could hear the engine ticking over, and, annoyed to find the Argentinian still at her side, she quickened her step.

Even as she was peering into the dark interior of the cab to have a look at the driver, the rear door opened from the inside and she felt a podgy hand from behind clamp over her mouth. The fat Argentinian lifted her bodily and bundled her onto the back seat where another man grabbed her. The moment the hand was off her mouth, Izolda attempted a scream, but the man in the car was too quick for her. Stifling her terrified cry, with brute force he held her struggling figure head down across his knees.

Quick as lightning the fat Argentinian jumped in; with

a spurt the taxi started off, the door slammed shut as they were moving away from the curb. Rapidly, the taxi left the Casino with its brightly coloured outline in electric bulbs, spurting away from the unsuspecting management. No one had seen the kidnap, not even those in the taxi rank talking unconcernedly amongst themselves round the corner. There was nobody about on the main roads to see the car speeding its way up to the Moyen Corniche.

Overwhelming terror seized Izolda. This was no nightmare such as she had suffered as a child of ghosts and vampires, but a real, living horror. She was lying on the back seat of a taxi between two sweating, foreign men, her head held downwards and smothered in the crotch of one, bottom up across the other's knees, with her shoulders, arms, legs held by four grasping hands in grips of vice that forbad any but the feeblest of wriggling movements from her. She could not scream now; she could barely breathe. Better . . . save . . . her . . . breath . . .

Half-smothered and gasping for air as she was, Izolda's brain yet stayed crystal clear. She saw with total clarity what was happening to her and why it had happened. She had not been dancing with the Latin Americans for well over a year without learning something about them. She knew these criminal abductors were not intending to hold her for ransom – she was from an unimportant family who had no money. They would have checked that out, damn them! Neither would they kill her; they wanted her alive for her uses. What they were after was her body. She knew only too well that the man into whose intimate parts her face was pressed, and the loathsome fat man at her legs whom she could feel fiddling around in his pockets for something, were part of a 'ring'.

It had all been documented in the French newspapers

The Order of the Star

how Latin American crooks, usually planted in England and Scandinavia, but now increasingly in the South of France, captured the slender, fair girls so admired by their countrymen in the South American continent. Society girls, officers', doctors' or lawyers' daughters from the middle classes were spirited away by one of these 'rings'. Not the titled upper-class girls who, if captured, would cause too much of a hue and cry with screaming banner headlines and every police force in Europe onto it, but unknown girls such as she. They were kidnapped, in far more numbers than the general public knew about, for the White Slave Traffic. They were snatched away as she was being snatched. They were taken to some small remote port along the French coast, were put on a sleazy cargo vessel which then sailed across to South America. Once there they were never likely to be seen or heard of again by their grieving families. They were used, used and re-used until, worn out, old and of no more use, they were cast out destitute into the gutter of whatever city they were in, like so many rag dolls who had lost looks and stuffing. Complete and utter simpleton that she was, Izolda saw now that she had put herself in the position of a sitting-duck, or, in the language of her hometown: a ripe lemon.

Though in those first, horrifying moments in the taxi, Izolda saw the situation in all its exactness, she was not expecting what came next. The loathsome fat men fumbling behind her, lifted her dress, and jabbed a painful, badly directed, needle into her thigh. She let out a muffled cry, squirmed and moaned. Her head whirled. Dope! They were anaesthetising her! She stopped struggling at the inevitability of what would happen. She would soon be powerless to fight back.

Evelyn Hart

Izolda did not immediately lose consciousness. She could feel the taxi climbing to the roar of low gears round one steep bend after another and guessed they were making for the Grande Corniche. The taxi stopped. A fourth man was there at the door. Broken French was rapidly spoken to the sound of paper money exchanging hands. Then she was roughly pulled out of the car and shoved onto the back seat of another, bigger one. She felt limp, nauseated, bruised by the rough handling. There was a small light on in the back seat but she found herself unable to focus.

With sickening terror, Izolda felt one of the men tearing at her sequined dress. Feebly she tried to brush him off, to no avail. She was left half-naked in her camiknickers. The man was going to violate her then and there . . . Perhaps all of them would violate her. How many men were there? Multiple rape, now, in the back of the car. Oh God, what a way to find out about 'It' . . . Like this . . . in a limousine with the light on, the engine smoothly purring . . . Moving off . . . on and on like Yvette could . . . violated while it sped . . . La Grande Corniche with its marvellous views of sea and mountains . . . Eze . . . The smell of new leather . . . accelerating . . . twisting, turning, turning . . . spinning . . .

Izolda passed out.

Chapter Twenty-Four

Lying awake in her bed waiting for Izolda to come home that Saturday night, Louise pondered on old age. She could never remember exactly how old she was when her birthday came round, and had to look it up in her passport; count the decades: seventy, eighty, even ninety perhaps, what difference did it make when it was all old age? She also had to remind herself about the present date by looking at the *Figaro*. It was getting on towards the end of September 1938; so much for Mademoiselle Blanche's prophecies! She had never believed them anyway. The Good Lord would take them all by surprise. The *mistral* was blowing great guns outside. Another hot summer come and gone with this last unpleasant blast which always set the dry timber ablaze from a carelessly discarded peasant's cigarette or the glint of sun on a broken scrap of glass, sparking up into huge fires on the mountainsides.

With the disabilities and slowness of body and mind which age brought on, it was hard to keep in sympathy with impatient youth, hard to have to become more and more dependant on Izolda's immature judgement and to cling to her impetuous arm for support. Hard too, on Izolda who had to learn to be patient with increasing feebleness, keep her vigorous strides down to age's teetering steps. Not having been away for two summers, she and Marie were tired and stale. The faithful *bonne* had opted to stay with Madame until they left for the East. What an amazing turnabout that was on DD's part! Going back into the Navy, that's what had done it. His great love. Good for him, but what a ridiculous business the plot of forcing his wife to shake hands with Izolda in front of a company of knowing friends. One-upmanship tit-for-tat, petty mindedness, she called it. She had written to Jimmy suggesting they go early next year. Deep down she was as excited as a girl. There was nothing like a long sea journey for putting one on one's feet again, always the cure in the old days. She had done so many sea journeys – and this time the haven of her son's home at the end of it. Truly the Lord had been good to her . . .

Shifting her position, Louise looked at her bedside clock. After midnight. Any moment now she would hear the taxi drawing up, and Izolda would come in to chat about the day's events including, no doubt, that lamentable parody of a wedding. The poor du Viviers; and the *mistral* hadn't helped. Here it was blustering at her window and threatening to burst it open. The clock ticked on, seconds lengthening into minutes . . . Not to panic . . . there was probably some perfectly valid reason for Izolda's lateness. She would give it another half-hour . . .

At a quarter to one Louise rose, put on stays, stockings, shoes and a coat over her long cotton nightgown. She picked up a torch from the hall, took her stick and let herself out of the front door. She walked along the path through the dark, empty compound towards the unlit road, her hair blowing in white silken strands about her worried face. In the distance she could hear the roar of the waves as they crashed on the rocks. She felt very much alone.

The Order of the Star

"Ah, if it isn't Madame Vintere, and in the middle of the night too," yawned Monsieur Bienvenue, awakened from sleep by repeated knockings. "What is it?" he shouted from an upstairs window. "*Tiens, la petite* not come home? *Un instant* while I strap on my peg-leg."

He said not to worry – he would look into the matter, he sent her back to the Villa and told her to go to bed. But Louise could no more go to bed than she could sleep. She sat in the dining-room where in the past her grandchild had sat at her knee to be read to. The Order shone out at her from the mantelpiece – and she waited.

Here was another crisis come into her life; she felt it in her old bones. That waiting business again . . . waiting for Izolda to come back . . . waiting for death. When one was old there was little one could do but wait, and waiting was the hardest thing of all.

Monsieur Bienvenue peg-legged it to the Casino, where the manager told him Mademoiselle had left at the usual time of midnight. Well, if that was so she had not arrived over an hour later at her home. Had anyone seen her get in the taxi? The manager went to enquire. No, he said on return, no one had actually *seen* her get into a taxi, but then they wouldn't. The taxi rank was round the corner, and if no taxi was waiting at the steps, Mademoiselle would walk round and beckon one to come. As a matter of fact a taxi *had* drawn up to wait at about that time. A croupier had looked out of the window and noticed it.

Monsieur Bienvenue questioned the croupier and was told it could not have been Mademoiselle's taxi as it was already engaged.

"How do you mean 'engaged'?"

"The engine was running and there was a passenger in the back seat."

"Was the passenger Mademoiselle Vintere?"

"No it was not Mademoiselle. It was a man," elucidated the croupier.

"But it was about midnight?"

"Yes, about midnight. I happened to look at my watch."

It was two-thirty am before Monsieur Bienvenue raised the alarm at the main Gendarmerie in the town. Leaving the search in their hands, he limped back up the Public Gardens to sit with *la vieille* until daylight, when Marie arrived with her black shopping bags strung about her.

"*Ta mignonne est manquante*," he informed. "Look after Madame well." And he made his way back to the Gendarmerie to take up the day's work.

"*Elle est bien malade*, our poor mother. We found her ill in Nice and are taking her home," the fat man excused at the ticket *guichet*. "We travel first class for her comfort."

"Tekt, tekt," the official clucked sympathetically. He handed over the tickets and observed the two lusty sons lugging their old mother between them onto the platform. She made a bunched figure in a black calico peasant's dress, a black shawl over her head covering all but the glimpse of pale skin revealed as they passed under the light of a lamp. It was still dark, and the *mistral* blew in gusts swirling pieces of paper and debris about the deserted platform.

The men propped the woman up in the far corner of an empty compartment, her head lolling forwards to rest in a dead weight on the lintel of the window. The early morning train hissed, waiting to get up steam. The fat Argentinian sat down heavily beside the figure and mopped his face with

The Order of the Star

a bandanna handkerchief. The sleekly moustached younger man slicked his hand over his blue-black hair in a gesture of relief.

"That's over then," the older man leant forward to offer his companion a reefer from a packet. "All going to plan. Boat's waiting in the bay. We'll be clear out to sea with our load before daylight."

"Windy. Rough riding at anchor in the inlet." The night train rumbled along the coast. It puffed billowing white smoke and shrilly whistled its way in and out of tunnels. Gathering speed it clickety-clicked along the straighter line further inland and then rattled along at a fair pace. The fat man glanced at his watch, turned off the overhead light, and settled down to doze.

A ticket collector, his cap worn well back on his head, tapped the glass door with the butt of his thick pencil. He came into the compartment hand outstretched, the light from the corridor illuminating the carpeted floor. He took the three tickets proffered, inspected them under the dim blue night light, and gave the black figure a cursory glance before handing the tickets back.

"*Elle dort bien*," he stated aimably while indicating the bundle which had let out a sound which could have been a groan or a snore.

"Si," the fat man replied shortly.

"*Elle est malade*," added the other.

"*La pauvre*," the ticket collector responded, who was none other than Ambere, erstwhile of the Garavan level crossing. Turning round he gave the recumbent figure a second glance from the doorway of the compartment. Then he stepped into the corridor, and, sliding the door shut behind him, left the passengers to sleep.

Evelyn Hart

"Not many on the train tonight," Ambere vouchsafed on his return to the guard's van, where he was sharing a bottle of wine with his friend Monsieur Delaroux. The latter was on his way with his wife (stretched out asleep on a third class bench) to the family farm in Frejus. Deftly, the one-armed conductor pulled the cork out of the bottle with his teeth. He took a swig, offered it to Ambere, and leaned back comfortably against the mailbags. He inspected his own two tickets.

"A good strong colour: grass green. I collect them for *la petite* Mam'selle. Since the other *vieille* Madame Vintere died we do not see so much of them, *hein*?"

"True. One misses the English. Things have changed for the worse in the Midi." Ambere took a slug of wine, wiped his mouth with the back of his hand, pushed his cap further off his head, handed the bottle back, and settled down on the mailbags beside Monsieur Delaroux. "Only three boarded at Nice. Two men and an old peasant woman in the first class for Hyeres; Spanish by their accent."

"Peasants travelling first class? Fancy that," mildly questioned Monsieur Delaroux. He tipped his head back, held the bottle a couple of inches from his lips, and expertly poured the wine into his mouth without spilling a drop.

"Come to think of it the men weren't peasants, *parbleu*. Smartly dressed dago types. Polished black shoes. Only the old woman was a peasant."

"Too many dagos in Menton these days. Those slick gigolos take our own young men's livelihood away by invading the casinos."

"There was something odd about that one," reflected Ambere.

"Which one, *mon vieux*?"

The Order of the Star

"The old woman; the peasant in black."

"What can be odd about a woman asleep in the train in the middle of the night? Your wife is one!"

"*Vous avez raison, mon ami,* nothing odd about that, *non,*" Ambere replied after taking another swig from the bottle. "They said she was ill. She slept like the dead. No, nothing strange about that though something odd caught my eye when I turned round to slide the door shut and leave them to sleep."

"Here, have some more wine, my friend. We might as well finish the bottle between us. You intrigue me with your 'something odd'; your National Service call-up has sharpened your wits!" Monsieur Delaroux smoothed down his empty sleeve with a chuckle. He liked taking the mickey out of the younger man. "Tell me, what branch you are in, you great *poilu* soldier you? Next year you will be promoted to the Intelligence Corps I shouldn't wonder, ho-ho!"

"*Enfin,* what was it that caught my eye?" Ambere continued the conversation after a pause, while he gurgled wine. He ignored the leg-pulling. Let the one-armed veteran have his fun. "Ah, yes, I have it."

"Have what, *alors*? Your brain appears addled tonight."

"The old woman's shoe. Under the black skirt I caught the flash of a shine . . ."

"What is odd about that? Perhaps she spits and polishes it!"

"I was about to say, if you would stop being so flippant, a flash of gold!"

"Gold? *Ma fois*! *Merde*, Ambere, the wine has truly gone to your head. You see things. An old woman in black with a gold shoe, ho-ho, what nonsense you talk, you young jackass. It was the light, I'll be bound."

"I tell you there was only the blue bulb on. The shoe shone gold in the dimness. *Oui.* By all the Holy Saints, *je le jure*, I swear it!"

Monsieur Delaroux looked at Ambere's face and saw that, though he looked flushed, he was not fooling. "*Ma fois*," he exclaimed "that is a strange thing, that is. Maybe, my friend, you should investigate further?"

"We shall be slowing down for the Cannes stop any moment now," Ambere looked at his watch. He retrieved his cap and put it on at its usual backward angle, "To be sure that I am not seeing things, I will take a closer look. It could be that something gold has dropped onto the carpet."

"I'd better return to the wife; if she finds I've been drinking there will be hell to pay." Heaving himself up, Monsieur Delaroux emptied the last dregs of wine into his mouth, threw the bottle into a corner, and, following Ambere across the metal floored coupling to the carriages, he bid his friend *au revoir*. He disappeared into a carriage to join his wife. The train began to slow down, brakes applied, released and then applied more strongly.

"*Excusez-moi*, Messieurs, Madame, I have to attend to the blind. We are about to arrive at Cannes. Not yet your stop," Ambere announced in the first class compartment. He switched on the light. The two men sat up blinking. The woman did not stir from her slumped position.

Ambere crossed the compartment and bent to adjust the lower part of the blind while he searched the floor. No gold brooch or ring there.

"She sleeps heavily," he observed, releasing the blind which went up with a rush. The two men on whom his back was turned, exchanged rapid glances. Doors opened and banged. Still not satisfied, Ambere brushed the old

The Order of the Star

woman's long black skirts to one side. Three pairs of dark eyes stared at the sight of limp, pink silk stocking-clad ankles ending in a pair of gold evening shoes.

"Sacred Mother! Run for it!" the fat Argentinian yelled, leaping to his feet and leading the way out. They doubled down the corridor and into the third class carriage from where Monsieur Delaroux looked up to see two men flash past, soon to be followed by his friend Ambere crying out:

"*Voleurs, au secours!*" Though the train was stationary, Monsieur Delaroux gave a great tug on the communication cord above his head. He then darted after Ambere. He caught a glimpse of the men leaping off the train on the side away from the platform, Ambere in hot pursuit. They disappeared up the line.

Monsieur Delaroux made his way back past his carriage and on to first class. In the compartment he found a crowd gathered round the slumped form in black. He pushed his way in and went up to the figure, who, with the shawl slipped off her head, he recognised immediately.

Ambere arrived panting heavily. "*Merde*, I lost them in the dark," he cursed. "Mon Dieu, if it isn't *la petite* Mam'selle!"

"Mam'selle, wake up Mam'selle," Monsieur Delaroux exhorted, kneeling beside Izolda and patting her face. "Look Mam'selle, it is your old friend from the tram, and here is Ambere of the level crossing. You are safe now, safe with your Mentonnaise friends."

Their anxious faces ballooned before Izolda. Blurrily she tried to speak: "Mons . . . Del . . . Amb . . . they?" But words would not form properly. Her tongue seemed too big for her mouth, lips dry and paralysed.

"*Oui, c'est nous, vos amis*. Remember the centimes you

placed on the line when you were *toute petite*? Remember old Madame Vintere and the *culottes* that fell off? Do not be afraid. We will look after you now."

Between stiff lips, Izolda managed a wan smile before dropping off again.

"Your Uncle has booked our passages on the *Chitral* for early next year," Louise announced, "I guess that gives us several months to sell up our things and get ready."

Izolda opened her eyes. She was in her dear little room with the communicating door through to her grandmother's. The sun slanted in through the slats of the closed shutters, and from her green-topped dressing-table her parents' faces smiled out at her. She had been back a week and every morning she had to throw off the nightmare that beset her in her sleep so that sometimes she woke up screaming and her grandmother had to come in to her. She sat up. She had a slight headache, otherwise she felt fine. "Where will we board?" she asked. A great liner instead of being battened down in a dirty cargo ship going in the opposite direction. She shivered at the thought.

"Marseilles. She sails from Southampton, but many passengers like to take the overland route to avoid rough seas on the Bay of Biscay."

"Does my father know . . . what, er, happened?" Izolda asked hesitatingly.

"No, honey. I can't see the need for him to be told. He'd only get in a flap and come rushing here and upset his wife." There was no harm done, except to her granddaughter's nervous system, which had certainly taken a bashing and with it the return of nightmares. Dr Pouget had gone over to the Cannes hospital to examine Izolda, and, thank the

The Order of the Star

Lord, had found her *intacta* and unhurt except for bruises and profound shock. Dear Mr Orange had gone from Monte Carlo to stay in a hotel nearby and visit her. So good of him when he was now well on in his nineties and almost blind. He had sat by her bed, patted her hand, and told her amusing stories about the time when her grandfather and great uncle had started work as lowly clerks at Jardines on the Yokohama Bund. It had helped to take her mind off her trauma.

"Has Daddy been called up yet?"

"I gather he's had his papers. In his last letter he approved of our plans to travel on the same ship with your uncle and aunt's friends Mr and Mrs Lauder and their daughter Maisie, of about your age, who is going out to marry her fiancé stationed in Hong Kong. Your father seemed as pleased as anything at the thought of going to sea again, though in what capacity at his age I wouldn't hazard a guess."

"Funny old Dick-O! That'll make him happy. What about Marie? Is it all settled for her?"

"The nest-egg has gone over big I can tell you! I wouldn't be surprised if Marie doesn't live to be over a hundred like her mother before her. Those Italian peasants are real tough. I shan't live that long, not after the fright you gave me."

"I wish you wouldn't go on, Grandma. How's Cousin Julia?" Izolda changed the subject.

"As well as can be. Did you know she came here to be with me when you went missing? Wasn't that just the sweetest thing? She was such a comfort. Quite like old times. In Japan we were always having to comfort one another for one tragedy or another," Louise sighed.

"Well, this *wasn't* a tragedy."

"No, by the skin of your teeth," Louise retorted huffily.

"Daddy with his Royal Navy, Cousin Julia with her nuns, Marie with her money, us going to the Far East; at last it's all working out well, isn't it?"

Izolda watched Louise, face pallid and drawn, deep lines etched between nose and mouth, her bushy eyebrows sprinkled with white, her dress soiled at the front where she had dropped her food at table and not noticed to change to a clean one. Fondly, Izolda watched her grandmother moving to the window with her little steps in their dainty strapped shoes, throwing wide the shutters to let the autumn sun stream in. And particularly on that day in the Villa Micheline in her remorse at the anxiety she had given, did Izolda notice how, despite old age and increasing infirmity, her grandmother's eyes stayed steadfast. Pale blue eyes like Diamond's could become icy; black eyes like the Latin American's could turn cruel. But her grandmother's brown eyes remained constant and stable.

"I reckon one has to learn through living," Louise, standing by the window, remarked, "but you would jump in with both feet!"

"*Le Bon Dieu* looks after us," snuffled Marie, limping in with a glass of her hot *tisane* for her *mignonne*. And then she called to mind the saying from Alphonse Kerr of whom she had never heard but nevertheless frequently quoted in her broad-toned nasal Mentonnaise:

"*Voila*," said Marie. "*Nom de nom de pas de Dieu, plus ça change, plus c'est la même chose.*"

Part Three
Eastward My Home
1939–1940

Chapter Twenty-Five

A crowd of spectators lined the decks of the great P&O liner SS *Chitral*, (15,000 tons and launched fourteen years previously) and one of a fleet of 'C' ships on the China route, to watch the passengers joining the ship at Marseilles. They themselves had caught the boat train that February at St Pancras Station for Southampton, had endured the rough seas through the Bay of Biscay, and enjoyed the comparative calm and warmth of the Mediterranean Sea. The ship had shaken down, côteries had formed.

All the passengers, most of whom were men, were leaving behind an exceedingly troubled Europe. They felt the pull to get on with their jobs in the East, and at the same time a reluctance to leave their homeland to its uncertain fate. Yet no one on the *Chitral*, not even the servicemen, had an inkling of what catastrophic events the journey eastwards was to lead them into. Unconcerned therefore about their future, the already seasoned travellers drifted away to the saloons to wait for afternoon tea to be served. A lone man remained on deck.

He stood leaning against the rails not far from the gangway. His tall, broad-shouldered figure was relaxed and yet suggested an alertness. On his strong-jawed and clean-shaven face was a speculative expression. He was not looking at a fresh faced young man with suitcase and kitbag who came bounding up the steps two at a time with assured ease, nor even at a pretty brunette climbing the gangway with her parents, but was surveying the thirteenth century Fort Saint-Jean with its ancient cannons by the entrance to the Vieux Port *bassin*. As a military man he was speculating on the workings of the strategic defences of the fort, and how invaders from olden times up to the Barbary pirates of the mid-nineteenth century had been successfully repulsed.

Shouted orders brought the man back to the present. He looked down to find that navvies were standing by to release the heavy ropes round the bollards. On the deck near to him sailors were grouped in readiness to remove the gangway and put to sea. All waited for the tail of the passengers to make their way up, and they seemed to be taking an uncommonly long time over it.

Looking more closely, the viewer saw that the pair of latecomers consisted of a small, upright lady, black straw hat firmly hat-pinned in place, one gloved hand holding a walking stick, the other tucked into the curve of the arm of her companion, a young girl of unusually graceful bearing who stood tall above the old lady. They were followed by a white-coated steward carrying some small pieces of hand luggage.

The sight of these two – while men on the docks stood by the ropes and sailors on the ship waited to weigh anchor – caused the man watching to find the scene touching in its very starkness of contrast between the age of one and the youthfulness and slender figure of the other who, with her shoulder-length golden hair, gave the impression of an out-of-door, sun-filled life. He found himself moved by the care he saw in the way the girl supported the old lady, and his

The Order of the Star

feelings in that moment were heightened by the cognisance of a whole great liner held up, tugs ready, all waiting patiently and politely for faltering steps to take their time.

Out of a certain curiosity that the couple engendered in him, and also out of courtesy for age, the man went up to give the pair a hand as they were about to step onto the deck. As the old lady smiled her thanks at him, orders were given to remove the gangway, and the girl looked up to see who it was standing in her shadow. For a moment she looked full at him from large, expressive eyes, but instead of the open smile of the old lady, the girl gave him a startled, wary look, and quickly turned away. The man stared at her, amazed at the depth of disquiet he glimpsed. She was afraid of him, as shy and nervous as a gazelle. Why should she feel so threatened when he was only trying to help?

"Come, honey," he heard the old lady drawl, "this nice steward is goin' to lead us to our cabin where I reckon we can get ourselves sorted out."

He watched them moving off. How extraordinary, he thought, the girl may have been physically supporting the old lady, but it was the latter, wobbly on her dainty feet though she might be, who was supporting the girl. Shrugging off the strange encounter, the man turned away to stride off along the deck in the opposite direction.

The siren hooted, and gently the tugs nosed the liner out into the Mediterranean.

Izolda took stock of their large, bed-cum-living-room de luxe cabin where their trunks were already installed. Besides outsize beds, a dressing-table and writing desk, two comfortable chairs and a sofa were grouped round an incidental table graced by a large arrangement of roses.

"What luxury," exclaimed Izolda as she buried her nose in the flowers.

"They're from Jimmy and Toni," Louise picked out the greeting card," 'Love and Best Wishes for the voyage', how sweet of them. And here's a card from Mr and Mrs Lauder, Jimmy's friends. They say the Purser has arranged for us to sit at their table, and that they and their daughter, Maisie, are looking forward to meeting us at dinner. Tradition has it that one does not dress in evening gowns on one's first night on board. You can put on an afternoon dress, honey. I shall wear a hat. I'm going to unpack the minimum, and then take a rest after that tiring journey."

An old hand at travelling by sea, Louise knew all the ropes. Hats in her day were worn in hotels and houses except when in evening dress, and ships came into the same category as hotels. "I'll come with you tonight," Louise went on, "facing the dining saloon for the first time on a voyage can be quite an ordeal, particularly when joining the ship after its point of departure. After tonight I shall only go to the dining saloon for luncheon; the rest of the time I shall stay here reading and playing my patience. I prefer to keep myself to myself on a long sea voyage. A mighty lot of gossiping and intriguing goes on on a steamer, but I want *you* to go right out there and have a good time. You'll be just fine with the Lauders," she looked up a little anxiously at her granddaughter, who had got in a flap on the train. So had she for that matter! It was the first train journey Izolda had taken since the kidnapping, and blow me down if they hadn't got stuck in a tunnel, lights extinguished. They had had to sit there in the dark, she thinking they were going to miss the boat, and Izolda thinking it was another kidnapping attempt! Thank the Lord that was over. They were on their

The Order of the Star

way at last. She could hear the drum of the liner's powerful engines, and felt again the thrill of a great ship under her. For the first time in years she could really relax, put all worries behind her, leave all to Jimmy. Now she wanted to be on her own for a short shut-eye . . .

"While I'm resting why don't you explore the ship," she hinted, "find out where the dining saloon is situated."

"Oh Grandma, are we away from . . . Being stuck in that tunnel really scared me."

"Yes, really away," Louise said firmly.

"I suppose the same sort of situation could happen in the East, couldn't it?"

"No it couldn't. As far as I know there aren't any Latins in Hong Kong." It was just as well that Izolda did not know there were plenty of pirates still on the high seas in China as well as bandits on land, and a great many drug addicts in Hong Kong. "Now run along and enjoy some fresh air on deck," she urged.

Izolda took her grandmother's advice and was walking smartly round the decks when a young man, coming from the opposite direction, passed her, stopped and turned round to look. "Good Lord, if it isn't Zol from the Villa Micheline," he exclaimed.

"Chippy!" Izolda gasped. "What are you doing here?"

"Travelling to Hong Kong. I've been posted there. What about you?" he appraised her. What a difference from the mousey – though spunky – small girl in the compound he'd led on their pretend travels.

"Same, with Grandma. Posted to what?"

"A ship. I'm in the Navy."

"Gracious. I imagined you'd have joined the Army like

your father." He looked just the same – only grown. Same blue eyes and that floppy fair hair.

"Thought I'd be different from Dad. Where's your cabin?"

"First Class somewhere. Hope I can find it again. I was just setting out to explore."

"What a coincidence you being here. I came on the overland route. First Class by His Majesty's bounty."

"Ours is by the bounty of my uncle in Hong Kong. He's a Banker. Deck level so Grandma doesn't have to cope with stairs."

"Remember how we used to go pretend exploring, me on my bicycle, you on your scooter; off to India, off to China, and here we are doing the real thing! I don't know my way around either. Come on, let's explore the *Chitral* together."

They went off chatting away. Old friends. It was lovely, Izolda found, suddenly relaxed; so easy the way the childhood friendship picked up as if it had been yesterday. It was the first time she had been able to talk to a man in easy terms since the abduction. She had been tied up in knots ever since that hideous episode. Her grandmother had said a long sea voyage was a cure-all. It augured well meeting Chippy right at the beginning. He was fun; he'd help her to forget . . .

"I met Chippy, he's also going to Hong Kong," Izolda burst into their cabin where she found Louise changing for dinner.

"Well now, isn't that real nice. Better hurry, honey." The dinner bells, played through the ship by a sailor, sounded down their corridor. When ready, Louise took Izolda's arm and they made their way to the dining saloon. In there, the chief steward looked down his list and led them to a round table where the Lauders rose to greet them with exuberant handshakes.

"My, Mrs Winter," Mrs Lauder gushed in a strong American accent once they had sat down, "Jimmy never tol' us he had a mother from the States. You can't hide it with that kinda voice."

"Georgia – long, long, time ago; funny how one never loses the accent of one's upbringing. I can tell you're from Boston."

"How cute your grandmother is," Mrs Lauder went into peels of laughter, long earrings and outsize pearls jangling.

"In Peking I much admired your son's grasp of Mandarin and Cantonese," Scot Mr Lauder addressed Louise in his rolling burr.

"He's had thirty years in China to learn it," Louise looked pleased at the compliment. "I gather you are going out to get married," she smiled at Maisie, a delectably pretty brunette with a *retrousée* freckled nose and periwinkle-blue eyes.

"Congratulations," Izolda joined in the conversation, "where did you meet him?" Envy of envies. She was all agog at this girl who was on pally terms with her jolly parents and seemed to treat them as equals. How long would it be before it was her turn to have a fiancé and then that family?

"Thanks," Maisie said, displaying her finger with sapphire and diamond ring for her to look at. "I met Hugh in Hong Kong again before Pa retired. We knew each other as children out there. Used to go to kindergarden hand-in-hand, rather sweet really. His parents are still out there; real old China hands, absolute ducks. They know your uncle and aunt well. Since Pa retired we spend half the year in Boston to be near Ma's parents. I'm half American, two passports."

"I've kept my dual nationality all my life," Louise informed. "Came in very handy in the Great War. It fairly foxed the customs people in Paris when we wanted to leave. Izolda's mother and I were living there for her singing training when the war broke out." The older generation began talking amongst themselves about the war and the danger of another breaking out in Europe.

"Funny," Izolda said to Maisie, "I've just met a man I used to know when we were children – rather like you and Hugh. He's sitting over there." She caught Chippy's eye and waved, at which he gave her a cheery thumbs-up signal.

"Knowing one another as children is not a bad basis for marriage, Hugh and I think. One doesn't change much, not underneath," Maisie pondered. "You'll love Hugh. Nice and tall. There's another man on board who matches him in height, a Gunner, friend of Hugh's. They were at the 'Shop' together. Hugh's a Sapper. It's lovely having Roger on board. We talk nothing but 'Hugh'!"

"So you're going to be Mrs . . . ?"

"Holden."

"Mrs Hugh Holden?"

"Yes. Why?"

"I was wondering . . . It couldn't be. Does he have a brother?"

"A younger one."

"There were two Holden brothers at a perfectly awful place I was in before I went to live in France, a Parsonage. I used to ball-boy for the eldest."

"Sounds like my lazy Hugh. Never disturbs himself unless he has to. He *was* at a place in England for the school holidays. They loathed it. There was an invalid wife of the Head and a perfectly beastly little boy . . ."

The Order of the Star

"—called Curly! Grandma, did you hear that? I know Maisie's fiancé! Hugh Holden, d'you remember him at the Parsonage?"

"Can't say I do. I recall one who couldn't get round to speakin'."

"This journey is full of coincidences," Izolda beamed. "First meeting Chippy and then knowing your fiancé who has an Army friend on board!"

"My," exclaimed Mrs Lauder," it sure is a small world. Fancy your knowing our Hugh. That makes you one of the family . . ."

"You'll *have* to be a bridesmaid," Maisie snatched from her mother.

"That's very kind of you I must say," Louise blinked at how rapidly the friendship was developing. She had forgotten how people who had lived in the East were so much more open and inviting.

"I've never been a bridesmaid. I'd *love* to!" exclaimed Izolda. It would do very nicely until she could get married herself.

"Ma," Maisie said exuberantly, "there's a dance tomorrow night. Let's get a party together to celebrate? OK Pa?"

"Good idea," boomed Mr Lauder, "I'll stand the drinks all round."

"We'll invite that nice retired Army couple in the cabin next door, dear," Mrs Lauder planned. "Let's ask Roger, and Izolda's friend to partner the girls. What about you Mrs Winter, you'll come and watch, won't you?"

"Thank you, but you can count me out," Louise stuck to her decision. Much as she had enjoyed the company that evening, she found the loud-voiced chatter tiring. In future she would not be seen for dust after tea time.

And in high spirits after the meal, Louise walked out of the dining saloon on Izolda's arm to relax in their cabin scented with Jimmy's roses, and where she only had to press a bell for her every want to be attended to.

The following evening, Izolda put on the long, green tulle evening dress with a bodice covered in sequins which she had worn at the Casino, and having discarded her flat shoes, put on a new pair of high-heeled silver sandals. Once dinner was over, the Lauders and Izolda foregathered in a saloon adjoining the dance-floor where a band on a raised stand had already begun to play. Chippy arrived and was introduced all round and then to the half-Colonel and his wife who were also joining them for the dance. Chippy, Izolda could not help noticing, gave each a rather limp handshake. The seven in the group stood chatting away until, after a while, Maisie said, "I wonder what's happened to Roger?"

"He'll be along in a minute, I expect," the Colonel's wife replied. "He's a busy man. Told me before dinner he had various duties to attend to first."

"Oh, what sort of duties?" asked Izolda.

"As the senior serving army officer on board from Southampton," explained the Colonel, "Roger was made officer in command of the army contingent on their way to India. Not his regiment. British troops. Poor bastards, sleeping in hammocks and stuck down there in the bowels of the ship. Vilely hot in the tropics. He's a Mountain Gunner. Brilliant man. Passed out head of his batch. Was my Adjutant at one time."

The 'brilliant man' at that moment walked into the saloon – all six foot four of him. Moreover, he was the same male who had frightened the wits out of Izolda on the

The Order of the Star

gangway when he'd loomed up from nowhere. Looking at him now, Izolda could not imagine why she had shied away in panic, for this man was the very opposite of the Latin Americans. She stood staring at the most magnificent specimen of manhood she had ever seen. She was amazed that anyone could be quite so beautiful with his height, his walk, his rugged looks, head well set on broad, slightly sloping shoulders, intelligent brown eyes taking in the company as he approached. And it was just as well that the company's eyes were not on Izolda, for anyone looking at her at that moment would have recognised the transparent emotions expressed openly on her vulnerable young face.

"How do you do," Izolda said precisely, to stop the trembling of her lips as she held out a hand when introduced, and a strong, firm hand grasped hers.

"Do you two young men know one another?" Mr Lauder enquired with raised eyebrow.

"No, I see you have not met," Mrs Lauder came in, "Mr Paine-Talbot of the Royal Navy, meet Captain Stamford."

"I seem to remember some matelots looking disgustingly healthy in the Bay of Biscay while we poor Pongoes were feeling distinctly green," Roger Stamford recollected.

"Not me," grimaced Chippy. "I embarked at Marseilles yesterday. Takes me twenty-four hours to get my sea legs." He shook hands with the Mountain Gunner who dwarfed him, though he was of good average height himself. Captain Stamford let the naval officer's hand go for a moment, and then, in front of them all he grasped the younger man's hand a second time with:

"Come on old chap, the Senior Service can do better than that!"

Izolda, her legs feeling like jelly, abruptly sat down on

the nearest seat, while a steward proceeded to pour the coffee for them. She found herself on a sofa next to the middle-aged man whom Roger Stamford had once served with. "Typical of him," the Colonel addressed her in an aside. "Extraordinary charisma. That young naval officer will be a better man with a firmer handshake for the encounter. Roger is the sort of born leader men follow gladly into battle. Bound to go far."

Chippy came to perch on the arm of the sofa beside Izolda, coffee cup in hand. "Phew, what a man! He reminds me of my father."

He hasn't taken umbrage. Chippy's so good natured, Izolda thought. "How are your parents?" she asked, and was surprised to find her voice sounded normal. "I'll tell you about the family sometime, Zol. 'Fraid it's not a happy story. Better do my stuff with the hostess first. Keep the next dance for me, won't you?"

Izolda nodded. The others paired off: Maisie with the Colonel, his wife with Mr Lauder, and to her consternation she found herself left alone with Captain Stamford, whom men would follow gladly into battle.

Quickly, she put down her coffee cup which had begun to rattle in its saucer. Idiotic to be so nervous, she remonstrated with herself, he's every girl's dream. Take Grandma's advice and go out and enjoy yourself. She folded her hands in her lap to stop the trembling. She looked up at the Captain expectantly with a shy smile. He came to sit beside her on the sofa. He seemed in no hurry to ask her to dance. She noticed how all his movements were deliberate and unhurried.

"I watched you arriving with the old lady," he said, amusement in his eyes, "I haven't seen her since. I hope she is well?"

The Order of the Star

"Yes, thank you. She stays in our cabin for the evening meal."

"Very wise. I'd spend my evenings there if it were not unsociable towards the Captain of the ship. I'm at his table."

"You're not sociable?"

"Not very."

"But . . . what would you do alone in your cabin all evening?"

"Read. I love reading; never have enough time."

"Oh? What sort of books?"

"About battles, mostly. History; military history. Anything I can lay my hands on. There's a very good library on board. Just now I prefer to be chatting to you," he said with a slow smile. He meant it. He had been intrigued by the contrasting pair – something unusual about them, a bit mysterious, good for a book. Besides, the shy girl next to him had a certain healthy, natural beauty which he found refreshing in the sophisticated modern era of blood-red fingernails and red lips, neither of which he cared for.

But Roger Stamford's words threw Izolda: *prefer to chat to her*? There was a pause during which time she simply could not think of one solitary thing to say in the face of his remark. They had nothing in common, certainly not in reading matter. She was more up in Molière, Shakespeare, Tennyson and Milton. Other than Waterloo at school – which Mademoiselle Blanche said *they*, the French, had won, though her grandmother had emphatically denied this – she had not read anything about *battles* and did not want to. Ugh! All that gore.

"You . . . you gave me a fright," she blurted out into the lengthening silence.

"On the gangway? I did wonder rather. I'm sorry."

"It wasn't your fault. I'd had a horrid experience. Some men . . ." her voice trailed away.

"I reminded you of them?"

"Oh no, never that," she answered vehemently. "It was just that, well, you appeared suddenly close from nowhere."

"Would you like to talk about it? Sometimes it helps with a stranger who can be objective."

Was he a stranger? She felt as if she had always known him: he had been at her birth and he would be at her death, even if she never saw him again. When she had gone to stay with Miss Sawtell in London after the disastrous visit to The Manor, the musical *Rose Marie*, starring Edith Day and Derek Oldham with its enchanting lyrical refrains of the Maid of the Mountain, '*You belong to me; I belong to you*', had turned her, at twelve years old, into an incurable romantic. Romance to her became *Rose Marie* on stage – a stage show. She never expected to encounter such heady romance in real life – and now she'd met Captain Roger Stamford and everything had changed. This was the real thing. The curates and the tutor she and Yvette had thought themselves in love with were as nothing compared to this man who effectively turned the hero of *Rose Marie* into a cardboard actor. And suddenly she wanted to tell the man beside her, wanted badly to pour the terrifying event out, to unburden herself onto someone with broad shoulders who was strong enough and uninvolved enough to not mind. She had kept much back from her grandmother so as not to distress her the more, and when the police had questioned her she had been in too much shock to remember afterwards what she had said.

So Izolda, unexpectedly in the middle of a dance party,

The Order of the Star

told an acquaintance of a few minutes the story of her attempted kidnap. It had a profound effect on their relationship by bringing down the barriers of not knowing one another, and it helped to distance the terrifying memory from Izolda's mind. At the same time it showed Roger Stamford the real depths of her character, depths which he suspected in her nervousness and shyness she herself was unaware of. He felt she must have considerable guts for an episode such as she related not to have had a far more adverse effect on her.

"Great heavens!" he exclaimed after hearing her out, "nothing half as exciting as that has ever happened to me. Did they catch the gang?" He noticed how white she had gone in the telling.

"No, at any rate not before I left. I'm rather glad . . . I, I suppose I would have had to give evidence. Only my grandmother knows about it here. You won't spread it round the ship, will you?"

"Certainly not. A confidence is a confidence as far as I am concerned." He watched her colour returning and waited for her to speak again.

"There is something *you* can tell me," she said brightly.

"Fire away!"

"I'm all at sea with these 'Sapper', 'Gunner', 'batch' and 'Shop' words Maisie bandies about. She told me you were at the Shop with Hugh Holden whom I used to know as a little girl."

"Really? He's an awfully nice chap. Well, the Shop is the soubriquet for the Royal Military Academy, Woolwich. Officers do eighteen months training there before getting their commissions. So it's no department store!"

"I thought Sandhurst was where the training was?"

"It is. Same exam for all. Only Sappers, Signals and Gunners go to the Shop. They call us three the 'brainy' Corps. Specialised I'd say, rather than intellectuals. I've known cleverer men at Sandhurst. You know what Gunners do?" Roger gave Izolda a smile, "Blow people to bits with their guns. Sappers do much the same thing, only with mines."

"It sounds perfectly beastly."

"I agree. I'm really not at all keen on blowing people to bits or getting blown up myself. Actually, we do a lot of useful and constructive things too, especially the Sappers. They are Royal Engineers, who as well as being fighting men, build bridges, mend water-works, lay pipes and make roads. A Sapper is a useful man to have around. Can put his hand to anything. Maisie has made a wise choice."

"She loves to talk to you about Hugh. They knew each other when they were small. Chippy – that's Christopher Paine-Talbot you've just met – and I played together as children."

"Really? That's nice."

Izolda could not help wondering why Captain Roger Stamford had gone into the forces if he did not like the idea of killing, or being killed. He seemed more sensitive than abrasive, as soldiers must be, but before she had time to pose the question the others returned and she took to the floor with Chippy. He was a bouncy dancer with an excellent rhythm who swung her along to the jazz tunes of the day.

Dancing with Chippy was great. She felt perfectly at ease with Chippy.

Chapter Twenty-Six

Izolda danced with the other men in the group, then Roger Stamford led her out on to the floor. She held her tumultuous feelings in check and tried to assess him objectively at close quarters. Smart in his dinner-jacket, white piqué shirt and black bow-tie, it seemed to her the whole military effect was set off by those braced-back shoulders – due to the training, she supposed. If he looked so good in civvy street gear, what must he look like in uniform?!

They did not talk. He seemed to be concentrating rather on the steps. She found him not strictly good-looking in the conventional sense. His jaw was too square, and his Roman nose looked as if it had been broken – in a boxing match perhaps? He had said he boxed as well as played rugger and rowed; obviously an athletic type. He had penetratingly keen eyes, altogether a tremendously strong face that exuded power and personality. 'Rugged' came into her mind again, lines already showing, yet he was a young man, in his mid-twenties, she'd have said. She felt totally inadequate to deal with such a character, totally overwhelmed at being in his arms. He smelt nice and fresh – unlike the South Americans, whose tuxedos exuded stale sweat – as if he had just taken a bath.

Bath! At the thought of this man lying in a bath, Izolda,

who danced as lightly as a feather and could follow any man's steps with ease, stumbled, so that her partner ended up by stepping on her toes. "Sorry," he apologised for the second time that evening. He held her up, their bodies touching. "I'm afraid I'm not much good at this sort of thing; you dance so well." He continued to hold her. They stood still in the middle of the dance-floor for a moment. She was young, naïve and altogether rather sweet, and had recently come through a traumatic experience. He felt a strong urge to kiss the top of her burnished head; if he did so, she would be covered in confusion! He refrained.

"It was my fault," Izolda got out, while standing there in his arms, "I'm not used to dancing in heels."

Flushing at the close encounter, she disentangled herself from her partner and made her way back to the saloon. With a pensive expression on his face, Roger Stamford followed. He stood looking at her as she flopped into one of the empty seats. She bent to rub her foot.

"I *did* hurt you," he said, looking at the slim ankle in the elegant silver shoe. Was it the shoe that had blown the White Slavers' gaff?

Izolda shook her head in answer to his statement of having hurt her foot, not trusting herself to speak. *Stop thinking about him lying in a bath*, she scolded herself. He's too big to fit into one anyway! A secret smile flitted across her face at the thought.

"This coffee's gone cold," Roger observed as he felt the pot. "Let's have some more while the others are dancing." He beckoned to a steward to bring a fresh lot. Pushing the used coffee-tray away from him, he sat forwards in his chair opposite Izolda. He studied her. He was used to summing people up – could sum up his men at one keen glance. He

The Order of the Star

was pretty sure he flummoxed her. He'd have said she was a complete innocent, despite having worked in a Casino. Bully to her for that!

The fresh coffee arrived; Izolda pulled herself together and confidently poured it out as she had hundreds of times for the Latins. She handed Roger Stamford his cup, and with expressive hand, gestured for him to take sugar and cream if he so desired.

"What a lovely ring," he noticed one of emeralds and diamonds heavily-set in gold on her right hand.

"My mother's engagement ring; the emeralds matched her eyes."

"They match yours, too. She must have died now that you wear it?"

"Yes. She was killed with one-eighth of the foreign community in the Yokohama earthquake of 1923. They call it the Great Kanto earthquake out there. I was lucky to have survived," Izolda informed in detail. She felt on home ground here.

"That earthquake. I remember hearing about it at my Prep school. Your hand gestures," he ventured, "you do not seem to me to be quite English?"

"It's my French upbringing," she smiled. "I am British, though a quarter American. My grandmother is an American from Georgia. She lived in Japan for most of her life and only came to France as a refugee after the earthquake. She lost everything, except that next day she found my grandfather's Order of the Star of the Rising Sun in the ashes of her home. It's her most prized possession."

So they were grandmother and granddaughter. He might have guessed. "Fortunate old lady to have a granddaughter to look after her," he reflected.

"*I'm* the fortunate one. She looked after me as a child; now it's my turn."

"I'd like to meet her properly and talk about the Japanese. To my mind the military there have got too big for their little boots."

"She'd enjoy that. We take tea in the small saloon before she disappears for the rest of the day. *Le five o'clock*, as the French call it. Join us tomorrow," she suggested.

The others returned from dancing. There was a buzz of conversation with long drinks all round, and then, as Roger did not ask anyone to dance and the pair seemed to be in deep conversation, the others disappeared again. "Do you mind? Not being a great dancer I prefer to talk. You've lived with your grandmother since the earthquake?"

"Not quite. To begin with, yes, and then my father married again and I went there. It didn't work. I was sent to a sort of Home, awful, from which my grandmother rescued me."

"And took you to live in France. Well done for her. My only claim to something French is my middle name."

"Oh?"

"I was christened Roger Edouard Colquhoun; Edouard because there were some Huguenots in the family way back."

"I daren't reveal all mine. You see my mother was an opera singer . . ."

"Come on. *I've* told all!"

"Izolda Carmen Violetta," Izolda said with a flourish. They both burst out laughing. "Chippy calls me Zol . . ."

"So I noticed," he interrupted. "I prefer Izolda."

"My mother used to call me 'Izarling'."

"I like that, too," Roger said.

"This ship," Izolda went on, a glow coming over her

The Order of the Star

(just think of being called 'darling' by him!) "is full of coincidences. I had an uncle called Edouard and a baby brother named after him. They died," she ended solemnly.

"People have a habit of doing that," he teased at her tone, and immediately kicked himself for being flippant: the poor kid's mother had been killed. That was not funny. "Generations of my family have died young," Roger hastened to repair his jocular remark. "We come from a long line of Army stock; Bibles in one hand, swords in the other they went into battle! God and the British Empire, good old Queen Victoria stuff. Yet when I look at the faded photographs of those lonely graves, I wonder if the sacrifice was worth it."

"And here you are following in their footsteps. Please don't leave your . . . body on a frontier," she said with a catch in her throat. She had nearly said 'magnificent' body, the body that would overfill a bath, left rotting in a lonely grave.

"No sane man wants war, but one has to draw the line somewhere, for instance at that megalomaniac Hitler occupying the whole of Europe. Can't have him ruling the British Isles and doing away with the monarchy, now can we? Besides, war has its excitements and its glories. I've seen shots fired in anger on the North-West Frontier; my uncles who survived tell me it was the best time of their lives. I shall take jolly good care not to get killed. I am not one of your blood and thunder types. It is a great life with travel, riding, mountaineering, fishing, shooting, sport – all the things I for one could never afford in England, and on top of that, the best kind of companionship a man can have."

He was still watching her. What a serious conversation

right from the start. He did not normally talk to females about his feelings for the Army, and females did not normally talk to him about kidnapping attempts! He noticed a basic robustness in the slender figure with the gracefully long neck, the small waist, hips curving out from that over-sequined top which his mother would have called 'bad taste'. He liked her sensitivity, and she was intelligent in a non-intellectual way.

Roger Stamford had no intention of getting involved with young girls at this stage of his career. On gaining his commission, his father, a retired Major, had warned him that to marry 'off the strength' – that was before he would be in receipt of a marriage allowance – would ruin his chances of early promotion. After the Shop, there had been some married women who had shown him plainly they were prepared to get into bed with him, and the sooner the better. He had fallen desperately in love with one; an affair, some years ago now, which had been killed dead by the husband declaring that if he did not stop seeing his wife, he would have him exposed and drag his name in the mud. That threat – he would have been cashiered – had been enough to cool him off in a matter of minutes. Since then he had steered clear of the opposite sex and was certainly not going to start up a shipboard romance before disembarking at Bombay. His devotion at present was given exclusively to his Indian troops, marvellous men all, the best soldiers in the world; he felt privileged to lead them.

"It goes without saying that you speak French fluently?" Roger Stamford sat back in his seat, wanting to distance himself from this undoubtedly attractive girl who had impressed him perhaps rather too much.

The Order of the Star

"I suppose I do," Izolda replied modestly, glad the Captain's intense gaze was no longer concentrated on her to such an extent. "I know a few words of Japanese, too. *Sayonara*, for instance."

"Humn. Nation of devilishly cruel soldiers. Crafty little yellow fighting-men who have to wear spectacles to see the target, so I'm told, not that I have met any."

"I warn you, if you ever make such a brash statement in front of my grandmother, you'll find yourself in the firing line, and will probably get some scathing riposte about the devilish Red Coats and their bestial behaviour in the States in seventeen hundred and something!"

"Point taken. I wouldn't dare," grinned Roger. "What does *sayonara* mean?"

"Goodbye. Literally 'till we meet again'."

"Till we meet again? That's nice, that's really nice," he said, intrigued by Izolda Carmen Violetta in spite of himself.

The journey continued into the heat of the Near East and through the narrows of the Suez Canal, where a hazy mirage gave the impression that the great P&O liner was floating on the desert wastes on either side. In the passage down the Red Sea, Roger Stamford became concerned for the welfare of the British troops in the ship and he arranged with the Captain for certain parts of first class to be barred off to passengers so that the men could come up and sleep on deck and enjoy the relief of a slight breeze made by the ship's wake.

It was during this stage that the gunner Captain showed his mettle. A Lascar working in the furnace-like heat of the engine-room, ran amok and tore through the ship attacking, with a lethal-looking knife, anyone who came into his path. Roger, hearing the shouts and screams, left the paperwork he was dealing with in his cabin, confronted the man, neatly tripped him up in a rugby tackle, and wrestled the knife from him.

Whether Roger Stamford was chasing Lascars who ran amok, or looking after the health of the soldiers, or was there to talk to or not, his presence was always with Izolda. Even when nowhere in sight, she hugged to herself the knowledge that he was there – somewhere – on the ship. Her face lit up when she saw his straight back striding along the deck in the distance, and her heart bounded every time she heard his voice. At night she dreamed of being with him in the moonlight, yet when she met him on board ship she found herself tongue-tied and with little to say.

The only time she could relax in his presence was when they were *à trois* with her grandmother for tea, which had become a daily meeting, so that the two could talk about the Japanese military. Then Izolda could sit back and listen to the conversation; then she could hug to herself the ecstasy she felt by just being in his presence.

The oddly assorted elderly lady and the upstanding young man discussed the way the Japanese had taken over Manchuria earlier in the decade, and how, in an attempt to disguise the move and hoodwink the rest of the world, they had installed Pu-yi, the ex-Emperor of China, who since fleeing from the Forbidden City in Peking, had been living under their aegis in the international port of Tientsin. If anyone was hoodwinked, Pu-yi was. Instead of finding himself reinstated in the northern part of China where his ancestors had come from, Pu-yi, together with his wife and entourage of Manchu nobles, found themselves

The Order of the Star

virtually as prisoners. In 1937, the Japanese army had gone on to take Peking, Tientsin, Nanking – where an appalling rape of innocents had taken place – and Shanghai. At an alarming rate they were now infiltrating down the coast. The Chinese, weakened by a network of communists, anarchists and Japanese collaborators within their midst, had resisted all the way along without much effect against the military might of the enemy. To Roger Stamford, the Japanese were behaving in the Far East in much the same way as Hitler was behaving in Europe, and he wanted to know what old Mrs Winter, with her knowledge of the Japanese, made of it.

"They were our staunch allies in the last war, Captain Stamford," Louise gave her opinion that though Japan was fighting China they were no enemy of the British. "The old treaties we have with them have not been abrogated. You notice how careful they have been to go *round* Hong Kong?"

"Isolated it," Roger said pensively. "Where will they stop? India?"

"They'll never stop until they are defeated, and who's to defeat them? Certainly not the Chinese, who are divided amongst themselves. Look back into their history, Captain Stamford. The Japanese and British have been attracted to one another since the former country was opened up to the West in the last century. They were drawn together in that they are both hardy, seafaring nations of small islands with very little room for expansion." Louise got into her stride, delighted to enlarge on her favourite subject. "Great Britain extended her rule by building an Empire, and the Japanese down the ages have wanted to go right in there and do the same to create their 'Great' Japan. I tell you straight out I saw the rapid development with my own eyes. They just lapped up what the expert English entrepreneurs and the Scots engineers who poured into the country, could teach them. They copied in exact minutiae the specifics of electricity, telephones, railways and shipping, and they particularly admired the British Navy. They founded their Imperial Japanese Navy to run on Royal Navy lines and called it 'The Mother of Navies'. Soon – that was in some forty years or so – they were competing with the West for world markets."

"Start by copying. Go on to compete. Next comes confrontation," Roger expressed thoughtfully.

"Confrontation with the Chinese and the Russians," snorted Louise. "They fought against the Germans in the Far East during the last war and took over the German Treaty Ports to relieve the China Fleet for action in European waters, and there is no reason to suppose they won't do the same again – unless, of course, they get the Victory disease, which goes to their heads as much as *saké*."

"How did you Westerners feel in Japan when all this progress and warfare was going on, Mrs Winter?"

"Proud," assured Louise, without hesitation. "I remember the tremendous pride we felt during the Russo-Japanese war at the beginning of the century in 1905, when news of the victory of Admiral Togo's sea battle at Tsu-Shima came through. The victorious fleet with their captured ships sailed into Yokohama harbour in line upon line, while we watched from the Bluff. For sure there was sadness as well, as there is in any war. My husband's oldest Japanese son, a naval officer, was lost in the sea battle, and another had been killed in the army in Korea during the previous Sino-Japanese war. The hospitals were overflowing with wounded. Many doctors came from England to help; I used to act as interpreter."

The Order of the Star

"I never knew that, Grandma. I mean about two of Grandpa's sons being killed."

"I told you when you were little. You've forgotten, I guess. The boys were brought up as Japanese and kept their mother's name; she was Sumuko, the daughter of a well-known Samurai."

"What happened to the third son?" persisted Izolda.

"Hojo? He fought alongside his brother in the Sino war, was wounded and came out of it covered in medals. Grandpa was very fond of Hojo's son. He loved children." Louise gave her deep sigh.

"So your husband was first married into the Japanese military. Do tell me what you know about the fighting forces?"

"I can tell you a little about the warrior class of Samurai," Louise answered, as pleased as anything, and proceeded to go into a long diatribe about these proud and heroic soldiers who were descended from a line of military and literary upper-class nobles that extended back thousands of years. Endowed with inherited position and wealth, they first had to undergo a stiff seven year's training, learnt by rote, to perfect physical and mental self-control of the highest order under the strictest discipline. The training turned them into the bravest, fiercest and most ruthless fighting-men, unequalled the world over. They were passionate nationals with a heady lust for power, who lived and died by the mystical *Bushido* code of honour.

"For sure they drink *saké* before going into battle," Louise went on, seeing she had the full attention of the Captain, who sat leaning forwards and was taking in her every word. "The Emperor is the head of the forces, and with a phalanx of Samurai generals strongly behind him what he, worshipped as the descendant of the sun god *Amaterasu*, says, goes! I dare say you could do with some Samurai to quell the tribes on the northern borders of India." Louise gave the English giant, with whom her granddaughter had fallen head-over-heels in love, a teasing look.

"We already have our own in the form of the Gurkhas," Roger replied, thinking Mrs Winter's description of the Samurai soldier did not fit in with the common one held by the British of the little Japanese man too big for his boots and wearing thick spectacles, and that he'd better revise that opinion. "The Gurkhas take *bhang* before going into battle, much the same sort of stimulant as *saké*, I imagine. So if Germany declares war, you don't expect the Japanese to side with them?"

"If by some blood-lust madness they *do* renege on the treaties, *I'll* have something to say to them!" Louise declared, eyes flashing.

"That'll be the day." Roger Stamford laughed heartily. And he rose to leave.

In contrast to her tendency to be subdued when with Roger, Izolda was overfull of put-on vivacity with Chippy. With him, she rivalled Maisie in fun and gaiety. She could have fallen in love with Chippy if she had not met Roger – the outstanding. Chippy was everything she liked. He still had that funny, childhood hair which fell over his high, domed forehead in an endearing fashion, to make her want to push it back from his face in a motherly way. He was so nice, so jolly, such fun, such an excellent dancer. He was the sort of person you could not be shy with – he got on well with everyone.

Yes, with Chippy Izolda felt thoroughly uninhibited, yet

The Order of the Star

she only cared for Roger, cared desperately what he thought of her, and it was obvious he did not think very much about her at all, so busy was he with the troops, or talking politics with the Lauders and the half-Colonel, or about the Japanese military with her grandmother, so that on the day before the liner docked in Bombay, she was almost glad it was the last time she would see him for the strain had been so great.

"I would like to keep in touch with you and your grandmother," he said on that day. "May I have your address in Hong Kong?" She gave him her uncle's box number, her heart leaping. He liked her sufficiently to want to write to her!

"*Sayonara*," he said later that evening, his hand strong and warm and altogether lovely in hers, "till we meet again."

Waking early, Izolda went out onto the boatdeck in time to see the dawn light tinge the stark outlines of the Western Ghats, and to follow the slow process of the liner through the narrows at Kolaba Point into Bombay's vast land-bound harbour, full of British warships and merchant vessels. She watched the crimson-streaked towers and flat roofs of the city whiten in the growing strength of the tropical sun.

On the dockside she saw the British troops, those who had been on the ship, assembling before being lined up to march off, and she saw Roger in their midst going round their ranks to say goodbye. He shook hands and had a word of cheer with each man. No wonder they would follow him into battle, she thought.

A fine-looking Indian Pathan in uniform, his *pugri* worn with an extra flair, elbowed his way with authority through the crowd, and, coming up to Roger, saluted smartly. This man too, Roger shook hands with. Behind the orderly

Evelyn Hart

followed a coolie who collected the luggage, and, talking animatedly, Roger and the Pathan disappeared into the long, low tin-roofed customs house.

He had gone. For a long while Izolda stayed on deck, her eyes too blurred with tears to take in the colourful, crowded scene below her.

Then she went down to the cabin to start the day, to start life again – without Roger.

TO BE CONTINUED